Caz Finlay lives in Liverpool with her husband, two children, and a grumpy dog named Bert. A qualified probation officer, Caz has always been fascinated by the psychology of human behaviour and the reasons people do the things they do. However, it was the loss of her son in 2016 which prompted her to rediscover her love of writing and write her first novel, *The Boss*.

cazfinlay.com

facebook.com/cazfinlayauthor
twitter.com/cjfinlaywriter
bookbub.com/authors/caz-finlay

Also by Caz Finlay

TRAITOR IN THE HOUSE

CAZ FINLAY

One More Chapter
a division of HarperCollins*Publishers* Ltd
1 London Bridge Street
London SE1 9GF
www.harpercollins.co.uk

HarperCollins*Publishers*
1st Floor, Watermarque Building, Ringsend Road
Dublin 4, Ireland

This paperback edition 2021
First published in Great Britain in ebook format
by HarperCollins*Publishers* 2021
Copyright © Caz Finlay 2021

Caz Finlay asserts the moral right to be identified
as the author of this work

A catalogue record of this book is available from the British Library

ISBN: 978-0-00-846333-5

Printed and bound in the UK using 100% Renewable Electricity
by CPI Group (UK) Ltd

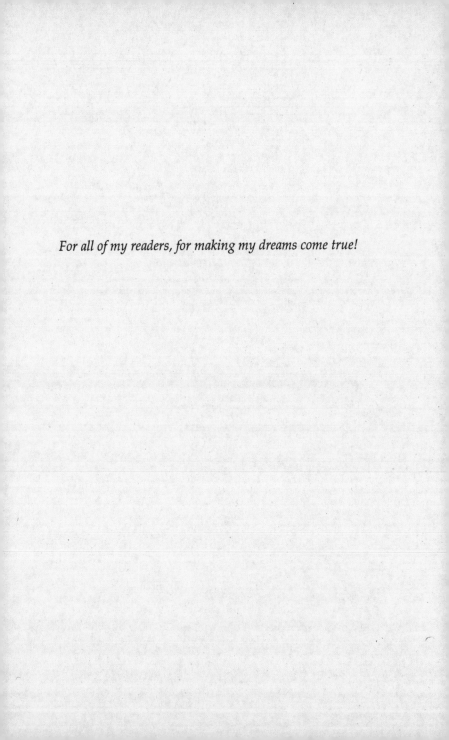

For all of my readers, for making my dreams come true!

Chapter One

DI Leigh Moss watched as the forensics team processed the crime scene. Their painstaking work would ensure the preservation of any evidence and, if luck was on their side, find something that would point them to the killer. Although Leigh didn't hold out much hope. This was the third murder in a month with the same MO, and so far they didn't have a scrap of evidence to identify the killer. What they did have was a serial killer who was targeting working girls.

After the second victim had been found two weeks earlier, the DCI from the Major Investigation Team had approached Leigh to collaborate on the investigation. Both victims had been well known to Leigh's Phoenix team, Merseyside Police's specialist rape and sexual offences unit, and both had also once been residents of Sunnymeade children's home. Sunnymeade had been closed down only two years earlier after an undercover investigation revealed a scandal of systematic abuse going back decades.

The latest victim, Nerys Sheehan, was also a former Sunnymeade resident. A young woman of twenty-one, with ash-blonde hair and eyes the colour of steel. She was as thin as a rake, and the couple of times Leigh had previously met her she'd had the urge to force a good pan of scouse down her. Nerys had been a likeable girl, with a dry sense of humour and an easy-going manner. After she'd ended up in A&E one time too many, one of the Police Constables from the unit had put her in touch with a local refuge. Nerys had managed to get clean and sort herself out, but it had only lasted a few short months before her pimp found her, and had her back on crack and back on the game within the week.

Leigh's heart broke when she thought about some of the women and girls they saw on a day-to-day basis. Each of them had a story to tell. All had been victims of some form of abuse, usually at the hands of the very people who were supposed to protect them. When she'd resigned from the Organised Crime task force, Leigh had planned to join the high volume crime team and spend the next part of her career dealing with burglaries and thefts. It had been her way of trying to minimise her usefulness to Grace Carter and her family now that she was even further indebted to the woman. A few months earlier, Grace and her firm had rescued DS Nick Bryce, Leigh's then boyfriend, from the clutches of an Essex gangster by the name of Alastair McGrath, who would have surely killed Nick if he'd had his way. But when the Assistant Chief Constable had approached her himself, and told her there was an opening in for a DI in the Phoenix team, she hadn't felt able to say no. Before she'd become a police officer, and after Grace had saved her from being murdered by Nathan Conlon, Leigh had worked with victims of sexual abuse and it was a cause still close to her heart. Whilst many people looked at a working girl and simply saw a prostitute, or a drug addict with loose morals, Leigh saw a woman who had survived through nightmares that such people couldn't even comprehend.

Thankfully, most of her colleagues in Phoenix thought the same way, and they did the best they could for the women they came into contact with. But for the most part, their best was never enough, and certainly not in the case of young Nerys or the other two young women who had met a similar fate. Leigh shuddered as she recalled her own past and how a few more months as Nathan Conlon's mistress might have led her down a similar path. Nathan was Grace's ex-husband and he had once been one of Liverpool's biggest gangsters. He had been as vicious as he was charming. Leigh had fallen for him hard and had thought her world had ended when he'd tossed her aside as soon as he'd got bored of her, as he'd done with most women. As much as she'd like to, Leigh could never forget just how much she had to thank Grace Carter for.

But there was one thing Nerys had in her favour, if you could call it that now that she was lying cold and broken on the ground just a few feet away. During a brief stint when Nerys's pimp had been inside and she'd managed to get herself off the crack, she'd worked at a knocking shop on the dock road – the aptly named Number 69. The place was well known to the Phoenix team. It was a well-established

Liverpool institution that had been around since the Sixties. Leigh's team raided the place from time to time, but for the most part, the punters and the employees of Number 69 caused little trouble and the management generally looked after their employees, ensuring they were paid a fair wage and worked in good conditions. It was a much safer place to work than the cold, hard streets of Liverpool.

It was often said that prostitution was the oldest occupation around and Leigh knew that there was no way of eradicating it entirely. Unfortunately, so long as women and girls were seen as a commodity, there would be men, because it was largely men, who would exploit that fact for their own ends. Places like Number 69 at least allowed some semblance of safety and enabled the girls to earn a decent income, and for that reason, Leigh and her team were willing to focus their attentions elsewhere. And with budget cuts, as well as policing some of the most deprived wards in the country, their attentions were always needed elsewhere. They never seemed to have the manpower or enough hours in the day to deal with everything that Liverpool's seedy underbelly threw at them.

The vibration of her mobile phone pulled Leigh from her thoughts. Pulling it out of her pocket, she glanced at the screen to see Grace Carter's number. Leigh answered it quickly. As much as it went against every instinct she had as a detective, she knew that if anyone could help her to shed some light on this case, it was Grace Carter – and Leigh was about to give her a reason to.

'Grace, thanks for calling me back,' Leigh answered.

'No problem. What's wrong?'

'It's delicate. Can I call round?'

'Here?'

'Is that a problem?'

'Not for me. But you're usually very reluctant to come to the house. Is this something I need to be worried about?'

'Maybe,' Leigh started. 'Probably not. To be honest, Grace, I need your help.'

There was a moment's pause and Leigh could imagine Grace frowning as she considered her request. If she refused then Leigh would have to mention the link between young Nerys and the Carter family, but she would rather do that in person if she could. The last thing she wanted was for Grace to go into defence mode before Leigh had even had a chance to plead her case.

'Okay,' Grace finally responded. 'Will tonight do? The kids will be in bed by eight. Call round then.'

'That would be great. I've got things I need to attend to here anyway. And thanks.'

'No problem. See you later,' Grace replied before ending the call.

Leigh slipped her phone back into her inside pocket and made her way back towards the crime scene as she saw one of the forensics signalling her. Her DS, Mark Whitney, was already there, peering at the victim's arm as the forensic officer held it outstretched.

'What is it?' Leigh asked as she reached the two of them.

'We can't be sure, Ma'am. But it looks like a tooth,' Mark answered.

'A tooth?' Leigh echoed as she brought her face closer to inspect the small white fragment which was embedded in a welt on the victim's wrist. 'Could it be our killer's? It's tiny. Is it a fragment?'

The forensic shook his head. 'We'll confirm when we do the post-mortem. But it looks like it's a child's.'

Leigh's blood ran cold. 'A child's tooth? What the hell?' she said with a sigh.

Mark shook his head. 'No idea, Ma'am.'

'She didn't have kids, did she?' Leigh asked, wondering if that was a snippet of information she'd forgotten.

Mark shook his head. 'Nope. Not as far as we know anyway.'

'Well, let's wait and see,' Leigh said to the forensic, who nodded and then resumed his work with his colleagues. 'In the meantime, check missing persons and make sure there are no kids missing too,' she said to Mark. 'God forbid.'

'Will do,' Mark replied as his own mobile phone started to ring and he slipped away to answer it.

Leigh closed her eyes and rubbed the bridge of her nose. This case got more sinister with each victim. There had never been any hint of any children involved up until now. She wondered if there was a perfectly innocent and reasonable explanation for the deceased to have a child's tooth embedded in her wrist when she was murdered – but couldn't think of a single one.

Chapter Two

G race put her phone on the coffee table and sat back against the sofa as she watched her husband Michael rolling around with their two youngest children, Belle and Oscar, and the newest addition to the family, their rescue Boxer dog, Bruce. She smiled absent-mindedly as she listened to their giggles. They loved nothing more than a game of Doctor Belle and her ticklish dinosaurs – a game which Belle had made up at the age of two and still three years later insisted on playing at every available opportunity. Oscar was by far the most ticklish of her dinosaurs, but Dr Belle could give him a run for his money.

'You okay, love?' Michael asked as he sat up, slightly breathless from his exertions. When Grace had seen the missed call from Leigh on her phone, she had left the game, and although she'd intended to return, the call had unsettled her and she realised she'd been staring into space for the past few moments. It was very unlike Leigh to want to visit them at home. On the one previous occasion she'd had cause to be there, at Grace's request, she had fidgeted the whole time.

Grace looked at her husband. 'Yes. I think so anyway. That was Leigh Moss. She wants to call round later.'

'Why?' he asked with a frown as he stood up, brushing the dog hair from his trousers.

'She didn't say exactly. Just that she needs my help.'

Michael walked over and sat beside her on the sofa, leaving Belle, Oscar and Bruce to continue playing without him. 'Anything we need to be worried about?'

Grace shook her head. 'I don't think so. She's going to call about eight after the kids are in bed.'

'Does that mean I'm making dinner again?' he said as he leaned back and put an arm around her shoulder.

'Well, you are a much better cook than me,' Grace replied.

'True.'

She gave him a playful nudge in the ribs. 'Don't get cocky, Carter,' she said with a laugh.

'Me? As if.' He returned her smile before kissing her on the forehead. Then he jumped up from the sofa. 'I'd better get going or I'll be late.' He picked up his coat from the back of the armchair and put it on.

'Be careful, won't you?' she said to him.

He walked back over to her and took hold of her chin in his hand. 'I always am,' he replied before kissing her again, this time on the lips. 'I'll be back before bath-time,' he said softly.

'Mine or the kids?' Grace replied with a smile, feeling the need to lighten the mood.

Michael grinned at her. 'Both. Most definitely both.' Then with a final kiss, he shouted goodbye to the kids before walking out of the door.

Michael climbed out of his Aston Martin and zipped up his Barbour coat as he walked across the road to the waiting transit van. He banged on the side as he reached it and the door was slid open.

'Evening, Son,' he said with a smile as he came face to face with his son Connor.

'All right, Dad,' Connor said with a smile before stepping aside and allowing Michael to climb in.

Michael sat on the wooden bench beside his stepson Jake and put an arm around his shoulder. 'You okay?' he asked.

'Sound.'

'Good,' Michael said as he looked at the bench opposite him and saw his business associates, Luke Sullivan and Danny Alexander, sitting quietly, holding baseball bats in their hands. Michael nodded to them both in greeting.

'We ready to go then?' Michael asked as Connor slid the van door closed again.

'Almost. One more pick-up, lads,' Connor shouted to the two men in the front of the van, whom Michael knew to be John Brennan and Jack Murphy – two of his and Grace's most trusted employees. Connor sat down beside him as the van moved away from the kerb. Michael leaned back and closed his eyes. It wasn't often he accompanied his sons on ventures like this any more. Especially not since Luke and Danny had joined the firm. They were the new Managing Directors of Cartel Securities and were already proving themselves to be assets. They were hard as nails and they were loyal. They worked closely with Connor and Jake and in a few short months had made themselves indispensable. Michael and Grace liked the fact that Luke and Danny could be trusted to have Jake and Connor's backs. It made them both able to sleep more easily at night.

This evening, Michael was tagging along because an old enemy had shown up and had made a play for some of their doors in the city centre. Joey Parnell had been a face back in the Nineties, long before Michael had been involved in the security game, but when he had worked for the likes of Sol Shepherd and Nathan Conlon. Parnell was a horrible cunt who would sell his own granny for the right price. Michael and his brother Sean had had numerous run-ins with Parnell and his lads back in the day, but over the years Parnell's firm had been outmanned and sidelined by the bigger and smarter companies that had taken over Liverpool. But now Parnell was back, and was slowly growing his empire again, making alliances with small two-bit factions across Merseyside who couldn't hope to make a mark on their own, and turning them into his personal little army. Now that Parnell and his new firm had made a move on some of Cartel's doors, it was time to slap them down before things got out of hand.

'Who else are we picking up?' Michael asked Connor as the van sped along the road, jostling the five men in the back up and down.

Connor grinned at him. 'Didn't he tell you?'

'Who? Tell me what?'

'Uncle Sean,' Connor replied.

'What didn't Sean tell me?' Michael asked with a frown. Sean was his brother, two years older than him, and they had always been as thick as the proverbial thieves. They'd had a good operation going, back in the day, and had been unstoppable. They had taken down anyone who stood in their way, and with his brother by his side Michael had felt invincible. But that had been a long time ago, before they had got themselves involved with Nathan Conlon, Grace's ex-husband and Jake's father, whose greed and ego had ended up in them all getting sent down for a long stretch. But as soon as Sean had finished that sentence eleven years ago, he had promised his wife Sophia that he'd go legit, for the sake of her and their three children. And apart from a few occasions when he'd taken a momentary hiatus from retirement, he had kept that promise, opening up a string of restaurants with Grace's help and becoming a successful businessman.

Jake put a hand on Michael's shoulder. 'He's coming with us.' Jake said with a flash of his eyebrows.

'Sean?' Michael said.

'Yep. When he heard we were visiting Parnell, he said he wouldn't miss it for the world.'

Michael smiled. It was always good to have his brother by his side. A few months earlier, Sean had come along when he and Grace had dealt with Alastair McGrath, a gangster from Essex, who had tried to muscle in on their business and fuck Grace over. Michael had seen the fire in

Sean's eyes when they had taken down the rival firm, and he'd wondered if his brother was getting a taste for action again.

Ten minutes later, Michael grinned as Sean climbed into the back of the transit van and sat beside him.

'All right, bro?' Sean asked.

'I am now. Although I'm surprised to see you here. Does Sophia know where you are?'

'I told her I was helping you and the boys out with a problem. I didn't go into the specifics.'

'She'll have your nuts if she finds out what kind of problem you're helping us with,' Michael said.

Sean laughed. 'What she doesn't know won't hurt her. So you'd better make sure I get home in one piece then, hadn't you?'

Chapter Three

J oey Parnell was putting the day's earnings into the
safe when he heard the commotion in the car park
outside. Instinctively, he reached for the metal bar
which he kept beside his desk. Joey and his firm had been
making waves in recent weeks, and he knew it was only a
matter of time before the Carters pushed back. Well, this
time he would be ready for them. He'd assembled himself a
small but loyal crew of lads, who were more than willing to
help him take back what was rightfully his. There had been
a time when Joey had run the most successful security
business in Liverpool, until Michael and Sean Carter had set
in motion a chain of events that had ended up destroying
his business and putting most of his workforce in the
hospital or in the nick. Well, now it was payback time.

'Lads,' Joey shouted into the back room. 'Get out here,
and bring your fucking weapon of choice with you. We've
got company.' He smiled as eight of his best soldiers

bounced out of the back room armed with baseball bats and machetes. 'You ready for this?' he asked them.

They nodded and grunted in response. Each of them had their own axe to grind with Jake Conlon or the Carter family. They stood in wait as they listened to the footsteps of Conlon and Carter's men running up the short flight of wooden steps. He and his lads would send them all packing with a few broken bones and a message that they were not to be fucked with. A few seconds later, the door burst open and Joey recognised John Brennan enter the room, closely followed by Luke and Danny. Joey smiled. He'd been expecting them now that they were the Carters' new muscle. A pair of arrogant little pricks who had been getting too big for their boots since they'd been taken on by Grace and Michael. But Joey knew where they came from and despite them walking around the city like they now fucking owned the place, he knew they were really a couple of pretenders to the throne. They didn't seem to realise they were simply cannon fodder to the Carters, who no longer deemed themselves worthy of getting their hands dirty.

Joey ran his hand up and down the metal bar as he glared at Luke Sullivan. He was about to show the little fucker exactly who he was. More bodies started to pour into the office and Joey looked up to see who they had brought for backup. He frowned as he saw it was Jake Conlon and Connor Carter. What were they doing there? He'd been assured that they preferred to stay out of the action these days. But if Joey was surprised at their presence in the room, he almost shat his pants when he saw the unmistakeable figures of Michael and Sean Carter walk through the door. Sean was last in and he closed the heavy iron door and bolted it behind him.

Joey swallowed as he looked around the room at the assembled men, all of whom were tooled up and carrying a bat or some sort of cosh. All except Michael Carter anyway. Joey glanced behind him at his crew who were equally armed and equally dangerous, at least he hoped they were. It also brought him some small comfort as he realised that he outnumbered the Carter firm, if only by two men. And as well as that, Michael was unarmed – wasn't he? It was only when Michael raised his fists that Joey saw the glint of the knuckledusters on them and his heart almost packed in. Michael stared directly at him. 'What the fuck do you think you're playing at making a move on our doors?' he snarled.

'They were my doors long before they were yours, gob-shite,' Joey snarled back. There was no way he was going to show any weakness. That was what the Carters and their ilk thrived on. Besides, if they played their cards right, maybe Joey and his men could give the Carters and their firm a run for their money. Sean and Michael hadn't been in the thick of the action for years and John Brennan was approaching fifty. Joey's men were all young and fit. Suddenly he felt sure they could take them on and send them packing.

'Gob-shite?' Michael asked with a flash of his eyebrows as he turned to Sean. 'Did Joey Parnell just call me a gob-shite?'

'I believe he did,' Sean replied. 'Cheeky fucker, aint he? Do you think he's forgotten about that night we found him banging that stripper?'

Joey blanched as he felt the bile rising in his throat. That had been the night that had ended his previous career. How was he to have known that the bird he'd been knocking off was Nathan Conlon's favourite bit on the side? Michael and Sean had been in league with Conlon back then and they had kicked seven shades of shit out of him. Not content that this was punishment enough, they'd told Conlon all about it too and Joey had been blackballed from working in every decent club in Liverpool. It had been the beginning of the end for him. The memory left a bitter taste in his mouth and ignited a fire in his belly.

'I fucking remember. You cunts!' Joey spat. 'Come on, lads,' he snarled as he lunged for Michael with the steel bar. Michael was still fast for a man in his forties and he ducked. Joey stumbled forward and looked up to see Michael's iron-clad fist barrelling towards his face. The force of the impact knocked Joey onto his arse. He barely had time to process the ringing in his ears when a second blow connected with his jaw and he heard the sickening crunch of bone as he was sparked flat out onto the floor. He tasted the blood in his mouth and began to cough as it trickled down his throat. He glanced up to see Michael coming for him again, but thankfully one of Joey's own men, Col, ran over and swung his bat towards Michael's head. Missing, he struck him across the back instead, but Michael stood up as though he'd been barely touched and he started laying into young Col until he too slumped to the floor and stopped moving altogether. Rolling onto his side, Joey looked around the room to see his men being overrun by the Carter firm – as though there were dozens of them in the room rather than just seven. He felt the throbbing in his temple and face intensify as the room started to spin. Joey closed his eyes and soon the shouts and screams of the men in his office started to fade until he slipped into unconsciousness.

CHAPTER FOUR

Chapter Four

Michael stepped out of the changing room of Eric's gym, freshly showered and in a clean set of clothes. He handed the holdall in his hand to Jack 'Murf' Murphy with a nod of thanks.

'Everything in here?' Murf asked as he scanned the sea of faces.

The men nodded. While Jake, John, Luke and Danny had headed straight to The Blue Rooms to get cleaned up, Michael, along with Connor, Sean and Murf, had made their way to Eric's gym to use the showers and changing rooms. They often used the place for such occasions and Eric never asked questions. He had given Connor and Jake a spare key each to use the gym whenever they needed to. In turn, Eric was well looked after, both financially and from any chancers who might try and take the piss out of a man who, while still hard as nails, was pushing seventy. Whereas Jake and the lads could get away with a quick clean-up at the club, Michael, Connor and Sean had kids at home and it just didn't feel right walking into their family home covered in someone else's blood. John and Murf had accompanied the respective groups because it was their job to make sure that any weapons, bloodstained clothes or any other incriminating evidence was cleaned or appropriately disposed of.

'Thanks, Murf,' Michael said as he approached Connor and Sean.

'No problem, Boss. I'll sort these now.' He disappeared out of the back door.

'Well, do I look presentable?' Sean asked as he held out his arms.

'Yes,' Michael replied with a grin. 'But I'm pretty sure Sophia will notice that you're going home in tracksuit bottoms and a T-shirt when you left in jeans and a completely different top.'

Sean shook his head. 'She'll be fine. She knows I was out with you. She'll be pissed off with me, but she won't ask too many questions.'

'If you say so, bro,' Michael said with a laugh. Sean's wife Sophia was renowned for her fiery Italian temper and he wasn't quite as convinced that she wouldn't rip his older brother a new one when she realised what he'd been up to.

Connor laughed too. 'I think you're going to be sleeping in the spare room for a week,' he said.

'What? No!' Sean insisted. 'She'll be fine. But let's get going, eh?'

The three men laughed as they started to head to the back door of the gym. Michael put an arm around Connor's shoulder. 'So, how's that beautiful grandson of mine doing?' he asked.

Connor's face broke into a huge grin. 'Oh, he's ace, Dad. He smiles all the time, and he's started laughing at this song Jazz sings him. He's so fucking cute.'

Michael smiled at his son. His grandson Paul was just over three months old and Michael loved to see his son so happy. A few hours after Paul's birth, there had been some complications with Jazz, she'd lost a lot of blood and had almost died. But the doctors had responded quickly and had saved her life, ensuring that she'd suffered no lasting consequences. But her ordeal had seemed to bring her and Connor even closer and they were planning their wedding for the following year.

'He looks just like you and Paul when you were babies,' Michael said as he felt a wave of sadness wash over him. Connor's twin, Paul, had been murdered twelve months earlier and his loss still hit Michael like a sledgehammer at unexpected moments.

'I know. He looks just like him,' Connor said quietly.

Michael pulled his son towards him and kissed the top of his head. 'I can't wait to see him and Jazz tomorrow then. You're still coming for dinner, aren't you?'

'Course we are. When do we ever miss a Sunday roast?' he said.

Michael said goodbye to Connor and Sean and climbed into his car as he prepared to head home. Joey Parnell and his boys had all been given a good hiding and would be licking their wounds for a while. Luke and Danny had suggested a more permanent solution to their Joey problem, but Michael had convinced them otherwise. After Jake and Connor had been arrested for murder a few months earlier, he was much more cautious about the way they dealt with their enemies. You couldn't just wipe out a new firm and not expect the plod to start sniffing around. Grace had managed to get DI Moss on side, but Michael didn't quite trust her. Once a copper, always a copper. And it wasn't like she was bent like the ones they had on their payroll. No, she was only on their side because she owed Grace a debt. Grace said that it was a better reason, because she wasn't motivated by money. Anyone who was willing to sell their morals and principles down the river for a few grand every month couldn't be relied on to remain loyal, in her opinion. However, someone who owed you their life, or the life of someone they loved, would remain loyal in the face of even the most difficult situations – and in DI Leigh Moss's case, she owed Grace both. Michael wasn't quite sure yet which side of the argument he agreed with, but he supposed that only time would tell.

Michael turned up the radio as he drove through the streets of Liverpool. He noticed it was almost seven and he would just about make it home in time to help Grace with Belle and Oscar's baths. At five and one, they were a handful together, and now they'd added a dog to the mix. He smiled as he thought about the home he was on his way to. Only five years earlier, he would have hardly believed it was possible. He'd been married to his second wife,

Hannah, and had been thoroughly miserable. Not that any of that was Hannah's fault – she was a good woman, attractive, kind and funny, but he had never loved her. She had been a rebound fling after Grace had rejected him years before. He had liked Hannah as soon as he'd met her. They'd got on well together and he had stupidly convinced himself that he would fall in love with her if he tried hard enough, and then he would forget about Grace. Except of course, that could never work. He still felt guilty about the whole thing. Hannah had wanted children but he had told her he didn't, then he'd gone on to have two with Grace – one of whom was conceived while he was still married. He swallowed and shook his head. As far as he'd heard, Hannah had remarried too and was expecting her first child. It gave him some comfort to know that she was happy now at least.

His thoughts returned to Grace and their kids and he realised he was driving with a huge smile on his face.

Chapter Five

Grace closed the door to Belle's bedroom and crept past Oscar's room before heading down the stairs where Michael was in the kitchen making dinner. Walking up behind him, she slipped her arms around his waist and laid her head against his shoulder. His shirt felt cool against her warm skin.

'That smells good,' she said as she inhaled. 'You smell good too,' she added as she planted a kiss on his neck. He'd showered before he came home and put on fresh clothes. She'd been bathing Belle and Oscar when he'd arrived home and hadn't had a chance to ask him how things had gone at Joey Parnell's yard. But the fact that, apart from some bruised knuckles, Michael was unharmed, happily cooking a curry, and had needed to change his clothes, told her as much as she needed to know for now. They would unpick the whole thing later after their visit from DI Moss.

'What time did you say she was coming?' he asked as though reading her mind.

'Eight, so she'll be here any time now. What time will dinner be ready?' she peered over his shoulder at the simmering pan of lamb rogan josh.

'It's ready whenever you are,' he said as he turned around. 'Get rid of her quickly and then we can eat.' He bent his head and kissed her. 'And then after we've eaten...' He kissed her again as he ran his hands down to the small of her back, pressing her body against his.

They were interrupted by the sound of the doorbell.

'She'll be out of here as soon as possible, I promise,' Grace said with a smile as she untangled herself from his arms.

Grace showed Leigh into the kitchen and sat on a stool at the breakfast bar. Leigh followed suit, placing her handbag and a manila folder down on the counter in front of her.

'Mmm, something smells good,' Leigh said as she looked around the spacious kitchen.

'Michael's made one of his amazing curries,' Grace answered as he made his way over to them, carrying an open bottle of Barolo and three glasses.

He planted a kiss on Grace's head as he sat down beside her and placed the wine and glasses on the counter.

'I didn't know you could cook.' Leigh said with a raised eyebrow.

'With all due respect, you know fuck all about me,' Michael said. There was no love lost between him and DI

Moss after she had arrested Jake and Connor for murder a few months earlier, but he tolerated her for Grace's sake.

Leigh stared at him, a smile playing on her lips as she appeared completely unfazed by his response. Grace noticed Leigh's gaze lingering on Michael's bruised knuckles – always on duty!

'Would you like a drink, Detective?' Michael asked as he started to pour a glass.

'Actually, I'd love one. Thanks,' Leigh answered as she rubbed the bridge of her nose.

Grace watched her husband pour three glasses of wine before handing one each to her and Leigh. 'So, what is it I can help you with?' Grace asked.

Leigh took a sip of her wine and shifted in her seat. 'I assume you've heard about the two murders of working girls this past month?'

'I read about them in the *Echo*. It was awful. Those poor girls.'

'Well, there's been another one. She was dumped early hours of this morning. Same MO.'

'Oh, God. That's awful,' Grace said with a shake of her head. 'Do you have any idea who's responsible?'

Leigh shook her head. 'Not a clue, unfortunately,' she replied with a sigh. 'Although please keep that to yourselves.'

Grace and Michael nodded. 'Of course,' Grace said. 'But what has any of this got to do with us?'

Leigh took another sip of her wine. 'The latest victim is a young woman by the name of Nerys Sheehan. Does her name ring a bell at all?'

Grace shook her head and she felt Michael bristle beside her. 'Should it?' she asked.

'Maybe. She worked at Number 69 for a few months last spring.'

'Number 69?' Michael asked.

'Yes,' Leigh replied.

Grace swallowed. Jake and Connor owned a stake in the place after acquiring it from a local no-mark, Ian the Thrush, after he had screwed them over on a drug deal. She had advised them to get rid of it – it wasn't the type of establishment that she wanted her family to have anything to do with. But shortly after they had obtained shares in the place, Paul had been murdered and Number 69 had become the least of her worries. She had no idea if the boys still owned a share, but she was sure the fact that Jake and Connor were connected to Number 69 was the reason Leigh was currently sitting in their kitchen with a large glass of red.

'It's that knocking shop on the dock road,' Grace said as she placed a hand on Michael's thigh. She felt his muscles tense as he too realised the connection.

He glared at Leigh. 'So what?' he snarled.

'Jake and Connor are part-owners of the place. Did you both know that?' Leigh asked.

'Of course we do,' Grace replied coolly. 'If you're here trying to make some tenuous link between our sons and the murder of these girls then you had better tread *very* carefully, Leigh.'

Leigh placed her glass on the counter. 'I don't believe for a second that Jake and Connor had anything to do with the murders, but there is no escaping the fact that their names are connected to the place and sooner or later someone will come asking questions about it. We are vigorously pursuing every line of inquiry. Some madman has killed three women in a month and I have every reason to believe he won't stop with Nerys.'

'So are you here to warn us that your lot will soon be sniffing around the boys? Or are you pursuing a line of inquiry?' Grace asked.

Leigh swallowed. 'To be honest, Grace, I'm here looking for your help.'

Michael took a deep breath while Grace stared at Leigh. 'My help?'

'Yes. As I said, we're pursuing all avenues but all I'm coming up against are dead ends.'

'I read that the first two victims were at that awful children's home together. Maybe this Nerys girl was there too?'

'She was.'

'Well, there's your answer then. That can't be a coincidence, can it?'

'I agree,' she replied as she began to rub the bridge of her nose again. 'But you remember that place was closed down a few years ago? And everyone involved with the scandal is in prison. We've tracked down all of the staff and the kids who would have been there at the same time as our victims and all of them are accounted for. A few of them live abroad now and the rest of them have concrete alibis.'

'Still. That's no coincidence, Leigh.'

'Like I said, I agree. But I've pursued every line I can via legal channels.'

Michael started to laugh and shake his head before he took a swig of his wine.

'I still don't understand why you're asking me for help.' Grace said.

'Because like it or not, Grace, your boys are linked to this case now—'

'A tenuous link, at best,' Grace snapped.

'Still a link though, and I'm sure they don't want the police looking into any of their business affairs.'

Michael slammed his glass onto the counter. 'Is that a fucking threat?' he snarled.

'Not at all,' Leigh shook her head. 'I don't think I'm explaining myself very well. We have a serial killer running around Liverpool torturing and killing young women. There is now a link to your family. I could do without my colleagues looking into your business affairs and finding out about our history together, but I also believe that you will be able to get information from the girls at Number 69 that they would just never dream of giving to the police. I'm just asking you to ask some questions for me. Do a bit of digging? See if you can come up with something that might lead us down a new avenue of investigation, or a snippet of information that might help us crack this case. Please, Grace?'

'I'm not sure you understand the terms of our arrangement, Leigh. I – we,' Grace said as she looked at Michael, 'don't assist the police with their investigations. *We* don't work for *you*,' she added pointedly.

'I know that. But this is a special case. I wouldn't ask if I wasn't desperate. I need to find this lunatic and quickly. He's going to act again. You told me once that this was your city. Do you really want this bastard running around here under your nose carving up young women?' Leigh stared at her defiantly.

Grace shook her head. 'Of course not. But you have no idea what you're asking of me.'

'I do. The same as you've asked of me. I know this goes against your principles. But these girls are innocent, Grace. You know that. Who else is going to stand for them if women like us don't?' Leigh picked up the manila folder and opened it. She spread out the three photographs of the victims. 'This is Tracy Rose, Ellie Castle and Nerys Sheehan,' Leigh said softly.

Grace flinched as she looked at the battered and broken bodies of the three women. She heard Michael let out a long slow breath beside her and when she turned to look at him he had closed his eyes. The two of them were no strangers to dead bodies, Michael in particular, but that didn't make seeing the images of the three women any easier to deal with.

'What was the cause of death?' Grace asked.

'Strangulation. We're still waiting on the full autopsy results for Nerys, but we're sure the result will confirm the same for her too. The first two victims also had incredibly high levels of opiates in their system, and I suspect Nerys's toxicology report will reveal the same of her. All three victims were well known to police and had ongoing drug issues, but the levels in Tracy and Ellie's systems were indicative of an incredibly large dose shortly before death. Perhaps as a way to keep them quiet and compliant? Some of the injuries you can see on the photographs were inflicted just before time of death, but all three victims had a catalogue of injuries that were up to one to two to weeks old.'

'What does that mean?' Michael asked.

'It means they were systematically beaten, most probably tortured, for one to two weeks prior to their deaths,' Leigh said sharply. 'There were ligature wounds on each of the victims' ankles and wrists, which indicates they were all bound to something, or someone, prior to death too.' Leigh picked up her wine and took a large gulp.

Grace stared at Leigh and, despite their differences, she couldn't help but feel some sympathy for her. Grace had read about the previous victims in the newspapers and had seen the reports on the rare occasions she watched the news. She knew that no arrests had been made and from the look of Leigh, the investigation was taking its toll on her. Grace wondered if, given Leigh's background, she felt any affinity to the dead women. Leigh herself had once told Grace she believed she'd have ended up dead in a ditch somewhere if Nathan had continued stringing her along.

'I will think about speaking to some of the girls at Number 69,' Grace said. 'But I want Connor and Jake's names kept out of this. You will look into their involvement in Number 69 personally and discover that they handed over their share to Opal Henshaw before Nerys ever even worked there. My solicitor will be able to produce paperwork to that effect should anyone care to see it.'

Leigh smiled. 'Thank you.'

'I haven't done anything to thank me for yet,' Grace replied.

Leigh downed the last of her glass of wine. 'Well, thank you for the drink. I needed that. I'll leave you both to your dinner.'

After Grace had shown Leigh out she walked back into the kitchen to find Michael dishing up two plates of lamb curry and rice. She sat at the table and he placed the food in front of her before sitting at the chair opposite.

'Do you think the boys are in any trouble with this?' he asked.

'No. I'll speak to Opal tomorrow. She'll be over the moon to have the boys' share in Number 69, especially as they're going to hand it over for nothing.'

'She'll think she's won the lottery,' Michael agreed. 'To be fair though, she deserves it after putting up with that cretin Harry for all these years.'

'Hmm, you're right about that.' Opal Henshaw had been responsible for the smooth running of Number 69 for years and was a part-owner in the business. She was the one who always made sure that the girls were well looked after, but her business partner, Harry, her former pimp and all round dirt-bag, whom she didn't always see eye to eye with, was more interested in profit than anything else. With Jake and Connor's stake in the place, Opal would be the majority owner. 'I'll speak to Faye tomorrow and make sure she backdates all of the paperwork.'

'And she'll definitely be able to sort that?' he asked.

Grace smiled at him. Her solicitor, Faye Donovan, was a miracle worker. 'Of course she will – for us.'

They ate in silence for a while before Michael spoke again. 'Are you really thinking about helping Leigh then?'

Grace swallowed a mouthful and looked at him. 'I'm honestly not sure yet. What do you think?'

'It's your decision. But you need to be careful if you do. If anyone gets a sniff that you're working with the plod, there'll be fucking uproar. You'll lose a lot of credibility with most of our associates.'

'I know. I'll be discreet. *If* I do anything, it will only be to talk to Opal and the girls.'

He smiled before scooping the last mouthful of curry into his mouth.

'What would you do?' she asked him.

He put his knife and fork down and rubbed a hand across his beard. 'I don't know. It goes against every instinct I have to help DI Moss with her investigation...'

'But?'

'But, there is a psychopath running around murdering women in our city and I wouldn't mind knowing who that was. I'm not saying we need to give any information we find to the police, but I'd still like to find out who the sick fuck is who's doing this. And it's true that Opal and the girls are more likely to talk to you than to a bunch of coppers.'

'I know what you mean. When I speak to Opal, there's no harm in asking a few girls if they knew Nerys, is there?'

'Okay. But be careful.'

'I always am. You know that,' she replied with a smile.

'You should take John with you.'

'John?' she asked with a laugh. Despite having no reason to, Michael seemed to have an issue with her and John working together so closely. Not that he'd ever voiced such concerns to her, but she could tell by the way his face changed whenever she mentioned John's name – a momentary scowl flickering over his face. 'You don't fancy coming down to Number 69 with me then?'

He started to laugh. 'No thanks. That wasn't my kind of place even when I was young, free and single. Besides, Opal terrifies me. I'm pretty sure she wants to have her wicked way with me, you know?'

'Well, I can't say I blame her,' Grace said with a flash of her eyebrows. 'If you weren't already my husband, I'd be trying to have my wicked way with you too.'

He stood up and walked around to her side of the table. Pulling her up from her chair, he wrapped his arms around her waist. 'I seem to remember you doing just that when I was someone else's husband,' he said with a grin.

Grace gave him a gentle shove and stared at him open-mouthed, feigning indignation. He had been married to Hannah when the two of them had had a one-night stand which had resulted in their daughter Belle being born. 'I can't believe you would even bring that up. Besides, you were the one who was married. I was a free agent. And you pursued me, if I recall?'

'I most definitely did. I have been chasing after you since the first day I met you, Mrs Carter. But you already know that. I'm just glad you finally came to your senses,' he said as he pulled her to him and silenced any potential comeback with a long, deep kiss.

'Do you remember that night?' Grace asked when they stopped for a breath. 'I still think about it sometimes.'

'Of course I do. It was the first time you ever called me Mike.'

She frowned at him. 'What? I never call you Mike.'

He leaned his head to her ear and whispered. 'Yes, you do. All the time. When you can't quite pronounce that second syllable.' He started to chuckle.

Grace blushed as she realised what he was referring to. She trailed her fingertips across his cheek and whispered. 'How about we go to bed and you can make me call you Mike then?'

Chapter Six

John Brennan opened the door of his BMW X5 and Grace stepped out onto the side street.

'You ready for this?' She grinned at him.

John rolled his eyes. 'As I'll ever be, I suppose.'

Grace laughed. 'Oh relax. Opal is a pussycat really, you know?'

'If you say so, Boss,' he replied. 'But I'd rather take my chances with a bunch of machete-wielding psychopaths than Opal Henshaw.'

Grace placed a hand on his arm. 'Don't worry, big guy. I'll protect you,' she said with a wink then she turned and started to walk down the street towards Number 69 with John following closely behind.

They walked until they reached the giant steel door which was the entrance to one of the oldest and most renowned knocking shops in Merseyside. Using his fist, John knocked twice on the door and waited for ten seconds before knocking once more – the agreed code for punters. A minute later the large door creaked open and a short woman with horn-rimmed glasses peered out.

'I'm here to see Opal,' Grace said with a smile. 'She's expecting me.'

'Grace?' the woman asked.

Grace nodded and the door was opened wider so she and John could step inside. They followed the short woman to the office at the back of the building, passing the crudely designed reception area that could provide at least some semblance of a legitimate massage parlour if the police ever raided the place, which they seldom did. The girls who worked at Number 69 were well looked after and the place rarely came to anyone's attention thanks to Opal's influence and her two strapping sons who worked behind the front desk. They passed through a corridor with numerous rooms leading off. Grace ignored the groaning and the banging noises coming from behind the doors and turned to John, who gave her a grin.

They were shown into Opal's office and the short woman closed the door behind them.

'Grace? John?' Opal said as she stood from her chair and walked towards them. She pulled each of them into a hug, enveloping them in a cloud of sweet perfume. 'It's very nice of you to visit,' she said with a laugh. 'Please, make yourselves comfortable.' She indicated the two plush purple velvet chairs opposite her desk.

Grace and John took a seat and watched as Opal walked back to her side of the desk. She sat down with an exaggerated sigh and smiled at them both as she flicked her purple pashmina over her shoulder. Opal Henshaw had once been a striking woman with jet black hair and olive skin. Years of working on the streets had hardened her and her appearance. She was in her late fifties now and her working days were well behind her, apart from the occasional exclusive client who was willing to pay through the nose for her services.

'How are things, Opal? I hear business is doing well?' Grace asked.

'It gets me and my girls by,' she replied. 'How about you?'

'Business is good. I can't complain,' Grace replied with a smile.

'And how about that handsome husband of yours?' she asked with a cackle. 'It's a shame you didn't bring him with you. Not that I don't appreciate your company, John,' she said as she licked her lips and batted her eyelashes at him.

John coughed awkwardly and Grace suppressed a laugh. 'Michael is good, thanks, Opal. He sends his regards.'

'So,' Opal asked as she leaned her elbows on the desk. 'You have some business to discuss, Grace?'

'Yes. As I mentioned earlier on the phone, the boys want to hand over their share in this place.'

'Just like that? Ten per cent of this place? And they want nothing in return?' Opal frowned.

Grace nodded. Opal was a shrewd woman.

'Why?'

'They should never have got involved in the place, Opal. I mean no disrespect, but this isn't our business.' She looked around the room. 'It's not what we know and that makes me uncomfortable. They took Ian's share as a punishment, and I understand that, but they never should have kept it. So, now it's time to hand it over.'

'I get that. But this place makes a decent profit. So why now?' Opal frowned.

'Did you hear the reports of a woman found dead near Cookson's Bridge last night?'

'Yes?'

'Well, it was another working girl. Her name was Nerys Sheehan.'

Opal blinked rapidly. 'God. Really?'

'Yes,' Grace whispered. 'She worked here, didn't she?'

'Yes, a while back now. But I remember her. She was a nice kid,' she said as she shook her head.

'The police know about her connection to this place, Opal. And I'm sure you'll understand that I can't have the police sniffing around my boys again. Not after what happened a few months ago. So, that's why I've persuaded Jake and Connor to sign their share over to you. My solicitor has drawn up some paperwork, making it all above board,' she said as she pulled a brown envelope from her handbag. 'I've had her backdate it. I hope you understand why?'

Opal nodded and took the envelope from Grace's outstretched hand. She took the papers out of the envelope and scanned them. 'This all looks legitimate,' she said with a raised eyebrow.

'Of course it is,' Grace said.

Opal nodded again. 'I know you're a woman of your

word, Grace. But you must understand it's not every day someone just hands over a gift like this.'

'I know that, and I would be sceptical in your shoes. But you have my word there are no strings attached. This benefits my family as much as it benefits you.'

Opal stared at Grace, and then at John, who had remained silent throughout the entire meeting. 'Do you ever speak, John? Or do you just sit there looking fine?' Opal said as she tilted her head to one side.

John's face flushed pink and he shifted in his seat. Grace suppressed a smile. 'He's my right-hand man,' she said to save John's embarrassment. 'He comes everywhere with me.'

Opal leaned forward and licked her lips. 'Well, you can certainly come everywhere—'

'I wondered if you could tell me any more about Nerys, Opal?' Grace interrupted her before she could finish her sentence and make John even more uncomfortable than he already was.

Opal sat back in her chair. 'I didn't know her that well, to be honest. Like I said, she didn't work here long. She kept herself to herself mostly. But she was a nice girl. The punters loved her, especially the regulars. You know? The ones who come here because they're lonely and too shy to find a proper girlfriend? She was always good with the real sad cases.'

'Can you tell me anything about her at all? Did she have any family?'

Opal stared at Grace for a few seconds before shrugging. 'I haven't a clue. But Donna, the lady who showed you in here, might. She and Nerys were pretty close. Nerys stayed in touch for a while, until that vile pimp of hers put a stop to it anyway.'

'Who was her pimp?'

'Leo Baines. Scum of the frigging earth.'

Grace frowned; she recognised the name but didn't know why. John leaned towards Grace and said quietly. 'Porter's daughter. The twins carved his face up.'

Of course. Paul and Connor had rescued a sixteen-year-old girl from his clutches a few years earlier on her behalf, and they had very helpfully carved the word 'paedo' into his forehead while they were at it. Funnily enough, he'd taken to wearing a hat after that.

'He's inside now anyway, where he belongs,' Opal spat.

'Oh?'

'Yeah. Got a bit too rough with one of his girls and ended up putting the poor mare in a wheelchair for the rest of her life. He got six years just before Christmas.'

He wasn't the man responsible for Nerys's death then, Grace thought. 'Do you mind if I have a quick chat with Donna before I go?'

Opal chewed her bottom lip as she appeared to consider the request. 'Okay, but just you. Donna gets a bit twitchy around big blokes like him. You can wait in here with me.'

John looked at Grace and she had to stop herself from bursting out laughing. John Brennan was a huge, intimidating bear of a man, who struck fear into the hearts of even the most hardened criminals. But he was staring at her like a rabbit trapped in the headlights with a look of fear in his eyes.

'Actually, John, I need you to phone Jake and Connor for me and let them know I need to see them later, if you don't mind. You can phone them from the car. I won't be long.'

'No problem, Boss. I'll wait in the car,' John said as he stood up and walked out of the room.

Opal started to laugh. 'He's a bit skittish for a big fella, isn't he?'

'Oh, behave yourself. You know you terrify him. You terrify most men, Opal,' Grace said with a smile.

'Well, I have to keep them in their place, Grace, or they'll think they can take the piss. You know that better than most.'

'I do. John is one of the good ones though.'

'They can all be good ones if you know how to keep them in line,' Opal said with a flash of her eyebrows. 'And you, my dear, have a knack for keeping them all in line. I don't know how you do it. Seriously.'

'Well, I wouldn't say all of them. I have my fair share of enemies.'

'Don't we all. But nothing you can't handle. I'm sure there are very few people who would dare to go head to head against the woman who took out Nathan Conlon!'

Grace bristled at the mention of her ex-husband's name. It was true that she had killed him. She had put a bullet in his chest and watched as he'd choked on his own blood. But that was only because he'd been about to kill her with his bare hands – after he'd already beaten and raped her. After he had subjected her to years of physical, emotional and mental abuse. There was no love lost between Opal and Nathan – she had been one of his many conquests. One of the many women he had used and discarded like yesterday's newspaper, only to go running back to Grace claiming his undying love. He'd been dead for five years but she was still reminded of him almost constantly. The city and its people had a long memory.

'So, it's okay if I have a quick chat with Donna?' Grace asked as she stood up.

'Of course, love. But don't keep her too long, will you? The rooms will need a clean before the afternoon sessions start.'

'It will only take a few minutes. Thanks, Opal.'

'No problem. And thank you, Grace. For the paperwork,' she said as she held the envelope aloft.

Grace stepped into the hallway and walked to the reception to find Donna, who was folding some towels.

'Hi, Donna,' Grace said as she approached.

Donna looked up with wide eyes. 'Hi, Grace,' she said quietly.

'Do you have a minute? I need to ask you about someone.'

Donna placed the towels on the nearby table. 'Of course.'

Grace took a seat on the plastic sofa and it creaked noisily as she sat down. She indicated for Donna to sit beside her. Donna took a seat, smoothing her dress over her knees as she did.

'Do you remember Nerys Sheehan?' Grace asked.

'Yes. She worked here last year for a few months,' Donna said.

'Is there anything you can tell me about her? Did she have any family at all?'

'Why do you want to know? Is she in some kind of trouble?' Donna asked as she fiddled with the hem of her dress.

Grace swallowed. 'Nerys was found dead yesterday.'

Donna stared at her. 'What?' she said with a gasp. 'How?'

'She was murdered.'

Donna's hand shot to her mouth and tears sprang to her eyes. 'God. No!' She shook her head in disbelief. 'Do you know who? What happened?'

'I don't know anything yet. But I'd like to find out.'

Donna frowned at her. 'But why? Did you know her?'

'No.' Grace shook her head. 'I didn't. But as my sons were connected to this place, I wanted to do a little digging myself, if you know what I mean?'

Donna nodded as a tear rolled down her cheek. 'I didn't really know her that well but we used to have a good laugh in between her punters. They loved her, you know. She had a nice way with people.'

'Why did she stop working here?'

'Her pimp, Leo, found out she was working here and he started hanging around outside for her and showing up every time she was on shift. Opal's sons warned him off but by that time I think he had his claws into her again. She started losing weight and turning up looking really rough. He'd obviously got her hooked on crack again and after a few weeks she stopped turning up for her shifts and Opal had to let her go.'

'Opal mentioned that Leo's in prison now.'

'Yes. So I heard.'

'Were there any of her regulars who stand out at all? Any who might have been obsessed with her? Or had been overly interested in where she'd gone? Or maybe they were just a bit strange.'

'Lots of our punters are strange. But no one stands out. No one that I think would murder her anyway.'

Grace sat back with a sigh. She wasn't sure she'd find out any information here. 'Did she have any family at all that you know of?'

'No. She grew up in care. No contact with her mum and dad. No relatives that she ever mentioned to me. She seemed to be a bit of a loner, if I'm honest. She didn't really talk to the girls in here much.'

'But she did talk to you?'

'Yes. We're both big fans of jazz music and we used to listen to some CDs when she was on a break.'

'Jazz? That's unusual for someone her age. Where did that come from?'

'She used to listen to it in the care home she grew up in. Her and her friend used to sneak up to the attic and they found an old record player with a load of jazz records. I think it was a way of escaping the place.'

'I can understand why she'd want to do that.'

'Hmm. Me too,' Donna said and visibly shuddered.

'Did she stay in touch with this friend?'

'Not that I know of. She never mentioned his name.'

'His?'

'Yeah. It was a boy, but like I said, she never told me his

name.'

'Thanks, Donna. Is there anything else you remember about her at all?'

Donna swallowed and looked around the room.

'What is it?' Grace asked.

Donna leaned forward in her seat. 'She told me once that she had a child. A daughter,' she whispered.

Grace smiled at Donna and admired the fact she was still being discreet about her friend's secret, even though there was no real reason to now.

'A daughter?'

'She would be about five now, I think. But nobody else knew about her. Nerys was ashamed, I think, that she'd basically left the kid with her dad as soon as she was born. But Nerys was only sixteen when she had her.'

'Did she ever see her?'

'I honestly don't know.'

'Where is the child?'

'No idea. She never told me who the father was. She didn't even tell me her little girl's name. I don't think she'd have told me at all except it just slipped out one afternoon when we were talking. I was talking about my own daughter and she said something about her little girl. But she clammed up straightaway, like she'd told me something she shouldn't have.'

Grace looked at Donna as the tears welled up in the girl's eyes again. 'Thanks, Donna. That's been really helpful,' she said although she had no idea if it was. She wasn't sure she'd garnered any information that the police couldn't have got themselves. Donna would have been

CAZ FINLAY

unlikely to reveal the information about Nerys's daughter, but Grace was sure the police could have discovered that information themselves eventually.

Grace walked out of Number 69 and down the street to John's waiting car. He smiled at her as she slipped into the passenger seat.

'Did you get what you needed?' he asked.

'I have no idea,' she replied with a shrug. 'Time will tell, I suppose.'

John put the car into gear and pulled away from the kerb. 'I'm just happy to be getting away from this place.'

'Opal scares the shit out of you, doesn't she?' Grace said with a laugh.

'Yeah,' he said as he started to laugh too.

Chapter Seven

Michael pushed open the door to Cartel Securities and walked down the hallway towards his old office, which was now occupied by Luke Sullivan and Danny Alexander. The door was closed and he almost walked straight in, before remembering that it didn't belong to him any longer. He stepped back and knocked.

'Come in,' he heard Luke shout.

He walked into the room and nodded a greeting to Luke and Danny. He was surprised to see Jake there too, perched on the window ledge. 'Hello, Son,' he said to Jake, crossing the room and giving him a brief hug. Michael turned around and noted that Luke was sitting in his old chair. He felt an unexpected pang of something and couldn't quite work out if it was nostalgia or resentment.

'You two okay?' Michael asked, noting Danny's split lip and the cut over Luke's left eye.

'Yeah, course,' they both replied in unison.

'Have a seat, Boss. What can we do for you?' Luke asked.

Michael sat on the unoccupied chair and stretched his legs. 'I just wanted to check how you were doing, and thank you for last night. You did a good job, lads.'

Luke and Danny both smiled at him. 'Thanks, Boss,' Danny said. 'I think Parnell will think twice about making a move on any of our doors again.'

'Well, I'd like to hope so, but I wouldn't count on it. He'll either back off or come back at us with everything he has. You'll need to be on your guard.'

'We will be,' said Luke.

'I thought it might be a good idea to take on some extra staff?' Michael added. 'It might be worth putting a few extra lads on all of the doors for a while, especially on Sophia's and The Blue Rooms.'

'Good idea, we'll get on it today,' Luke said and Danny nodded eagerly while Jake started laughing.

'What's so funny?' Michael asked.

'I told them you wouldn't let go of this place so easily. You can't help yourself, can you?' Jake replied.

'Fuck off, you cheeky bugger,' Michael said good naturedly.

'He's still the CEO,' Danny said with a shrug.

'Oh, stop arse-kissing,' Jake said as he patted Danny on the back. 'Anyway, I've got to meet Connor in half an hour. See you all later.'

———

Michael waited until Jake had left until he spoke again. 'You two have had some trouble with Parnell before, haven't you?'

'Yeah, a couple of months before we approached you and Grace with our proposal to merge,' Luke replied.

'What happened?' Michael asked with a frown as he sat back.

Danny and Luke exchanged a glance before Luke replied. 'We set up Sable Securities with just the two of us and a few bouncers working a couple of local pubs. We started to get a good reputation and it wasn't long before we started taking on other contracts with some local building sites and quite a few pubs and clubs. We had our share of issues, as you can imagine, with other firms trying to take the piss because we were new and small, but we had a really good bunch of lads and we built up a really good business.'

Michael already knew all of this. He and Grace had done their homework before they'd gone into business with the two of them.

'Then last year, this new firm turned up at a few of our boozers and tried to force us out. We held our own and sent them packing but they kept coming back so in the end we had to take more decisive action, if you know what I mean?'

'What did you do?' Michael asked.

Luke looked at Danny again before he went on. 'We found out they where they were operating from and we torched the place. Then we kidnapped a couple of them...'

'Oh? And?'

'We returned them to their boss,' Luke stopped and looked at Danny.

'Slightly worse for wear?' Danny suggested.

'That's when we met Parnell. He went feral when he saw what we'd done to his lads and pulled a gun on us. But for some reason, he didn't use it. He let us walk away and then everything went quiet for a few months. That's when we had the idea of approaching you and Grace about you buying us out and keeping us on. We knew that the takeover attempts would just keep on happening but we knew that we had a good set-up and with some backing we could do so much more.'

Michael sat back in his chair.

'If we've brought trouble from Parnell to your door, then we're sorry,' Luke said sincerely.

Michael held up his hand to stop Luke from apologising any further. It was unnecessary. 'The security game is full of trouble. We knew we were taking on your enemies as well as your business. Besides, I pissed Parnell off a long time before you did, lads,' he said with a grin. 'He's been around for a long time. At least he was around a long time ago anyway. He disappeared though and I'm wondering what's brought him back to these parts.'

'You've got history with Parnell?' Danny asked.

'Oh, yes, we certainly do. Me and Sean both knew him back in the day.'

'I wondered why Sean tagged along last night,' Luke said. 'Couldn't resist one for old times?'

Michael laughed. Although he had been shocked that Sean had tagged along last night, it had been good to have his big brother at his side again. 'So, Parnell has an issue with you two as well as some old grudge against me and Sean, and we all know he's a stupid cunt, so I'd expect that once he's had time to lick his wounds, he might make another move.'

'We'll look into those extra staff today,' Luke assured him. 'And we'll put all of the lads on extra shifts until we get some.'

'Good,' Michael said. 'And I don't mean to step on any toes here, it's just a suggestion. I trust the two of you to manage the business as you see fit, but as Jake told you, I can't help myself from sticking my oar in.'

'It's fine. We appreciate your input, don't we, Dan?' Luke said.

'Good. Because I meant what I said before. You two impressed me last night. I knew you could handle yourselves, but you did a great job.'

Luke and Danny couldn't hide the pride on their faces and it made Michael smile. 'It makes Grace and me feel better to know that you two are at the helm, and also that Connor and Jake can call on you when they need to.'

'And they can,' Danny assured him.

Chapter Eight

G race sipped her glass of Diet Coke as she sat at a small vinyl-topped table at The Old Bank pub on Stanley Road. It was late afternoon and the place was quiet except for a few men sitting at the bar and dotted around the place, whom she assumed to be the regulars. Suddenly she was filled with an overwhelming sense of nostalgia – the smell of a pub could always do that to her. She had grown up in a pub not too dissimilar to this one. Then she had become the owner of it at the tender age of eighteen when her father passed away. Shortly afterwards she met Nathan Conlon. Despite his best efforts to run the place into the ground, she had made a huge success of it when he'd gone to prison for twelve years. It was the place where she'd first met Pat Carter, and subsequently his sons Michael and Sean. It had broken Grace's heart to burn her pub to the ground five years earlier in a bid to finally be free of Nathan and break the hold he had over her.

Grace looked up to see the unmistakeable figure of DI

Leigh Moss walking towards her. She weaved her way through the tables until she reached Grace. Removing her coat, she took a seat opposite. 'Thanks,' she said, indicating the untouched glass of Diet Coke on the table in front of her.

'You're welcome. I'm afraid there's no shot of brandy in it though,' Grace said with a smile. 'I have to pick the kids up from their grandparents shortly.'

'That's fine. I have to get back to the station soon anyway.'

'No rest for the wicked, eh?'

Leigh half-smiled. 'Something like that,' she said before taking a sip of her drink.

The two women sat in silence for a few moments.

'Did you speak to the women at Number 69?' Leigh eventually asked.

'Yes. I didn't get much information about Nerys though. It seems she was quite shy and kept to herself mostly. I assume you know all about her pimp, Baines?'

Leigh nodded. 'Oh yes. Benny Baines – nasty piece of work. He would have been high on my suspect list, except he's in prison.'

'Benny?' Grace frowned. 'I thought his name was Leo?'

'He is, but we call him Benny because he always had one of those Benny hats glued to his head. We never knew why until we arrested him,' she said with a smirk.

'Scarring on his forehead, perhaps?' Grace grinned back.

'Yes. It just looks a mess from a distance, but up close...'

'You can make out the word paedo?'

Leigh laughed. 'Exactly. Now, how would you even

56

know about that?' Grace was about to answer when Leigh help up her hand. 'Actually, forget it. I don't want to know. Did you find anything else out about Nerys?'

'Only that she had a child.'

'A child?' Leigh asked with a frown. 'There's nothing in her medical records to indicate that.'

'Well, that's what I was told,' Grace replied with a shrug. 'Perhaps she lied?'

'Do you know anything else about this child?' Leigh asked, her brow furrowed.

'A daughter. She's about five and probably lives with her father. But that's all I was told. Nerys apparently let it slip to one of the girls she was close to. But then she clammed up and wouldn't say any more about her.'

'Five? So Nerys would have been sixteen when she had her?'

Grace nodded.

Leigh frowned again and shook her head. 'It doesn't make sense. You can't just have a child and there be no record of it.'

'Maybe she lied? Or was confused? Or delusional? Who knows what that poor girl had been through?'

Leigh rubbed her temple and closed her eyes.

'Why does this information about a possible child have you so rattled?' Grace asked.

Leigh opened her eyes and stared at Grace. 'It doesn't. It's just a surprise.'

'Don't bullshit me, Leigh. I can tell this has you spooked. What is it you're not telling me?'

'I really can't say. I shouldn't be talking to you about the pertinent details of the case.''I think it's a bit late for that now, don't you? If you want my help at least have the courtesy to

be honest with me,' Grace said.

'It's not that easy, Grace,' Leigh said with a sigh. 'I haven't told you anything yet that couldn't easily be gleaned from the media reports, but this information could be crucial to the investigation. And for that reason, it's being kept from the public.'

'I'm not exactly the public though, am I?'

'You're not police either though,' Leigh reminded her.

'Yet you still came to me for help. So, do you want it, or not?' Grace snapped.

Shaking her head in defeat, Leigh leaned forward. 'This can't go any further. Promise me.'

'You already know I can keep a secret, Leigh,' Grace replied pointedly.

'I suppose so. Nerys had something secreted on her person when we found her. It was a child's tooth.'

Grace frowned. 'A tooth?'

'Yes. I know. Weird, isn't it?'

'Very,' Grace replied. 'Do you think it could have been her own child's then? If she does have one, that is?'

'Could be,' Leigh replied with a shrug. 'We don't know whether it was something of significance to the killer or her. Either way, it must have meant something to her. She forced it into one of the welts on her wrist.'

Grace felt a shudder run along the length of her spine as she thought about what poor Nerys must have endured. 'Is there any way to identify who the tooth belongs to?'

'Sadly not. Not using any scientific methods anyway. This will take good old-fashioned police work. Or someone who has a knack for getting information out of people,' Leigh said, tilting her head and looking at Grace.

'I have to admit I'm intrigued,' Grace said. 'The possibility that Nerys had a daughter there is no record of, and the tooth ... they have my interest piqued, but you have a team of trained detectives to look into this. I'm not sure I can help you any further. I'm not even sure I want to.'

'I'd ask you to reconsider but I understand, and I appreciate you speaking to the women at Number 69 for me. And if you hear anything else at all that you think might help, I'd really appreciate you letting me know.'

'Okay,' Grace said as she picked up her drink and took a sip. 'So, how are things with you and that Sergeant now that you're no longer working together?'

Leigh rolled her eyes. 'Don't ask.'

'Oh? Trouble in paradise?'

'Well, it was never really paradise to start with. But...'

'But?'

'It was as close to a decent relationship that I'll ever get. But things were different after what happened. Every time I looked at him, I just felt so much guilt. If he hadn't been following my orders... If I hadn't been so obsessed with bringing Alastair – and you – down, then it wouldn't have happened, would it?'

'Leigh, you can't think like that. He's a copper. He was doing his job. You lot put your lives on the line every day, don't you? I'm sure he doesn't blame you at all.'

Leigh shook her head. 'That's just it. He doesn't. He was

so bloody nice about the whole thing that I could hardly stand to look at him. If he'd just been angry with me, or made my life a little less easy, or we could have had a huge argument, maybe I would feel a little better?'

'So, are you two over then?'

Leigh looked down at the table before she answered. 'Yes,' she said with a sigh. 'If the guilt wasn't bad enough, then it would only be a matter of time before he discovered that I had come to you to rescue him. He'd eventually have found out about our connection, and he would never look at me the same again. I don't think I could handle that. And he deserves so much better.'

'Isn't that up to him to decide?' Grace asked.

'Maybe. But I've decided I'm not cut out for relationships. I'm better off on my own. It's much less hassle that way, anyway.'

'I get you. I used to think that,' Grace said as she stared at the woman who was so much like her, but so very different.

'What changed?' Leigh asked.

'Michael Carter,' Grace said with a smile. 'He was someone worth breaking all of my rules for. Maybe one day you'll meet someone worth breaking all of yours for?'

Leigh snorted and downed the last of her Diet Coke. 'Thanks for the drink and the pep talk,' she said as she flashed Grace a sarcastic smile.

'Any time,' she quipped back.

'I do appreciate the information though,' Leigh said seriously as she fastened up her coat. 'Thanks again.'

'No problem,' Grace replied and then she watched Leigh

walk out of the bar. Grace sat back in her seat and again inhaled the unmistakeable aroma of an old-fashioned pub. It was soothing to her. She felt a brief twinge of guilt over Leigh's relationship ending. The truth was that it was Grace who had arranged for DS Nick Bryce's kidnapping a few months earlier. He'd been leverage in her plan to get Jake and Connor out of prison for murder. As it turned out, he was leverage that she hadn't needed in the end, when she had persuaded Bradley Johnson to take the fall for his brother Billy's murder instead. It was the least he could do for the family that he had continually, and royally, shafted. But although Grace felt a brief pang of guilt for the impact it had had on Leigh's relationship, she wouldn't lose any sleep over it. She would do anything to protect her family. She always had and she always would. It was one of the ways that she and Leigh were very different.

Chapter Nine

Grace sat on the small sofa next to Michael in their office in Sophia's Kitchen. She leaned back against the soft leather and he put his arm around her shoulders. Sean sat on the chair behind the desk and turned to face the two of them.

'Do you think there will be any comeback from last night then?' Grace asked.

'Maybe,' Michael replied with a sigh. 'I've just spoken to Luke and Danny and they've had trouble with Parnell before. Let's hope last night was enough to warn them off.'

'We certainly proved our point last night,' Sean said. 'But...'

'But what?' Grace asked.

'But Parnell is a prize fuck-nugget,' Sean said with a grin.

'I've spoken to Luke and Danny about taking on some extra staff and increasing bodies at all our venues, especially here and The Blue Rooms. If Joey decides to rally whatever troops he has and wants to make a statement—'

'You mean wants to sign his own death warrant?' Sean interrupted with a frown.

Michael nodded in agreement. 'If he does, then he will target our highest-value and most high-profile venues. As well as that, they are the two places where us or the boys are most likely to be, and that would be the icing on the cake for him if he could get to any one of our family.'

Grace shook her head. 'He'd have to be crazy to try. Or completely stupid?'

Sean leaned back in his chair and sighed. 'Unfortunately, Grace, Joey Parnell is both of those things.'

Michael rubbed a hand over his beard. 'I think we're missing something else.'

'What?' Grace asked.

'I think someone else is backing Joey. Someone with a lot of clout given that he's managed to get a foot in the door so quickly.'

'But we know all of the people with clout in this business,' Grace said. 'Most of them work for us,' she reminded him.

'I know. Maybe it's someone we don't know? Someone from another area who wants to move in on the Liverpool security business and is using Joey to do it? I do know that he's been building himself a small army of recruits, which mostly seems to consist of all the people we've ever pissed off, sacked or had a major falling-out with. How he's managed to get some of them their SCA licences back I don't know.'

'Which adds weight to your theory that he's got someone with some power to wield behind him,' Grace said.

'Hmm,' Michael said, seemingly deep in thought.

'Well if he's hoovering up all of the dregs of society that you two have ever crossed, I'd suggest it's not so much a small army as a fucking huge one.' Sean said with a flash of his eyebrows.

'If there is someone big behind him, do you think they'll make a move on Jake and Connor's business?' Grace asked as she thought about the possible implications of yet another gangland war.

Michael and Sean both shook their heads. 'Parnell dabbled in a bit of dealing back in the day. He and his bouncers used to sell some tablets and a bit of coke on their doors, but he never really had the stomach or the brains to make a success of it, and I'm not sure that's changed. Besides, I've not heard anything at all about any new players moving in. On that score at least, the business seems to be running smoothly,' Michael said.

'Good,' Grace said with a sigh of relief. 'At least that's one less thing to worry about. We could do without another war.'

Michael and Sean looked at each other.

'What?' Grace asked.

'You realise a dispute over the doors will be just as bloody and brutal as any over drugs, don't you?'

'Of course I do. But at least the security business is legitimate. There are things we can do out in the open too.'

'Such as?' Michael asked.

'We can use our contacts in the licensing commission. The police. The council. We have the best team of lawyers in the North West. There are lots of ways we can disrupt our competitors' business legally too.'

'The lady has a point,' Sean agreed.

'She always does,' Michael said with a smile before kissing Grace on the forehead.

Sean rolled his eyes and grinned.

Michael stood up. 'I'm going to go and order us some coffee and cake before we go over the plans for the new place. I've seen some of Grace's ideas already, bro, and I think we're going to need something to take the edge off when we see how much it's going to cost us,' he said with a grin as he patted Sean on the back.

'Oi, you cheeky sod,' Grace said.

'God, I remember the days when a business meeting would be powered by whisky and cocaine, and now we're taking the edge off with coffee and cake?' Sean started to laugh as he shook his head.

'Well, we're too old for that now. And I've got two kids to pick up in a few hours,' Michael said, and laughed too. 'Besides, you could never handle your whisky, or your coke, if I recall?'

Sean stuck his middle finger up in response and Michael disappeared out of the office.

Grace laughed at the two of them. It wasn't often the three of them got to sit down together for long any more. They had five restaurants and a wine bar together already as well as the new venture Grace was working on. In addition, Grace and Michael still oversaw the running of

Cartel Securities and kept an eye on Jake and Connor's businesses too. Sometimes it felt like there weren't enough hours in the day. Grace sometimes wondered how much easier and less stressful life would be if she and Michael could just focus on the restaurants with Sean. It would have a positive impact on all of them as Sean often had to pick up the slack on some of the restaurant business that Grace and Michael just didn't have the time for.

Grace and Michael had plenty of people they could delegate to, but she found it hard to trust that someone was as capable of the task as they were, and as a result, she trusted very few. It ended up that she, Michael and Sean were left to do everything and she knew that something had to give soon. She sensed that something was about to change though. Grace had a good feeling about Luke Sullivan and Danny Alexander. They had proven themselves to be loyal, hardworking and a great fit for Cartel Securities. There was just something about them. Plenty of charm and charisma, which was handy when negotiating a business deal, but also when persuading a group of drunks or wannabe gangsters that they really had chosen the wrong firm to pick a fight with. Luke, in particular, used his head to sort out problems just as much as his fists and Grace really liked that about him. In fact, Danny and Luke reminded her a little of Michael and Sean when they were younger.

She realised she was smiling to herself when Sean spoke.

'You're looking very pleased with yourself, Grace. What are you up to?' he asked.

'I'm just looking forward to showing you and Michael

the plans for the new place. It's going to be stunning,' she said as she walked over to the desk and perched on the edge of it.

'It's nice to see you and Michael so happy,' he said and she detected a hint of something in his voice.

She placed a hand on his shoulder. 'What's going on with you?'

He looked up at her. 'Nothing. Why?'

'Why on earth did you go with Michael and the lads last night?'

'Because Parnell is a nasty cunt and I thought my brother and my nephews might need some backup. Is that a problem?' he said with a frown.

Grace shook her head. 'Not for me it's not. In fact, it makes me feel better to know that you've got their backs. But you promised you'd left all of that behind. I don't understand why you're allowing yourself to get sucked back in again.'

'Except when you need me?' Sean snapped. 'Then it's okay?'

Grace blinked at him. 'That is completely unfair, Sean, and you know it. I have only asked for your help once and that is when your brother and my son were kidnapped and almost tortured to death,' she snapped. 'You decided to help us deal with Alastair McGrath all on your own.'

He didn't respond and continued to glare at her.

'Unless you're talking about the time when I was kidnapped? I didn't exactly ask for your help then either,' she said.

His face softened then and he ran a hand through his thick, dark hair. 'Of course I didn't mean that, Grace.'

'Then what did you mean?'

He sat back against the chair and sighed. 'Nothing. I'm just looking for someone to blame. It's easier than admitting that I miss it all. I loved going out with the lads last night and getting stuck in. I miss working with Michael – and you. I hardly see you both anymore. I miss the old days,' he said with a wry smile and shake of his head. 'Maybe I'm having some kind of midlife crisis?'

Grace smiled at him. 'I know we haven't been around as much as we used to be. But we're working on that. As for the other stuff, are you crazy? Sophia will kill you if she finds out. You promised her you were done with all of that. For her and your girls' sake,' she reminded him.

'I know. But the girls are older now. Sophia is working in Antonelli's with Steph and she's loving it. So, she's less bothered about it than she used to be.' Steph was Sean and Sophia's oldest daughter and, having inherited both her mother and father's flair for cooking, was an incredible chef. She devised and oversaw the menus in all of their restaurants, but Antonelli's was her favourite and where she chose to base herself. Sophia had started working there a few months earlier too, now that their younger daughters, Nicola and Louise, were in high school.

'Has she told you that?' Grace asked.

He looked at her.

'Has she?'

'Not in so many words, no.'

Grace stared at her brother-in-law. She loved him dearly.

Even before she had married Michael, Sean had been one of her closest friends. But she loved his wife Sophia too, and they had always seemed like the perfect couple. Before she and Michael had got together, she had always envied Sean and Sophia's strong relationship.

'Are you and Sophia okay?' she asked quietly.

He looked into her eyes. 'Yes,' he said firmly. 'It's nothing like that. I just miss being in the thick of it, that's all.'

'Your brother wants out and you want back in? What are you both, some kind of tag team?' she said with a laugh.

He laughed too and she was relieved that there was no further tension between them. Just then, Michael walked back into the room carrying a tray loaded with coffees and cake.

He placed the tray down on the desk.

'How much cake did you get?' Grace asked as she eyed the tray full of pastries and gateaux.

'Yeah. Just how much is this new place going to cost us?' Sean asked as he stared at the tray.

Michael laughed. 'They're not all for us. They were about to be binned. I'll take what we don't eat to Dad and Sue when I pick the kids up.'

Sean nodded. 'Right, show me the plans for our new gaff then.'

Chapter Ten

G race walked into the offices of Cartel Securities. She and Michael had handed over the day-to-day running of the business to their new business partners, Luke Sullivan and Danny Alexander. Grace and Michael were still the CEOs but they left most of the operational decision-making to Luke and Danny. Grace liked to call in from time to time to see how things were going. Luke and Danny were a great fit for the growing Carter/Conlon empire. They were proving themselves to be assets and had become indispensable to Jake and Connor, which only made them go up further in her estimation.

The door to Michael's old office, now Luke and Danny's, at the back of the building was closed. Grace tapped lightly on the door.

'Come in,' she heard Luke shout.

Grace stepped inside to see Luke, Danny and a young woman whom she'd never met before. The three of them looked slightly awkward, making her wonder what she had walked in on.

'Hi, Grace,' Luke said with a smile as he crossed the office to stand in front of her, leaving Danny to scowl in the corner and the woman looking similarly annoyed.

'Hi,' Grace replied. 'I've just called in to pick up that paperwork for the new contract. Have you both signed it?'

'Of course,' Luke said as he walked towards the desk and picked up an A4 envelope from the top of a pile.

Whatever look passed between him and Danny obviously snapped Danny from his bad mood. 'Nice to see you, Grace,' Danny said with a flash of his charming smile. 'I don't think you've met my little sister, Stacey?'

Grace looked at the young woman and saw the resemblance to her older brother. 'No, I don't think I've had the pleasure,' she said as she stepped forward and offered her hand.

Stacey shook it warmly and smiled, whatever annoyance had been bothering her momentarily forgotten. 'Hi, Grace. It's so lovely to meet you. I've heard so much about you.'

'Well, don't believe everything you hear,' Grace replied with a laugh.

'Oh, it's all been good, don't worry.' Stacey laughed too. 'Luke and Danny love working for you.'

Grace looked over at the two men. 'Glad to hear it. They're a great addition to our team.'

They both smiled appreciatively. There was still tension in the room and Grace decided she'd take the paperwork and leave, not wanting to get involved in any family drama. She knew that Luke was an only child and that he and Danny were like brothers. She wondered how Stacey fitted into their relationship. Was she close to Luke too?

'I'll take those papers and head off,' Grace said.

Luke handed them to her. 'You're not going to stay for a coffee?' he asked.

'Not today, thanks. I'll leave you all to it.'

'I'll walk out with you, Grace,' Stacey said as she picked up her handbag. 'I really need some air.'

'Stace!' Danny snapped.

'I'm done arguing with you,' she said as she lifted her bag onto her shoulder.

'At least let one of the lads take you home,' Danny said with a sigh.

'I can drive you,' Luke added.

'I can look after myself,' she snapped.

'I can offer you a lift?' Grace said.

Stacey smiled. 'That would be great. Thank you.'

That seemed to satisfy Danny. 'I'll call you later,' he said to Stacey.

Grace and Stacey had said their goodbyes and were sitting in Grace's car on the way to Stacey's flat in Aigburth when Stacey spoke. 'Do you have any annoying older brothers, Grace?'

'Nope. I'm an only child. I always wanted a brother though – or a sister.'

'I'm sorry. I know I'm lucky to have a brother who cares

about me so much, but sometimes it feels like he still treats me like I'm fourteen instead of twenty-four. It's suffocating.'

'At least you know it comes from a good place?' Grace offered, although the truth was she knew little about Danny and Stacey's background. He had mentioned a sister who had recently returned to Liverpool, but he hadn't talked a lot about her.

'I know it does, and believe me, he has good reason to feel protective, at least he did when we were kids, but he doesn't seem to realise that I'm a grown woman who can look after myself,' she said with a shake of her head.

'He went to prison when you were young, didn't he?'

'Yeah. I was only thirteen. He still feels so guilty about it.'

'About what he did?' Grace asked. She knew that Danny had killed his abusive stepfather in a fight, and wondered why he would feel any guilt over that.

She shook her head. 'No, not about killing that rotten excuse for a human being. For me having to go into care.'

'Oh, I see. It seemed like you were in the middle of something when I walked in. Everything okay?' Grace asked.

Stacey paused before answering. 'I have such a complicated back story, it's hard to explain, to be honest. But let's just say my ex is a real nasty piece of work and he's on the missing list. The police are looking for him and before he disappeared a couple of months ago, he made contact with me again. There's been nothing since, and I have no idea what's happened to him, but Danny and Luke are convinced that I'm in some sort of danger.

They would keep me wrapped up in cotton wool if they could.'

'Well, that's understandable, I suppose. Protecting people is their job after all.'

'I know you're right, and for the most part I accept that, but when they try to interfere in my life, well, it really pisses me off,' she said with a sigh.

Grace glanced at her watch and saw it was almost lunchtime. 'Do you have anywhere to be?' she asked.

Stacey shook her head. 'No. I lost my temping job last week, so I'm a free agent.'

'Do you fancy grabbing a quick bite to eat? I'm meeting Michael at one of our restaurants in an hour or so. We could get some lunch first? My treat.'

Stacey turned to her and smiled. 'That would be lovely. Thank you.'

Thirty minutes later Grace and Stacey were sitting at one of the best tables in Sophia's Kitchen waiting for their food to be delivered.

'Thank you for this, Grace. I love this place,' she said with a beaming smile. 'It's not the easiest place to get a table at though.'

'What? Just ask Danny or Luke and they can get you a table any time.'

'I know. But I'd rather not ask them for favours. It kind of undermines my argument that I don't need anything from them,' she said wryly.

'I suppose so. Well, now that you know me, you can always ask me instead.'

'Oh, thank you, Grace. That's so kind of you. But to be honest, I don't have that many people I can go to places like this with. When I do go for dinner, it's usually with Danny anyway. I don't really have any friends as such.'

'Oh?' Grace was surprised. In the very short time Grace had known Stacey she had found her to be bright and funny, and generally good company.

'I find it hard to trust people that I don't know,' Stacey replied. 'Which makes this a bit odd, because I feel like I could talk to you for hours,' she said. 'I suppose I feel like I know you. Danny and Luke talk about you a lot,' she said with a grin. 'They absolutely love working for you.'

'What are you going to do now for work then? You said you lost your job?'

'Yeah. It was only a temping job working as a receptionist at an accountant's. I was providing maternity cover, so I knew it wouldn't last. But I'd been there for six months and I was really starting to enjoy it. I got a good reference though and I'm sure the agency will find me something else, but I'd like to find something permanent. But I have so little experience. I've never really worked since leaving college – which is a whole other story – so most girls my age have been doing this for years already. That's kind of what I was arguing with Danny about.'

'Oh? Why?'

'I was looking at some jobs in hospitality. I do have some qualifications, but I'd like to work my way up, so I was thinking waitressing or bar work just to get some experience under my belt before I started applying for the more senior-level jobs.'

'Why were you arguing about that?'

'Oh, I don't know. I think they'd prefer me to stay in a quiet little office somewhere. And that would be fine, but there are no quiet little office jobs around. Not that I can find anyway.'

'Well, I can't offer you a quiet little office job,' Grace said. 'But I do have an opening for a waitress in one of the busiest and most exclusive restaurants in Liverpool.'

Stacey stared at her. 'What? Here?'

'Why not?'

Stacey shrugged. 'I heard competition is fierce to get a job here, that's all. I've never done waitressing before, you know.'

'You mentioned that. But it would be a week's trial. If you don't cut the mustard, you don't get the job and you move on. No harm done.'

'But why? Why would you give me this opportunity? Don't get me wrong, I'm grateful, but I'm happy to work my way up from the bottom. I don't want any special treatment,' she said as she looked down at the table.

'It's not exactly special treatment. I need a waitress. You need a job. I like you. I like your brother and if you have his work ethic then you'll be fine here. My gut very rarely lets me down, and I have a good feeling about you, Stacey.'

Stacey looked up with a smile. 'I don't suppose Danny and Luke can protest too much about *you* offering me a job, can they?' She started to laugh.

'Can you start tonight?'

Stacey nodded eagerly.

'Good. I'll introduce you to Lena after we've eaten. She's our new head waitress. She will tell you all you need to know and give you your shifts for the next week.'

'Fantastic.' Stacey beamed. 'I won't let you down. Promise. I'm so glad I bumped into you today. A slap-up lunch and a job, that's not a bad afternoon.' She raised her glass of iced water in a toast. 'To new beginnings.'

Grace raised her glass too. 'Indeed,' she replied with a smile. She had a good feeling about Stacey Alexander.

Chapter Eleven

Leigh Moss was in her office sifting through the evidence of what was now being colloquially referred to as the Liverpool Ripper case. She knew there was a vital clue left by the killer. There always was, but for now, it was eluding her. The killer was clever, or at least one of them was. The theory that there might be more than one perpetrator was one she'd been mulling over since Grace had first mentioned it a few days earlier. She supposed it would make sense. Three bodies in just over a month was a lot to deal with. Not only that, all three victims hadn't been seen for two to three weeks prior to their deaths, and their wounds indicated they had been bound and abused for some time prior to being killed. That was a lot for one man to cover up on his own.

Leigh sat back in her chair and rubbed the bridge of her nose. It was dark outside and she was alone in the office. She switched on her desk lamp and took a swig of her lukewarm coffee. She would give it another half an hour before heading home to her empty house. She missed Nick. When it was cold out, he'd always have the central heating on by the time she got home. The kitchen was always filled with the smell of food – whether it be a takeaway or something he'd picked up from the supermarket that he could bung into the oven. He wasn't a great cook, but he could follow instructions on a packet.

The shrill ringing of Leigh's office phone echoed around the empty floor and snapped her from her melancholy. She wondered who it could be at this time of night.

Picking up the receiver, she placed it to her ear. 'Hello?'

'Leigh,' she heard the voice of her colleague from Greater Manchester police, DI Natalie Smith. 'I thought I'd probably catch you still at your desk. You're a workaholic like me,' Natalie said with a laugh.

'Hi, Nat,' Leigh said, thankful for the distraction. 'It's lovely to hear your voice. How are things?'

'Oh, you know, same old, same old. I was thinking before how I haven't seen you for ages, so thought I'd give you a call and see how things are.'

'I know. I'm sorry I cancelled our last night out, but we got this case—'

'Oh, God, don't worry about that, Leigh. I know how it is,' Natalie interrupted her. 'How is your investigation going anyway?'

Leigh sighed heavily. 'Not as well as I'd like it to, let's just put it that way.'

'Oh, like that, is it?' Natalie asked sympathetically.

'Yep.'

'I read the newspaper reports and saw your interview on the news. You were very good.'

Leigh cringed at the memory. It should have been the DCI leading the briefing but she'd been involved in a minor car accident on the way and Leigh had to step in at the last minute. She'd had the appropriate experience and training to talk to the press, but it wasn't a role she particularly enjoyed. 'Thanks, Nat. But I hated every second.'

Natalie laughed. 'I can imagine. Anyway, I wanted to tell you about another case it got me thinking about. It was about six months after our trafficking case wrapped up, so two years ago. The victim was Melanie Simmonds.'

Leigh listened intently as Natalie gave her the details of the case in Manchester, which had some similarities to the Liverpool Ripper, enough at least to raise Leigh's suspicions as well as her colleague's.

'And you never caught the perp?' Leigh asked after Natalie had given her the case summary.

'No. She was naked and there was evidence of recent sexual activity as well as penetration with a blunt object, which we believe was non-consensual due to the other injuries, but the cause of death was strangulation.'

'So there was DNA on the body?'

'Yes, there were traces of semen in her vagina. But there were no matches on the databases. Because of the strangulation and the sexual activity, it was assumed we were looking for a disgruntled customer or her pimp. We interviewed dozens of suspects and collected DNA samples but no matches.'

'Perhaps the DNA wasn't from the killer?'

'It's a possibility, but like your victims, Melanie hadn't been seen for a couple of weeks prior to her death and she had ligature marks on her wrists. It was suggested that they could have been made during the course of her work – she was known for being willing to engage in bondage – but it could well have been that she was being held somewhere beforehand.'

'There are similarities, Nat,' Leigh said with a sigh. 'But there are stark differences too. Our killer hasn't left any DNA for a start and there was no evidence of sexual activity, at least immediately prior to death. Perhaps it was a heat-of-the-moment act?'

'Perhaps. Or perhaps efforts were made to try and make it look like one?'

'Maybe? I feel like my judgement is clouded with this one. I'm so desperate to catch this bastard, I don't want to be seeing links where there are none.'

'I get that. Let me send you the case file and see what you think.'

'What do you think? You know the case and I trust your judgement.'

'If I'm honest, Leigh, my gut tells me that this has something to do with our trafficking case.'

'What? How?'

'Melanie Simmonds mixed in the same circles as some of our trafficking victims. She was often the *entertainment* for the same parties. At least one of her former pimps was one of the men we put away. Perhaps she was a loose end?'

Leigh picked up her pencil and started scribbling notes on the yellow notepad beside her.

'Did you pursue that line of inquiry?' Leigh asked.

'Not officially. As you know, any suggestion that we didn't get the whole trafficking ring isn't welcomed by the powers that be. But I looked into it as much as I could, not being one of the officers on the case. But from the little digging I was able to do, I wouldn't put it past our very own Teflon Ted to have had a hand in it.'

'Shit!' Leigh breathed. Teflon Ted was the name the two of them had given to Sol Shepherd, one of the biggest gangsters Manchester had ever seen, and who they believed was one of the big players behind the trafficking ring they had helped to bring down years earlier. Despite Leigh and Natalie's efforts as the two Detective Sergeants on the case, they were never able to provide any concrete evidence of his involvement, and despite him being arrested and questioned, his expensive brief had ensured he'd never been within two feet of a courtroom. Then there had been threats of legal action for harassment and defamation of character, and Chief Superintendent Barrow, who had been in charge of overseeing the strategic elements of the joint investigation between Greater Manchester and Merseyside police, had warned them off.

'Exactly,' Natalie said.

'Send me what you can then please, Nat. And thanks.'

'No problem. I hope you catch the bastard anyway, Leigh, even if it's nothing to do with Melanie.'

'Thanks, Nat. I'll give you a call soon.'

'Bye, Leigh.'

Leigh put down the receiver and leaned back in her chair. Her brain had kicked into overdrive as she started to formulate ideas about this whole new angle on the case. She felt the adrenalin starting to course around her body as she considered the implications and possible connections to the trafficking case. If there was a connection, why was the killer now targeting women from Liverpool, and in particular from the Sunnymeade children's home?

Chapter Twelve

Joey Parnell walked up the steps of the small wine bar in Birkdale. He winced and held his ribs as he pulled open the heavy glass door. He was still in considerable pain from the kicking Michael Carter had given him a few nights before. He hated that cunt and one day soon he would kill the arrogant fucker, his cock of a brother and his stuck-up bitch of a wife too. Joey walked through the empty bar towards the small table at the back where the man he worked for was sitting, cradling a glass of whisky.

'Have a seat,' his boss, whom Joey was only ever allowed to refer to as JB, said.

Joey sat down opposite him, noting the other glass on the table but not reaching out for it until he was given permission to.

'What the hell has happened to you?' JB snapped with a frown as he stared at Joey's bruised face.

Joey touched his lip gingerly and winced. 'That cunt

Michael Carter and his firm paid me a visit. Don't worry, I'll pay him back.'

JB's face turned bright red and he brought his fist crashing down onto the table. 'You're lucky that's all you've got, you stupid little prick! Didn't I teach you how to dispose of a body properly? How to clean it to make sure there was no evidence left?' he scowled.

Joey felt his heart jump into his throat. 'I did clean it, Boss. There was no trace of anything!' he insisted, hoping he was right.

'Really? You didn't notice that she had a tooth embedded in her fucking arm?' he hissed.

'A tooth? No! Whose tooth?' he asked as he unconsciously ran his tongue around the inside of his mouth checking for any missing teeth, despite knowing there were none.

'A child's tooth. But not just any child. Hers!' JB spat.

Joey looked at his boss and watched the vein throbbing in his temple. This was bad. 'She didn't have a kid,' he insisted.

'Well, it seems she did, Joseph. So now not only is this a murder investigation, it has also become a hunt for a child who up until yesterday didn't even exist. And all because you are a stupid fucking cretin! So, forgive me if I don't give a rat's arse about you getting a bit of a slap from Michael Carter. I did not bring you back here so you could start a fucking squabble with the Carters. You're being paid to do a job, not to mess about trying to exact your petty revenge over something that happened over twenty years ago.'

'I am doing my job, Boss,' Joey pleaded. 'I overlooked the tooth—'

'Because you got careless and cocky!' he snarled.

Joey looked down at his hands. God, he hated fucking up, especially when working for JB. 'Yes. But it won't happen again. I'll make sure this next one is thoroughly checked before I dump her.'

'You'd fucking better. And leave the Carters alone!'

'But they started it—'

'They started it? What are you? Twelve? You're a bloody disgrace,' he spat. 'Haven't you screwed up enough? How could you not notice that she had a child's tooth?' he spat in disgust.

The insult stung, but Joey shrugged it off. 'She hid it, Boss. I didn't see it. Besides, it was just a tooth. It was probably just something to remind her of her kid. She must have had it with her all along. It's not a big deal. It's not like it could tie us to anything.'

'Fortunately for you!' JB snapped. 'If you screw up like that again, it will be your teeth they'll be picking out of something with a pair of tweezers! So, do me a favour, and concentrate on the job I'm paying you for.'

'Okay, Boss. But you did say I could set the security firm up again. It's the perfect cover—'

'Set your poxy little firm up, or don't, I don't really care. But if you draw any unnecessary attention to me and what we're doing, then you'll regret it, Joey.'

Joey swallowed. His boss didn't have to spell out what would happen to him. He knew.

'So, tell me where we're at. Did you get any information at all from the last one?' JB asked.

Joey shrunk back in his seat, knowing that his answer to this question was not the one his boss was going to want to hear. 'No. She said she didn't know where it was, and if she did, she wouldn't give it up.'

He leaned forward, both fists on his desk now, as his face turned purple with rage. 'You promised me you were good at this, Joey. That's three of those little whores you've tortured and killed now, and we're no closer to finding out where this bloody memory card is. What the hell have I been paying you for if you can't get me answers?' he snarled. 'Do you have any idea what would happen if that were to fall into the wrong hands?'

'I know, Boss. But you told me not to keep them at the house for more than two weeks. You said people would start looking for them. So, I did what you said and once the two weeks was up, I got rid of them. And I did everything you told me to so there was no evidence on the bodies.'

'I know what I said, you ignorant little turd, but I assumed that two weeks would be enough for you to get the information you needed from them. I thought you were a professional?'

Joey swallowed again. 'I am. But if someone doesn't know anything, no amount of torture will make them talk. They were babbling all kinds of nonsense at the end, but not one of them could tell me where that memory card was.'

His boss scowled at him and sat back in his chair. 'Maybe I should have approached one of your competitors to help me out instead,' he snorted. 'I bet Michael or Sean Carter could have got those whores to talk.'

Joey frowned but didn't respond.

'But I don't suppose they go in for that line of work?' He grinned at Joey then, a twinkle in his eyes. 'It takes someone with a certain skill set to be able to torture a woman like that, doesn't it, Joseph?'

'Yes.'

'And I'm not sure those Carter boys have the stomachs for it.'

'Pair of pussies,' Joey spat.

His boss started to laugh then and poured himself and Joey a glass of whisky. 'When this is all over, you can tell me how much they screamed,' he said, the glint in his eye all too evident to Joey, who understood the reason for it better than most. 'So, you still have number four. Is she talking?'

Joey shook his head. 'She says she knows nothing about it. But I've only had her for a week. Give me a bit longer?'

JB scowled. 'And then what? What's your next move then? Tell me how you're going to get this memory card for me.'

Joey took the glass of Scotch and downed it in one. His boss's mood could change at the drop of a hat and he wanted to get out of there before it changed again. 'Simon Jones. He's the key to all of this. He's the one who said one of the girls had the card, but it looks like he was just trying to throw the heat onto them.'

'No shit!' JB said with a shake of his head.

'He's been on the missing list for two months now, but I'll find him, boss,' Joey went on.

'And how are you intending to do that?' JB asked as he sipped his whisky, his eyes burning into Joey's all the while.

'His ex-girlfriend has moved back to Liverpool. I've been keeping tabs on her. He's made contact once and it's only a matter of time before he does it again.'

'And we're just going to wait for this to happen?' JB asked.

Joey nodded but sensed he was about to get another bollocking.

'So your plan is for you to hang around scratching your balls and wait for Simon to fall into your lap, is it? Do you think I have time for that? I'm a very busy man, Joey, and I want this whole mess dealt with. If you don't come through with something for me soon, I'll be forced to take my services elsewhere.'

Joey's heart began to race as he realised the threat implicit in that statement. 'I'll sort it, Boss,' he assured him.

'Use the ex-girlfriend as bait if you have to. But find me that bloody card or you'll be on a general population wing in HMP Walton faster than you can blink. And when that lot find out what you've done ... well, I don't have to spell it out for you, Joseph, but you'll be shitting via a bag within the week.'

Joey felt the bile rise in his throat, as he always did when he thought about going back to prison.

'I'll find the card,' he said, with more confidence than he felt.

'You better had. Now get out of here before someone sees you,' he barked.

Chapter Thirteen

Grace walked into Sophia's Kitchen and noticed Stacey sitting near the bar. It had been three days since she'd offered her a job as a waitress and initial reports were that she'd been an excellent addition to the team. She hadn't put one foot wrong yet, and providing there were no major calamities between now and the end of the week, she would be offered a permanent contract.

Grace walked over to her. The restaurant was quiet after the lunchtime rush and Stacey was reading the *Liverpool Echo*.

Grace walked up and stood beside her. 'Hi, Stacey. How's it going?'

Stacey looked up and blinked and Grace noticed the tears in her eyes. 'Oh, hi, Grace,' she said as she wiped her cheek with the back of her hand and sat up straight on the stool.

'What's wrong?' Grace asked.

Stacey glanced back at the newspaper. 'I was just

reading an article about that girl they found last week. I knew her, that's all.'

Grace frowned. This was certainly an interesting development. 'Oh? How?'

'We went to the same children's home. She was a couple of years younger than me and we weren't really friends. But I remember her...' Stacey shook her head and wiped another tear from her cheek.

Grace put an arm around the younger woman's shoulder. 'Why don't you come on into the back.'

'My break finishes in a minute,' Stacey said with a sniff.

'That's okay. I'm sure they can manage without you for a little longer. Come on.'

Stacey slipped off the bar stool before following Grace into the back of the restaurant. Grace saw Lena as they passed. 'I just need to speak to Stacey about something. Can you manage without her for half an hour?'

Lena flashed her megawatt smile. 'Of course. No problem, Grace,' she replied as she walked away with a swish of her flaming red hair.

———

Stacey was sitting in the chair opposite Grace with a glass of brandy in her hand when Grace finally asked her the question that had been bothering her for the past ten minutes. 'So, how did you know Nerys Sheehan?'

Stacey took a sip of her brandy and then placed the glass on Grace's desk. 'I didn't know her that well, really. I spent a couple of years at Sunnymeade when Danny went to prison. I was fifteen when Nerys arrived and she was probably about eleven or twelve then. I didn't have that much to do with the younger kids, I didn't have much to do with anyone to be honest, but I remember her because she had an unusual name and she used to try and run away all the time. There were plenty of kids who tried to leg it, but she was persistent. She thought of all kinds of ingenious ways to get out of the place – but they always found her. Poor kid. I think she was one of the ones who really suffered there, if you know what I mean?' Stacey sniffed.

Grace assumed that Stacey was alluding to the allegations of physical and sexual abuse that had dogged the place in the years before it had finally been closed down by the council amid a huge court case involving the warden and his wife. 'Were you ever targeted in there?'

Stacey stared at Grace and picked up her glass, taking another sip of the brandy. 'Once. I'd only been there for a couple of months. He cornered me in the kitchen late one night when I'd sneaked downstairs for a drink. I had a sore throat and I couldn't get to sleep.' She shook her head. 'Anyway, he put his hand up my nightie, but thankfully the caretaker came in and disturbed him. He acted like nothing had happened and then he told me to get to bed and patted me on the backside.' She shuddered. 'God, he was a vile creep. I don't know how him and his wife managed to get away with what they did for so long. But everyone in that place was terrified of them, especially him.'

'But it never happened again?' Grace asked.

Stacey shook her head. 'Never. The next day Luke paid a surprise visit to Sunnymeade. He used to visit and take me out to the cinema or shopping every other Saturday, but he'd never visited on a weekday before. I wouldn't have even seen him if I hadn't been sent home from school early because I had tonsillitis. Anyway, I saw him coming out of the office and he pretended he was there to see me. Whatever he'd said or done, that creep left me alone after that.'

'How did Luke know what had happened?' Grace asked.

'Tony, the caretaker, I assume. Luke and Danny both had reputations even back then, and I think Tony was a little in awe of them.'

Grace nodded.

'Anyway, did you know her too?' Stacey sniffed.

Grace's mind was racing with questions and Stacey's question threw her. 'Who?' she asked.

'Nerys?'

'Oh, no.' Grace shook her head. 'But she used to work at a place I know of, that's all. Do you remember anything else about her? Anyone she was close to? Any visitors?'

'She was always hanging around with this other kid. I always thought he was a bit odd, but I suppose he was just quiet. No one really liked him – no one except Nerys and a couple of the other young girls anyway.'

'What was his name?'

Stacey sucked on her top lip and appeared deep in thought. 'God, I can't remember. Maybe Steven? Or Stuart?'

'When was the last time you saw Nerys?'

'It would have been the day I left that God-awful shithole, on my sixteenth birthday. She gave me a hug and I remember thinking how sad and small she looked. I'm sure she'd have climbed into my backpack and snuck out of there if she could. I almost wanted to stuff her in there and see if she'd fit. If I had, maybe she wouldn't have ended up on the front page of the *Echo*.'

'Do you think what happened to her had anything to do with the home?' Grace asked.

Stacey paused briefly before answering. 'Not directly. Collins and his wife are in prison, aren't they? But who knows? I don't doubt that being in that place and what she went through there played a huge part in the path she chose in life, don't you? I'm not sure anyone got out of there unscathed,' she said as she looked down and started picking her fingernails.

'Not even you?' Grace said quietly.

Stacey looked up and held Grace's gaze. 'Not even me,' she said with a resigned smile. Then she picked up the glass of brandy and downed the last of her drink before standing. 'I think I've bored you enough with my childhood stories. I'd better get back to work before Lena comes looking for me.'

'It was nice chatting, Stacey.'

Stacey smiled. 'Yeah. It was. Thanks, Grace.' She indicated the empty glass on the desk.

Grace sat back in her chair and closed her eyes after Stacey left her office. Despite what she had told Leigh about no longer wanting to be involved in the murder investigation, she couldn't stop thinking about the case. And now Stacey's disclosure had stoked her interest even further. There was something she was missing, she was sure of it. She wondered if the police had identified Nerys's childhood friend, Stuart or Steven. Had they spoken to him and ruled him out? Did they even know about him? Grace shook her head. This was none of her business. It was for the police to deal with, and despite her obvious issues with Merseyside's finest, she knew that they were perfectly capable of cracking the case without her assistance – even if it might take a little longer. Would that mean another young woman murdered in the meantime? Three women in just over a month, with the time between each murder growing shorter. Had the killer already identified his next victim? Was she already in danger – already silently pleading for someone to come and rescue her?

Grace shuddered, remembering the time a couple of years earlier when she had been kidnapped, held prisoner and almost raped. Her kidnappers had intended to kill her, of that she'd had no doubt. Fortunately, her ordeal had lasted only eight hours. Her disappearance had been noted and Michael had pulled out all of the stops to find her, but it had felt like a lifetime and it had left an indelible mark. She was still prone to bouts of claustrophobia in small, dark spaces and, due to the disgusting condition of the flat where she was held, the smell of stale food or weed made her gag. Was there some poor woman out there going through a similar ordeal, or about to? And was there a possibility that Grace could help to stop that happening?

Grace opened her eyes and scanned the room, looking for something that might perhaps jolt her brain into activity. She couldn't shake the feeling that there was something she wasn't seeing. She suddenly realised why Leigh enjoyed her job so much. There was something fascinating about taking a collection of obscure and seemingly unconnected, insignificant clues and piecing them together to solve a crime. She imagined that the feeling when you did was incredibly satisfying and addictive.

Grace had just switched on her laptop when her mobile phone started to vibrate on the desk beside her. She glanced at the screen and saw Leigh Moss's number.

Picking it up, she swiped the screen to answer. 'Hi, Leigh.'

'Grace. There's been a development. Can we talk?'

'What kind of development?' Grace asked.

'I'd rather not say over the phone. You'll want to hear about this though. I can promise you that.'

'Is there something I need to know about right now?' she asked sharply.

'Can we meet this afternoon?' Leigh suddenly started to talk in a whisper making Grace wonder if one of her colleagues had come within earshot.

Grace glanced at her watch. 'I have to pick Oscar up from nursery at five. I can give you an hour. Where do you want to meet?'

'How about one of your quieter restaurants?' Leigh asked. 'Stefano's?'

Grace considered the time. It was after the lunchtime rush at their restaurant on Hope Street on the other side of the city centre. Stefano's did most of their business in the evening, so she supposed it would be quiet enough for them to sit at a table and be relatively unnoticed and undisturbed.

'Okay. I'll meet you in fifteen minutes. If you get there before me, ask them for my usual table.'

'I will, and thank you, Grace.'

Grace ended the call and rubbed her temple to stem the throbbing of the headache that had been threatening for the past half-hour. She rummaged around in her desk drawer and found a box of paracetamol. Popping two into her mouth, she washed them down with the remains of the glass of water on her desk. What the hell did Leigh have for her now? Grace had a sinking feeling in the pit of her stomach. From the tone of Leigh's voice and her desire to meet as soon as possible, Grace had a feeling that she was about to be dragged further into the ongoing murder investigation, whether she wanted to be or not.

Chapter Fourteen

Stacey walked through the back of the restaurant to the bar area.

'You okay?' Lena, the assistant manager, asked with a sympathetic tilt of her head.

'Yeah, I'm fine, thanks,' she replied. 'What do you need me to do?'

Lena smiled. 'Table fourteen are waiting to order.'

Stacey pulled her notepad from her apron. 'I'll go and take that now,' she said before walking across the restaurant to the table near the window where the grey-haired couple in the finely tailored clothes were sitting. Stacey forced her warmest smile and began to take their order. She noted it down and passed it to the kitchen before taking some cleaning materials and starting to wipe down some of the tables in her section. She had done it earlier after the lunchtime rush, but the restaurant was quiet and she needed something to focus on – something that didn't require too much brainpower. Her conversation with Grace had her rattled. Anything to do with Sunnymeade made her feel on edge. Then she thought about Nerys. She remembered the scrawny little freckle-faced girl from Wales who'd arrived at Sunnymeade with the loudest voice of anyone Stacey had ever met before. Little Nerys could have cleared a room with the gob on her, but her time in the home soon knocked that out of her, as it knocked out most of the spirit of anyone who was unlucky enough to be sent there.

She wondered if Nerys had ever regained some of that fighting spirit she had once been renowned for – if only for a few short months. Did she fight her attacker? Or had she simply tried to comply with any demands, in the hope that it was the surest way to keep herself safe?

Stacey supposed that she had been lucky to escape Sunnymeade relatively unscathed, at least compared to a lot of the kids there. But the place had left its mark. When Danny had been released from prison when she was fifteen, he had fought to get her back, but children's services said he was unfit to be a guardian after his stint in prison. How bloody ironic! She had finally managed to leave when she turned sixteen and had lived on her own for a few months, until her little flat had been broken into and Danny had convinced her to move in with him. She had enjoyed being back living with her older brother. It had been nice to see Luke almost every day too as she'd had a massive crush on him back then. But soon, the guilt of what Danny had done to protect her started to eat away at her. Every time she saw his face, she was reminded of the sacrifices he had made for her. He had come out of prison a very different person to the one who had gone in. She supposed he'd just been a child when he'd gone away, and had become a man whilst he was in there. He was still her loving big brother, but he was different too. He no longer had any patience for anyone except her and Luke, and he was constantly getting into fights. If that wasn't enough to contend with, he had become so protective of her, it was almost unbearable. He questioned her every move. He interrogated every boy she so much as spoke to. It had been suffocating.

In an attempt to escape both her guilt and her overbearing brother, she had enrolled in college in Manchester and moved there when she was eighteen. It should have been the end of her worries – the start of a new, exciting life. Except it had been the start of a nightmare.

'You're going to remove a whole layer of wood from that table if you clean it any longer.' The voice snapped her from her thoughts. She looked up to see Lena standing beside her. 'You sure you're okay?'

'Yeah. Sorry, I'm just a bit distracted.'

'Well, speaking of distracted, here's your fine-looking brother and his hot mate,' she said as she gave Stacey a gentle nudge in the ribs.

Stacey looked up to see Danny and Luke walking through the doors of Sophia's Kitchen, smartly dressed in suits and looking every inch the pair of respectable businessmen they claimed to be. 'Oh, and look who else is making an appearance,' Lena said as she sucked the air in through her teeth. 'Jake Conlon,' she said, almost panting his name. 'God, he is fit,' she said as she started to adjust her blouse to ensure maximum cleavage.

Stacey started to laugh. 'It's a pity he's gay, isn't it?'

Lena stared at her open-mouthed. 'What? No way,' she gasped.

Stacey felt her cheeks redden. Danny had told her that and now she couldn't recall if it was supposed to be a secret. She didn't think so. She was usually so discreet. God, she hoped she hadn't just outed Jake Conlon. 'Maybe I misunderstood?' Stacey offered.

'Well, if it is true, what a waste of a man,' Lena said as she continued staring at the three men as they stood talking to the maître d'.

'What's a waste of a man?' their colleague Jamie suddenly piped up behind them.

Stacey groaned inwardly and wanted the ground to swallow her whole.

'Jake,' Lena whispered. 'Stacey reckons he's gay.'

'I never—' Stacey started but Jamie interrupted her.

'That is incredibly offensive, you know. I think most gay men would disagree with you.'

'That he's gay?' Lena asked.

'That it's a waste if he is,' he said with a roll of his eyes.

'You'd just be happy that a fitty like him was less competition for you, Jay,' Lena teased him.

'Can we stop talking about him being gay,' Stacey whispered as Danny, Luke and Jake started to walk over to them.

'Hey, sis,' Danny said with a flash of his trademark smile before nodding a greeting to Lena and Jamie.

Luke smiled at her and she felt her skin flush pink again.

'Do any of you know where my mum went? Did she say if she was coming back?' Jake asked them.

Stacey shook her head. She hadn't even noticed that Grace had left.

'She never said where she was going, but she said she'd see us tomorrow, so I don't think she's planning on coming back,' Lena replied.

'Shit!' Jake muttered.

'Anything I can help you with, Jake?' Lena said with a flutter of her eyelashes and her killer smile. If Jake noticed her flirting, nothing in his demeanour suggested it. 'Nah, it's okay, thanks,' he replied as he turned to his companions. 'We'll have to catch her later at home. Fancy a quick bite to eat while we're here?'

Luke nodded.

'Yeah, okay. I'm sure our Stace will be happy to wait on us hand and foot, won't you?' Danny said with a grin.

Stacey forced a smile in return. 'Of course, Sir,' she replied sarcastically. 'Sit wherever you like.'

Danny laughed and the three men walked to a table near the bar.

'He must be gay,' Jamie said with a laugh. 'You gave him your best come-on then, Lena, and not even a flicker.'

Lena gave Jamie a gentle shove. 'You just get back to work,' she said good-naturedly.

Stacey listened to her colleagues chatter as they walked away and she made her way over to Danny, Luke and Jake. God, she really hoped that she hadn't blown Jake's secret.

Jake looked over the menu as Luke and Danny placed their order with Stacey. His cousin Steph was the head chef and she was constantly changing the menu. He wished she'd stop. He couldn't find his favourite dish and he frowned.

'And for you, Jake?' Stacey asked as she smiled sweetly at him.

'I want the steak and mushroom tagliatelle,' he said.

Stacey frowned at him. 'I'm sorry,' she stammered, 'I don't think we do that dish.'

'Just tell the chef it's for me. They'll be able to knock it up,' he replied with a smile.

She blushed. 'Okay, I'll ask,' she said before taking their menus. 'I'll be back with your drinks soon.'

Jake sat back in his chair.

'What do you think your mum will say about our proposal?' Luke asked.

'She'll be fine about it. It's business, isn't it?' he said with a shrug. 'I'm more bothered about where she is. She's not answering her phone and I just texted Michael and he didn't know where she was either. She's always at this place during the day and it's too early for her to pick up Belle and Oscar.'

'I'm sure she's fine. She's probably gone to see a mate,' Luke offered.

'You're probably right. But I told her we might call in, and it's just unusual for her to not let me know if she's not going to be around, that's all.'

'Do you want to go and look for her?' Danny offered.

Jake shook his head. 'Nah. She'll kill us if she thinks we're checking up on her,' he said with a roll of his eyes.

'I'm sure she's fine, Jake,' Luke repeated.

'Your sister seems to be enjoying working here,' Jake said in an attempt to change the subject.

'She fucking loves the place. And at least she's working somewhere I know she'll be looked after if there's a kick-off.'

Jake was about to answer when Stacey walked back towards the table. 'The chef said he can't make your dish if it's not on the menu,' Stacey said as the flush crept over her cheeks again.

'Who is the chef today?' Jake asked.

'Tony,' Stacey said quietly.

'For fuck's sake,' Jake muttered as he stood up from the table. He stormed into the kitchen, flinging open the door with such force that he almost knocked over a waitress. 'Get out,' he barked to her and she scurried out of the kitchen.

'Tony!' Jake shouted. 'Do you have steak?'

'Yes,' Tony replied defiantly as he stood there staring at Jake, his muscular arms bulging through the sleeves of his chef's whites.

'Do you have mushrooms? And tagliatelle? And every other fucking ingredient that goes in that dish?'

'Of course I do,' he snapped.

'Then why won't you make me my fucking dinner then?' Jake said as he took a few steps towards him.

'I love it when you get angry,' Tony answered with a grin.

'Is that why I'm back here?' Jake snarled.

Tony nodded. 'Let's face it, I need to take any chance I can get to see you these days.'

'Tony,' Jake said with a sigh as he ran a hand through his hair. 'I told you I don't do this. We had a bit of a laugh together, but that's all it was.'

'I know,' Tony said. 'But it would be nice if you could not pretend like I didn't exist next time you come in here, Jake. A few weeks ago you could hardly keep your hands off me. Right in this very kitchen.' He gestured towards the steel counter. 'And today you come in here and don't even bother saying hello. I have to find out you're here from the waitress.'

'I've only been in here ten fucking minutes! Now stop acting like a like a tool and making me look like a cunt and just do your fucking job!'

'Okay. Point taken,' Tony said with a sigh. 'I'll make your bloody steak and mushroom.'

'Thank you!' Jake said as he straightened his jacket and walked out of the kitchen.

Jake arrived back at the table and took a seat. The assistant manager, Lena, had made her way over to their table now and was openly flirting with Danny. Jake laughed to himself; it made a welcome change from her throwing herself at him.

Luke caught Jake's eye and grinned. Danny must have seen the look they exchanged as he turned his attention back to them. 'We've got some business to talk through,' he said to Lena. 'I'll catch up with you later,' he said with a wink.

'Later, Danny,' she purred as she walked away, sashaying across the restaurant and back towards the bar.

'You're such a slut,' Luke said to him good-naturedly.

'Can we not go anywhere without you trying to pick up some poor unsuspecting woman?'

'To be fair, I'm not sure you can entirely blame Danny for this one,' Jake said with a laugh. 'You want to be careful with her, she'll eat you alive, mate,' he warned.

Danny shook his head. 'No need to worry about me. Nothing I can't handle, lads. Anyway, are you getting your dinner, or what?' he said to Jake.

'Yeah. Tony has a bit of an issue with me ignoring him after me and him had a bit of a thing a few weeks ago.'

Luke started to laugh. 'Fucking hell. You're even worse than he is. So, you and Chef Tony, eh?'

From the corner of his eye, Jake thought he saw the flicker of a scowl cross Danny's face, but when he looked directly at him, Danny was smiling. 'There is no me and fucking Chef Tony,' Jake said.

'But you were fucking Chef Tony?' Luke said with a flash of his eyebrows.

'Fuck off!' Jake snapped as Stacey approached their table with some small plates of tapas. 'Compliments of the chef,' she said.

Jake glared at Luke before he had a chance to comment. Luke heeded the warning and simply grinned at him instead.

Danny remained quiet for most of the meal while Jake and Luke talked about football.

'You okay, mate?' Jake asked him when Luke went to find Stacey to pay the bill.

'Yeah,' Danny said. 'I'm fine.'

'You going to get Lena's number then?' Jake said as he finished the last of his bottle of Budweiser.

'Nah. Maybe some other time.'

'Wise move.'

Danny smiled at him and Jake wondered at the change in his mood. It had happened after he'd come back from the kitchen after seeing Tony. Surely Danny didn't have a problem with him being gay? No. Jake had told him shortly after they'd started working together and Danny had been fine with it, not that Jake would have cared if he hadn't. He didn't give a shit if people objected to his sexuality. He'd spent far too long denying who he really was and as far as he was concerned, if other people had a problem with that, then it was entirely theirs. But he'd worked closely with Danny and Luke these past few months, and they were good business partners. But they were more than that, they were good mates too – or so Jake had thought. So why did Danny seem to have an issue with him and Tony? Only one other possible explanation popped into Jake's head and he dismissed it as quickly as it had occurred. Danny loved women. All women.

Chapter Fifteen

Grace arrived at Stefano's just over fifteen minutes later to find Leigh already seated at Grace's favourite booth at the back of the restaurant. It was quiet and discreet and the perfect place to have a private conversation. She noticed two steaming cups of coffee on the table too and wondered how long Leigh had been there. Grace frowned. She must have been close to the place to get there so quickly and order coffees. Had this meeting in fact been planned well in advance rather than appearing like a last-minute arrangement?

'Hi, Grace,' Leigh said with a faint smile.

'Hi,' Grace replied as she slipped into the booth opposite. 'You been here long?' she asked, indicating the two coffees.

'I was on my way back to the station and I was only around the corner from here. It was why I suggested the place. I figured you'd be at Sophia's, so it seemed ideal.'

That made sense. St Anne's Street police station was just

up the road and that was where Leigh and her team were based. She picked up her coffee and blew on the hot liquid before taking a sip. 'So, what's this new development I need to know about?' Grace asked.

Leigh sat forward in her seat. 'I was chatting to a DI friend of mine from Manchester, and they had a case like this about two years ago. Melanie Simmonds. Similar MO but there was only one victim. They never caught the perp and assumed they were looking for a disgruntled customer or pimp with a grudge.'

'And you think this is connected to the girls in Liverpool?'

'It's a strong possibility. Manchester is only up the road. Maybe it was the killer's first time? A trial run?'

'But why wait so long before striking again?'

Leigh shrugged. 'Lots of reasons. Maybe that first kill sustained him for a while. Maybe he was in prison for something else? Maybe something happened to trigger him again? We can't be sure about why, but I think there's a good chance we're dealing with the same perp. There are too many similarities to be a coincidence.'

Grace took another sip of her coffee before she spoke again. 'That's all very interesting, but I'm still not sure why you think this particular bit of information is of relevance to me.'

Leigh took a deep breath. 'I worked on a case a few years ago. A people-trafficking ring. It was a huge collaboration between Merseyside and Manchester police and it was a huge success for the most part. We put a lot of people away for a very long time...'

'But?'

'I was never confident that we got them all. From what my colleague tells me, this Melanie Simmonds had connections to the trafficking victims. She was known to be provided as entertainment for some of the same parties as them. The investigation into her murder didn't focus on a potential link to the trafficking case, because most people believe that all of the major players were put away, and also because it appeared to be an isolated incident and an emotional, impulsive crime rather than one that was planned. But we now know that this is the killer's MO. We know that the victims were abused, possibly even tortured, for at least a week prior to their deaths, and the fact that there is so little evidence left behind by the killer suggests a high degree of planning. However, if you were to look at each case as an isolated incident, then they could well be perceived as crimes of passion, where the perp had simply made a good job of covering his tracks. The strangulation and blunt force trauma each of the women suffered could well point to an impulsive act.'

'How does this link to the trafficking case though?' Grace asked as she sat forward in her seat.

'Well, I don't believe in coincidences. Melanie had a link to the trafficking victims. She may well have known things that she shouldn't have. Crucial information about people who would do anything to stop that ever coming out.'

'So, she was killed before she could talk?' Grace said as the pieces of the puzzle Leigh was laying out for her slowly started to slot into place. Whether that was the right place was another matter entirely.

'Exactly,' Leigh said. 'Melanie turns up dead in some alleyway just a few months after the trial ends. Apparently, she hadn't been seen around her usual haunts in the months preceding her death. Rumour was that she checked into rehab and got herself clean. But when her body was discovered she had excessive amounts of crack cocaine and heroin in her system, just like our victims. The investigation assumed she had relapsed and gone back on the game to fund her habit. But what if she'd been in hiding and they found her?'

'That's an interesting theory, Leigh,' Grace conceded. 'But I still don't understand what any of this has to do with me?'

Leigh's face flushed and she took a quick sip of her coffee. 'Right. Let me get to that. I believe one of the ones who got away was none other than our mutual friend Sol Shepherd.'

'Sol?' Grace said as she sat back against the leather seat in the booth. 'But he's dead,' Grace said with a frown. Sol Shepherd had once been an associate of Grace's, and Michael had even worked for him back in the day. But last year, he had been responsible for ordering a hit that had cost Michael's son Paul his life, and Michael had sought him out and put a bullet in his head. Connor had in fact been the intended target, not that that fact was common knowledge, but it had been Paul that the shooter had seen that day and assumed was his identical twin. It had intended to be payback for Connor's affair with Jazz, who was married to Sol at the time.

'I know he is. But he wasn't when Melanie was

murdered. And I think he had something to do with Melanie's murder. If we follow the trail of breadcrumbs from Sol Shepherd, I think we'll eventually find our killer.'

'I wouldn't put it past him. He was involved in all kinds, including trafficking from what I'd heard. But he's dead! Where are you going to start?' Grace asked, fearing she already knew the answer.

'Jasmine?' Leigh said quietly, confirming Grace's suspicion.

'Jazz doesn't know anything about any woman being murdered,' Grace said, feeling suddenly very protective of her soon-to-be daughter-in-law.

'How do you know that? How do you know what she does or doesn't know about her former husband's empire? She was married to him for seven years.'

'But that doesn't mean she knows anything. Sol wasn't likely to tell her. Did you ever meet him? He was a misogynistic pig.'

'That may be, but Jasmine strikes me as a smart woman. Don't tell me you honestly believe she didn't make it her business to have some dirt on her husband should she ever need it? I appreciate that she's been through a lot these past few months, but I only want to speak to her. You can even be with her if that would make you both feel better. She may know something that she doesn't even realise is important. You know as well as I do that sometimes the most seemingly insignificant information can be the key missing piece of a puzzle.'

Grace looked at Leigh as she considered what she was asking of her. It was true that Jazz had had a tough couple of months. She had almost died after giving birth to Paul junior. She was adjusting to becoming a new mum. She was dealing with the aftermath of Sol's death whilst processing the guilt, albeit misplaced, that she was responsible somehow for the death of Connor's brother and Michael's son. She had been present when Michael had killed Sol, and they had both sworn that they would never tell Connor that he had been the intended target for the paid hitman that day. But Grace also knew that Jazz was indeed very astute. She was bright and shrewd and savvy, and Grace had no doubt that there was a strong possibility that Jazz would have known more about Sol's business than some of his closest associates.

'I'll speak to her, but I'm not promising anything. If she doesn't want to talk to you then I'm not going to force the issue. She's not a fan of the police, as you can imagine.'

Leigh rolled her eyes. 'Are any of your family fans of the police?'

Grace smiled at her. 'I suppose not.'

Grace drained the last of her coffee and was about to leave when she remembered her earlier conversation with Stacey. She assumed Stacey's name was on the list of children who had been at the home when Nerys and the other victims were, so she didn't want to drag her into the investigation if the police hadn't, but she did think it was worth telling Leigh about Nerys's childhood friend. 'I meant to mention. Did you interview anyone called Stuart or Steven about Nerys's disappearance?'

'I'd have to check my notes. The team did most of the

interviews. I can't recall a Stuart or a Steven standing out. Why do you ask?'

'Apparently Nerys was friendly with him, that was all. They used to listen to jazz records together in the attic.'

'Oh? How did you come by this information?'

'It's not important,' Grace said, feeling the need to protect Stacey for some reason. 'I'd tell you if I thought it was.'

Leigh frowned. 'But how do you know it's not important, Grace? It could be.'

'It's information from someone who wouldn't be likely to give it to you. That's all I'm prepared to say.'

'I suppose I should be grateful for any information?' Leigh said with a hint of sarcasm.

'Exactly,' Grace replied. 'Now, I need to go and pick up my children.'

'Speaking of which,' Leigh said. 'We put a rush job on the DNA of the tooth we found embedded in Nerys's wrist. It belonged to her daughter.'

'So she was telling the truth then? But how could she hide the birth of a child? And where is the little girl now?' Grace asked.

Leigh shook her head. 'I have no idea. But Nerys must have been in contact with her recently to have had the tooth in her possession.'

Grace felt the bile rise in her stomach. 'Oh, God, you don't think—' she started, but was unable to finish the question. It was too awful to contemplate. Leigh had just been talking about trafficked women and children and now here was a child who for all intents and purposes, didn't even exist. Grace was aware she was no angel and she knew of the lengths that some of her employees would go to in order to ensure that her businesses continued operating smoothly. As a rule, violence against women was something she didn't tolerate and she made that known. But anything involving children was a line that she would never cross, and if any of her employees did, then they would find themselves on the receiving end of her wrath. Suddenly, she thought of Belle and Oscar, and the idea of someone hurting them, or any child, made her feel sick to her stomach.

'Right now, I don't know what to think,' Leigh said.

Grace shook her head. She could have stayed and talked longer, but she really did need to pick Oscar up. 'I'll speak to Jazz,' she said as she stood up.

Leigh nodded. 'Thank you.'

Chapter Sixteen

Joey Parnell pulled the car into the dirt track that led to the old farmhouse. The building loomed into view as he approached and he cursed under his breath as he realised he hadn't left the torch outside the front door. The whole place was in darkness and without his torch, he struggled with the mortice lock. He would have to use the light from his phone instead.

The old farmhouse was a huge stone structure, built some time in the 1820s and set in the middle of two square acres of land. It was a one-storey building with a large concrete basement complex. In short, it was the perfect place to hold a prisoner – or two. The property belonged to JB and had been in his family for generations. Joey had first visited the place eight years earlier for a 'party' hosted by a mutual acquaintance of theirs, Sol Shepherd. It was the kind of party that not just anyone got an invite to; in fact invites cost upwards of a few thousand pounds and JB was paid very well for the use of his property. Not only that, he liked to partake himself. The women and girls for such events were provided by Simon Jones, whom Joey had been padded up with for a few months in Strangeways. It was during this stint inside that he and Simon had discovered they shared certain predilections, including a fondness for teenage girls and bondage.

Joey had been serving two years for breaking his girlfriend's jaw. She'd tried to claim rape as well, but they hadn't been able to make that stick. She'd been seventeen, which was perfectly legal in the eyes of the law, but nevertheless, the other prisoners had had it in for him from the minute he'd stepped foot inside the place and he'd ended up on the vulnerable prisoners' wing, where he'd met Simon.

Simon had bragged to him all about the work he did and talked about his bosses being incredibly powerful men. It was Simon's job to procure women and girls for his employers and their associates. Having been forced to leave Liverpool, Joey had been struggling for work and money, so Simon promised an introduction to one of these men. That was how, just two months after he got out, Joey had ended up working for Sol Shepherd, one of the biggest gangsters in Manchester's history. Sol had his finger in every single pie there was. But he didn't particularly like being known for his part in the sex-trafficking trade, so he distanced himself from it, and paid other people to handle that side of his business. As it happened, Joey had been released from prison just as an opening had arisen. His job was to ensure that the girls they loaned out were returned relatively unharmed, at least unharmed enough that they wouldn't be out of action for more than a day or two. He ferried them to the various parties where they were provided as entertainment. He was basically their bodyguard and their chauffeur, and he was paid well for his services. Not only that, he got to sample the merchandise himself whenever he fancied. Joey had thought he had it made. Then he had met JB, and his sexual proclivities made Sol and Simon look like choirboys.

JB was the most charismatic and powerful man Joey had ever met. Even Sol was wary of him. Joey could sense as soon as he met him that JB was the man with the real power. It wasn't long before Joey had attracted JB's attention with his diligence and love of his job, and soon he was working for both Sol and JB – and that was where the real money was to be made. Before long, it was Joey who was organising the parties. Simon Jones continued to provide some of the girls for entertainment, but for certain clients, Sol and JB also drafted in some of their own – women who had been smuggled into the country illegally, and who wouldn't be missed should they happen to disappear.

JB had always looked after Joey. When he'd been sent down again for another assault, this time against a man who'd tried it on with one of his girlfriends, JB had made sure his time inside had been comfortable and passed without incident.

Joey turned off the engine of his car and stepped out into the rain. Using the flashlight on his phone, he managed to open the locks on the door without dropping his keys in the mud. Pushing open the door, he stepped inside, stamping his muddy boots on the raffia welcome mat. He switched on the electric light beside him and made his way over to the hearth to light the fire. The house was always freezing cold when he'd been away for a few days, but the large coal fire soon warmed the small room he had made his living quarters. He didn't stay at the farmhouse every night. He was trying to establish his security business again and he couldn't operate from the farmhouse. There was a very poor phone signal for a start and he couldn't exactly give out the address. While its remoteness came in handy for some tasks, it wasn't a place he could run a business from. He had his own flat in Crosby with glorious views of the sea, and as much as he enjoyed the job he was undertaking for JB, he preferred his creature comforts.

Joey lit the fire and rubbed his hands together for warmth. He looked over at the large steel door and smiled. There was only one girl left, and she would be downstairs waiting for him. He had left a small light on and a few days' supply of water and snacks. He wasn't a complete monster. It was almost time for him to see if Anna Martinez knew where this damned memory card was. He doubted that she did. In the days he'd been holding her captive, she had told him everything about her life, but she insisted she knew nothing about any video recording and Joey believed her. He was beginning to believe that Simon Jones had thrown the four women who'd been there that night under the bus to save his own skin. Joey shook his head in disgust. How had he let himself be blagged by Simon Jones? It was bloody infuriating. Not only had Simon now disappeared without a trace, he quite probably had in his possession a memory card that could put both Joey and JB inside for a very long time. And if that wasn't bad enough, Simon had made Joey look bad in front of JB, and that just wouldn't do.

Chapter Seventeen

Grace looked down at the sleeping face of her grandson Paul – the newest addition to the Carter family. He was adorable. His long dark eyelashes rested on his chubby cheeks as he snored softly.

She felt a warm hand on her back as Michael came up behind her. 'Are you going to put him down so we can eat?' he said softly in her ear.

'But he's so cute and cuddly,' Grace protested.

'He certainly is,' Michael said as he kissed Paul's cheek gently. 'But you've been hogging him all evening, and your dinner's going to get cold.'

Grace smiled at her husband. 'Okay. Point taken,' she said as she placed Paul in his Moses basket near the dining table.

Grace sat down at the table with Jazz and Connor, while Michael and Jake placed the hot dishes of food onto the table. Everybody helped themselves until they were all sitting with a plate full of food. As was their usual Monday evening routine, they slipped into easy conversation. Grace listened intently as Jake and Connor talked about business and particularly enjoyed hearing how well Luke and Danny were working out. Jazz talked about how much she enjoyed being a mum and they all laughed at the latest schoolyard tale Belle had told them earlier in the evening before she and Oscar had gone to bed.

When the plates were cleared, Grace sat back in her chair with a glass of wine in her hand and smiled at her family. She had once thought there would only ever be her and Jake, then Belle had come along, and now she had the big family she had always dreamed of. They all looked happy and relaxed and the wine flowing freely suggested that they would all be spending the night. She had come to treasure their Monday evenings together. The whole family always got together on a Sunday, but Mondays were just for them. She took a deep breath as she realised she was potentially about to ruin everybody's good mood. She would speak to Jazz alone, but if she agreed to speak to Leigh, then Grace was going to have to tell them all that she had been helping out the very same DI who had, not so many months ago, arrested both Jake and Connor for murder.

It was another hour before Grace had the chance to speak to Jazz alone. She was in the kitchen making herself a cup of peppermint tea after giving Paul what would hopefully be his last feed until morning. He was turning out to be a good little sleeper.

'Want one?' Jazz asked as she noticed Grace walking towards her.

'No thanks,' she replied with a smile.

'Dinner was delicious. I think I'm still stuffed. Do you think Connor will ever learn to cook like his dad?' Jazz asked with a laugh.

'Well, Michael has taught Jake how to make spaghetti carbonara and that boy could barely boil an egg, so there's definitely hope.'

The kettle clicked off and Jazz poured the boiling water into her mug. 'Here's to hope,' she said as she raised her mug in a toast.

Grace laughed. She loved Jazz and was looking forward to her and Connor getting married in a few months' time. She was already one of the family and Grace loved spending time with her.

'I need to talk to you about something, Jazz,' Grace said as she took a seat at the breakfast bar.

'Okay,' Jazz replied as she took a seat next to her. 'What is it?'

Grace took a deep breath and told Jazz about her involvement with the murder investigation, her conversation with Leigh and the possible connection to Sol.

Jazz stared at her open-mouthed for a few seconds as she digested the information. 'Do Michael and the boys know you've been helping that DI with her investigation?'

'Michael does, of course. But I haven't told Jake and Connor yet. I was hoping I wouldn't have to. I hadn't intended to do any more than sort out the whole business with Number 69 and have a chat to the girls while I was doing it. But this case has got under my skin and I can't stop thinking about it.'

'I understand. It's hard to walk away from someone who needs your help. Especially when you're used to fixing everyone's problems.'

'What do you think about talking to Leigh?'

Jazz blew onto her mug of tea as she considered the question. 'The thing is, Grace, I know a hell of a lot about Sol's business. However, I'm not sure I want to be discussing any of that with some DI. But –' she took a sip of her tea and stared at Grace '– I trust you. So, if you trust her, then I'll speak to her. As long as you come with me too.'

'Of course I will.'

'And we go for some dinner and a few cocktails afterwards,' Jazz said with a wink.

Grace laughed. 'Deal. We'll have to tell Connor and Jake though?'

Jazz raised her eyebrows. 'I know,' she said as she slipped off her stool. 'Let's get it out of the way then, eh?'

Jazz peered into Paul's Moses basket and smiled at her beautiful sleeping boy. He looked so much like Connor, although he had her dark skin. When she was in her twenties, and had met her ex-husband Sol, she had thought she never wanted kids. The fact that Sol was seventeen years older than her, and had previously had a vasectomy, had seemed like the perfect combination. He had been her escape from a life of struggle and hardship. She had been a dancer at a club in Manchester when she'd first met him and although she was used to being groped by drunken punters on a regular basis, Sol had rescued her from one such chancer and had broken his fingers for daring to touch her. She had thought she'd found her proverbial knight in shining armour. It was only once she'd married him that she'd realised he was more a dragon than a knight.

It was only when her sister, Rose, had had children that Jazz had started to wonder if she had made the right decision in marrying a man who couldn't and wouldn't give her any of her own. She had pleaded with him to consider other ways of having a child but he had refused to listen. She had hated him by then anyway, but had thought at least a child would have made her life worth living. She had been lost and lonely, and wondering how she would ever make it through another week of being married to Sol, let alone the rest of her life, when she'd met Connor. Although he was nine years younger than her, they got on so well that she'd ended up talking to him for the whole night when she was supposed to have been out for a rare night out with his sister. She had met him again a few days later and when he'd kissed her, she had realised that she had never really known what it was to be in love. She had fallen for him hard. And then she had fallen pregnant.

Sol had always kept her on a very short leash, and he already suspected she'd been having an affair. He had beaten her regularly anyway, but had ramped up his efforts once he'd realised she was slipping away from him. But it had been worth it to keep seeing Connor. When her pregnancy had started to show, Jazz had known that Sol would kill her, Connor and their unborn baby when he found out, so she had planned to kill him herself. It had seemed like the only way out. She had a gun, and although she'd planned it all out to the last detail, and had an alibi in her sister Rose, she was prepared to be caught. Going to prison for murder was still a better option than staying with Sol, and it would protect Connor and their child.

The night she had been planning to kill Sol, Connor's father Michael had turned up and killed him instead. Michael had saved her life that night and she would be forever in his debt because of it.

Jazz continued smiling as she walked over to the bed. She loved Connor more than she had ever thought possible. She adored their son. And she adored her new extended family: Michael, Jake, Belle, Oscar and especially Grace, who although only ten years older than Jazz, felt like the mother figure she had always craved but never had.

Jazz pulled back the covers and climbed into bed beside Connor, who lay with his arms behind his head, staring at the ceiling. She could feel the tension in his body as she ran her hand down his chest. He hadn't taken the news well that Grace was helping out the DI who had arrested him and Jake a few months earlier for murder. He had been even less impressed when Jazz told him that she was going to speak to DI Moss too. She could understand his feelings, but this was important to her and something she felt she needed to do.

'Are you angry with me?' she asked softly.

He turned to look at her. 'No. Yes. I suppose I am a bit, Jazz,' he said with a sigh.

'But you understand why I need to do this? If Sol was involved in that woman's murder? I know he did the other things that detective thinks he did, and no one can do anything about that now. But if I know something that could help find out who is killing these women, Con, then I have to help. That could have been me,' she said as her eyes filled with tears.

He turned on his side and looked into her eyes. 'No, it couldn't,' he replied with a frown.

'It could, Connor. I told you about my past and where I came from.'

'But you didn't go down that road, did you? You could have, but you didn't.'

'Only because I had some good friends around me and I ended up dancing. But it was a slippery slope, Connor. I saw lots of the girls I worked with doing extras just to make ends meet.'

'I'm just worried about you, that's all,' he said as he placed a hand on her cheek and rubbed her skin with the pad of his thumb. 'Leigh Moss is a copper, and I don't trust her at all.'

'Neither do I. But I trust Grace. And she wouldn't let anything bad happen to me – to any of us. You know that?'

'I know. I love you so much, Jazz. If anything ever happened to you...'

'Nothing is going to happen to me, Con. I'm only going to talk to her. It will be a one-time deal and it will all be off the record.'

'Just make sure it is a one-off, Jazz. If anyone gets a sniff of you and Grace talking to the filth, it could cause a fucking war.'

'I will,' she said with a smile before she leaned forward and kissed him. 'I love you too, Con. I would never do anything to jeopardise our family.'

He wrapped a strong arm around her waist and pulled her closer to him until she was pressed against his chest. 'You have me wrapped around your little finger, don't you? How do you do that?' he said with a grin.

Jazz laughed. 'Well, I do have my charms.'

'Is that what you call them?' he said as he looked down at her breasts.

'You're such a boy, sometimes.' She laughed again as she pushed him onto his back and moved to straddle him.

'A boy?' he said with a flash of his eyebrows. 'Well, let's see about that, shall we?'

Jake sat in the back of the car while one of his bouncers drove him to The Blue Rooms. He'd left his car at his mum and Michael's house. He had planned on staying the night, but his mum's revelation that she was helping out that copper Leigh Moss, the very same one who had arrested him and Connor, had pissed him off no end. He'd had to get out of there before he said something he'd regret. He could hardly believe she had just sat there and casually told them that she was helping out the filth with their investigation. He could understand, to some extent, why she *might* want to help find out whoever was killing prostitutes in her own backyard, but doing it by helping out Leigh fucking Moss – he couldn't fathom it. And now she was trying to drag poor Jazz into it too. And Jazz was going to do it.

Jake stared out of the window and wondered what the hell had got into her. His mum was usually the person who had all of the answers. He could go to her with any problem and she would help him work out the solution. She was one of the most level-headed and logical people he knew. Nothing fazed her. Nothing was too big an issue for her to solve. So, why had she suddenly lost her mind?

'You okay, Boss?' Timmo, his driver asked.

'Yeah. Nothing a few whiskies won't fix, mate,' Jake replied.

Timmo nodded and returned his attention to the road. Jake hoped he was right about feeling better after a few whiskies. He didn't drink a lot any more. Not since losing Paul had almost turned him into an alcoholic and junkie. He was much more measured and restrained these days – but tonight he would make an exception. He hated drinking alone though and had phoned Danny and Luke to see if they fancied joining him. They didn't work the doors on a Monday night as a rule, so he knew they were free. He'd woke Luke up and received a yawned 'No thanks.' Danny, however, had been up for a night out and was also on route to The Blue Rooms.

Jake walked through the entrance of The Blue Rooms and into the bar. The music thrummed loudly in his ears, but the place was quiet as it always was on a Monday. He saw Danny sitting at the bar with a blonde hanging off his arm – and no doubt on his every word. Jake grinned. Danny Alexander had a different woman for almost every night of the week. Not that Jake blamed him. He was young, had no ties, and he was good-looking. If that wasn't enough, he filled a suit like a sausage filled a roll, and he was the new Managing Director of Cartel Securities. All of that rolled into one package made him a fanny magnet.

Jake patted Danny on the shoulder when he reached him and Danny spun around on his stool with a look that Jake could only describe as pure relief.

'Jake. I thought you'd never get here,' he said as he removed the blonde's hand from his thigh.

Jake laughed. 'Relax. I'm here now, mate.'

Danny slipped off his stool. 'Sorry, babe, but we've got to get to work,' he said to the blonde.

'Oh,' she said with a pout. 'Call me later, Danny.'

'Yeah, will do,' he said as he looked at Jake pointedly.

Jake played along. 'Come on then. We haven't got all night,' he said and walked through the club to his office in the back with Danny close behind him.

'What was that about?' Jake asked when he and Danny were in the safety of his office.

Danny shook his head. 'I took her home on Friday night and she's been back here every night since hoping for another round.'

'But Danny doesn't do seconds?' Jake started to laugh.

'I do – sometimes!' he protested. 'But she's really not my type.'

'Well, you've made me forget about my shitty night, anyway, mate,' Jake said as he picked up the half-empty bottle of Johnny Walker Black Label from the small bar in his office.

'Oh? What's up?' Danny asked as he sat down.

Jake poured two large whiskies and handed one to Danny. 'Oh, nothing. Nothing that I can be arsed talking about anyway. Family drama.'

'At least you have family to have drama with,' Danny said as took a swig of his whisky.

Jake nodded. Danny only had his sister, Stacey. Although he and Luke were as close as brothers. Jake knew that Danny would have liked to be part of a big family, as he'd told him one night after he'd had a few too many whiskies. 'I just wish my mum would think about how what she does affects us all sometimes,' Jake said.

Danny put his glass on the desk and stared at Jake open-mouthed. 'Are you kidding me?'

'What?'

'I would literally kill to have a mum looking out for me the way yours does for you. She does nothing but put you lot first.'

Jake stared at Danny and realised there was some truth in what he said. He noticed that the anger he'd felt when he'd left his mum's house earlier had already eased. He always found himself relaxing around Danny. He was easy to talk to. He reminded Jake a little of Paul and that made him feel both happy and sad at the same time.

'It doesn't mean I don't get to be pissed off with her on occasion though,' Jake said.

Danny laughed. 'Well, of course you do, mate. But, if you don't want to talk about it, how about we get pissed and talk about the footy instead?'

Jake raised his glass. 'Sounds good to me.'

Danny smiled at him and Jake had to remind himself that Danny liked women.

Grace watched as Michael closed the door to the bedroom and started to undress.

'Are you okay?' she asked.

He stared at her for a few seconds, his jaw clenched shut as though he was carefully considering his response.

'What is it?' she asked. Her revelation that she'd been assisting Leigh with the Liverpool Ripper investigation had gone down like the proverbial lead balloon after dinner. Jake and Connor had taken it particularly badly. And then Jazz had told them she was going to speak to Leigh too and it suddenly felt like someone had sucked the atmosphere out of the room with a giant vacuum.

Grace had fielded all of their questions, explaining why

she felt the need to help Leigh find the killer, and had thought they'd at least understood, even if they didn't agree with her decision. Jazz had persuaded Connor to stay the night as Paul was fast asleep but Jake had left, unable to hold his tongue. It was better than then arguing about it, Grace supposed. Her son could be a stubborn bugger when he wanted to be. But she would speak to him in the morning and smooth the whole thing over. What she hadn't counted on was Michael's sudden issue with it. He'd been aware of her decision to help Leigh, and while he didn't fully agree with it, he'd supported her anyway, as he always did. So why was he looking at her like that?

'It's one thing you getting yourself embroiled with that copper, Grace, but dragging our kids into it is an entirely different matter,' he snapped.

'I'm not dragging our kids into anything!'

'Oh, really?'

'Yes! Really! I asked Jazz if she wanted to speak to Leigh and she agreed to of her own free will. They're going to have a quick chat and that's it.'

Michael shook his head and stalked past her towards the en-suite.

'I didn't drag anyone into anything,' Grace went on.

Michael turned on his heel and Grace saw the anger in his face. It made her take a step back. 'Do you honestly think she would ever say no to you, Grace? You, of all people?'

'What's that supposed to mean?'

He walked back towards her and threw his T-shirt onto

the bed. 'It means that people don't say no to you. They can't!'

She blinked at him. 'Of course they can.'

He started to laugh then, but not his usual laugh that she loved – the one she felt in her bones. It was full of sarcasm and anger. 'You really think Jazz had a choice when you asked her to do this for you?'

She scowled at him. He was starting to piss her off now. Making out like she was some sort of tyrant. 'Of course she did!' she snapped.

Michael frowned at her as he took another step towards her. He towered over her. 'Do you have any idea what will happen if anyone finds out you've been speaking to Leigh Moss? Maybe you might be able to smooth-talk your way out of it, but Jazz and the boys won't. They will be the targets if this ever gets out. Not you!'

Grace closed her eyes as his words washed over her and she felt the anger swell inside her chest. She inched closer to him and craned her neck to look into his eyes. 'Are you seriously suggesting that I would put our children's lives at risk?'

His eyes darkened as he glared at her. 'You already have.'

She shook her head. 'But you knew what I was doing. You were fine with it.'

'You told me you were going to speak to the girls at Number 69. You never said it would go further than that.'

'So, what am I supposed to do now? Just walk away when there's a chance I could help?' she asked.

'Yes Grace!' he shouted. 'You cannot fix everything for everyone. When are you going to realise that?'

His words stung and she felt her hackles rise. He knew how to push her buttons so well. 'Maybe when people stop asking me to fix things, Michael! Don't you think I'd love to run away from it all? I tried that once. Don't you remember? And look how that worked out for me!'

'Oh, right? Are you talking about the time you fucked off to the other side of the country without telling me you were pregnant with my child?' he snarled. 'That time?'

'Yes,' she hissed. 'Sometimes I wonder why I ever bothered to come back!' She regretted her words immediately, as soon as she saw the hurt flash across his face. She had gone too far. But she couldn't back down now. The adrenalin and anger were still coursing around her body and her heart pounded in her ears.

'Is that so?' he growled.

No, of course not, she thought, but didn't say. Instead she glared at him, furious that he would suggest she would put Jazz and the boys at risk.

'Well, maybe you should fuck off back to Harewood then. But the kids will be staying with me!' he snarled before he stormed out of the room.

'The hell they will,' she shouted after him.

It was a few hours later when Michael finally came back into the bedroom. Grace lay still, wondering whether he would make any attempt to wake her. Or whether he would slip his hand over her hip and onto her stomach as he always did when he came to bed later than her. Then he would pull her body against his and kiss her shoulder blade and she would nestle against him.

He didn't. He lay facing away from her and soon she heard his breathing slow as he fell asleep.

Chapter Eighteen

Grace and Jazz walked into the back room at Stefano's, where Leigh Moss was already waiting for them.

Leigh stood as they entered the room. 'Hi, Grace,' she said.

'Hi, Leigh. This is Jasmine.' She indicated the younger woman behind her and sat down at the table.

'Thank you so much for agreeing to talk to me,' Leigh said as she extended her hand.

Jazz shook it lightly before removing her coat and taking a seat next to Grace.

Leigh sat down and Grace ordered the three women a cappuccino each from the waitress. When she had walked away to get their order, Leigh spoke.

'I assume Grace has told you why I wanted to speak to you?'

'Yes. You want to know if I know anything about Sol's

139

possible connection to the murder of a young woman in Manchester two years ago?'

'Exactly that.'

'If I know anything about that, then I'll tell you. But that is all I'm here to talk about. My ex-husband had many allies and many enemies, Detective Moss, and I don't want to give any of them a reason to come after me or my family.'

'Of course. I understand.'

'I hope you do. This is all off the record?' Jazz asked.

'Yes,' Leigh replied.

'And this is a one-time deal.'

'Okay,' Leigh said.

'Good.' Jazz smiled then. 'Let me start by telling you that Sol was definitely more than capable of murdering that girl, but he didn't. He may have been involved, but he didn't actually kill her.'

'Oh? How do you know that?' Leigh asked.

'Because I did my homework, Detective. I googled Melanie's murder and Sol wasn't in the country the day she was killed. We were in Morocco.'

'That's a good memory you have,' Leigh said.

'Don't patronise me, Detective,' Jazz said with a sweet smile. 'It was two days after Sol's fiftieth birthday. We were in Morocco for his birthday and we didn't get back until the following week.'

Grace sat back and smiled. She had accompanied Jazz to this meeting at her request, but she was starting to realise that Jazz didn't need her there at all; she was proving herself more than capable of holding her own.

Leigh smiled too. 'I'm sorry, Jasmine, I didn't mean to patronise you. I slip into interview mode all too easily.'

Jazz shrugged. 'It's okay. And you can call me Jazz. Only Sol and my dad used to call me Jasmine.'

'Okay, Jazz. Please call me Leigh.'

They were interrupted by the waitress bringing their coffees. They each thanked her before Leigh resumed her questioning.

'The reason I think that Sol may have been involved in Melanie's murder, Jazz, is because I suspect it may have been something to do with a trafficking case that I worked on a couple of years ago. I always suspected that Sol was involved but I could never prove it.'

Jazz remained silent, waiting for the question.

Leigh stared at her for a few seconds, no doubt wondering if her face was going to reveal something, but Jazz remained impassive.

'Do you know anything about him being involved in the trafficking of women and girls, Jazz?' Leigh eventually asked.

'I wouldn't put it past him to be involved, but I don't have any information to prove that he was.'

'Did he ever bring any of the girls or women to your house?'

'No. He wasn't stupid.'

'Did you ever hear talk about a girl called Melanie?'

'No. He screwed lots of women behind my back, but he never talked about them. Like I said, he wasn't stupid.'

'To be honest, Jazz, I'm clutching at straws here. Is there anything you think might help me with this investigation?

Or any link that you can think of, no matter how tenuous, to Melanie Simmonds?'

Jazz leaned forward in her seat and Grace sensed that Leigh had finally asked the right question.

'I do remember that a few weeks before his birthday he'd been moodier and more angry than usual. He was always a bit of a bastard, to be honest, but he was extra cruel. He snapped at everything I said or did. I remember because I was beginning to dread our holiday away together. Anyway, his right-hand man, Milo, was always at our house for one thing or another, and around this time they kept talking about this *problem* that needed dealing with and how *he* was going to go ape-shit when he found out. Now, Sol and Milo were always talking about *problems* they had to sort out, and I expect most of those problems ended up dead in a ditch somewhere, but this stood out to me because Sol actually seemed scared. Whoever *he* was, he had Sol rattled, and I don't know if you ever met him, Leigh, but Sol was scared of *no one*. I even started to hope that Sol wouldn't solve this particular problem and he'd be the one who ended up in a ditch for a change.'

Leigh sat back in her chair. 'And that was just before your holiday, and before Melanie was murdered?'

'Yes.'

'What happened afterwards? Did you ever hear him talk about this man again, or whether this problem had been sorted?'

'No. But shortly after we arrived in Morocco, he suddenly seemed more relaxed. He spoke to Milo a few times while we were away, and he always seemed to be in a good mood when he did. But he never mentioned *him*, again, whoever he was. At least not in my earshot anyway. And to be honest, by that time, I tried to spend as little time with or around Sol as possible, so I stopped hearing much of anything.'

'Thank you, Jazz,' Leigh said with a smile. 'You've been really helpful.'

'Have I? I hope so. I hope that you find the man responsible for killing these women, Leigh,' Jazz said as she reached out and gave Leigh's hand a squeeze.

'Oh, we'll find him. I promise you that,' Leigh replied.

Grace had just dropped Jazz off at home when her phone rang in her hand. She saw Leigh's name flash up on the dashboard of her car and groaned. What did the hell did she want now?'

'Hi, Leigh,' Grace said.

'Hi, Grace. I wanted to thank you again for speaking to Jazz for me. I started to do a little more digging into the Melanie Simmonds murder and found out she did a couple of shifts at a strip club called Jezebel's. She didn't last long because she couldn't keep her drug habit under enough control. But you'll never guess who used to be a silent partner in the club?'

'Sol Shepherd?' Grace said.

'Exactly.'

'Well done, Detective. Seems like you might be onto something.'

'Hmm,' Leigh replied. 'I've been told to keep my beak out of the Simmonds case and focus on the Liverpool murders, so I can't exactly go there in an official capacity, or send any of my team.'

'Okay?' Grace said, with a feeling that she already knew where this was headed.

'I don't suppose you fancy a recce with me tonight?'

'Me?' Grace laughed. 'Why on earth would I?'

'Oh, come on, Grace. You hated Sol as much as I did,'

'But he's dead,' Grace reminded her. 'Nothing we dig up on him will make a blind bit of difference.'

'But wouldn't you like to know who he was working with? Whoever this man is that Jazz talked about him being scared of? And don't think I haven't noticed how you get that little twinkle in your eye whenever we discuss the case. You want to get to the bottom of this as much as I do.'

'Even if that were true, you seem to be forgetting that I'm not a police officer, Leigh.'

'And I'm not asking you to be. All I'm asking is that you come for a drink with me tonight to Jezebel's. We'll have a few cocktails, use our considerable charm to get a bit of information about our old friend Melanie, and then leave without anyone being any the wiser.'

Grace sighed. 'Will this get you off my case for a few days?'

'Yes. Scout's honour,' Leigh said.

'Okay. I'll pick you up in the car park of The Rocket pub at half past eight.'

'Great. Wear something sexy. The fewer clothes, the better. We need information,' Leigh said with a laugh.

'Sod off! It's bad enough I have to tell Michael you're taking me to some dodgy strip club, without leaving the house in a miniskirt and a boob tube.'

'Okay. A little black dress will do,' said Leigh, still laughing.

'See you later, Leigh,' Grace said with a smile before hanging up the phone. She sat back in her seat as she waited at the traffic lights on Allerton Road. How was she going to tell Michael what she and Leigh had planned? Particularly after his outburst the previous night. She'd hardly spoken to him all day, except to make sure he was okay to pick up the kids from school. It was a good job he already wasn't speaking to her, she supposed.

Grace walked into the living room and saw Michael sitting on the sofa. Their boxer dog Bruce was curled up asleep next to him, but hearing Grace walk into the room, Bruce jumped up and ran towards her, wagging his tail excitedly. She scratched behind his ears and gave him a peck on the head. At least someone was glad to see her.

'Where are the kids?' she asked.

'I took them to Sean and Sophia's after school and they wanted to stay over.'

'Oh, okay. Have you eaten?'

'No,' he replied.

'Want me to make us something?' she asked.

'There's a lasagne in the oven,' he replied, barely glancing up in her direction.

'Right,' she said and left the room.

Grace went upstairs to shower, leaving her husband to sulk on the sofa. She hated arguing with him. They rarely had disagreements and her world felt completely out of kilter when they did.

Grace picked up a fluffy towel from the warmer and wrapped it around herself. Walking out of the en-suite, she found Michael sitting on the edge of the bed.

'How did it go today with Jazz? he asked.

'Fine,' she replied.

'Just fine?' he snapped.

'Leigh asked her a few questions about Sol and his involvement in the murder of a young woman in Manchester. Jazz answered them. None of it was on the record. Nobody saw us. It was fine. Jazz doesn't need to see Leigh ever again. Happy?'

'Not really. But it's done now. Isn't it?' He glared at her.

'Did you just come up here to argue with me?' Grace asked as she took the clip from her hair and let it fall loose around her shoulders.

'No,' he said with a sigh. 'Have you spoken to Jake? He seemed pretty pissed off when he left last night.'

'Yes. I saw him earlier. He was pissed off, and I completely understand why. But I talked to him and he's okay. We're okay. So it seems it's just you who's still annoyed with me.' She tilted her head to look at him.

'I'm just worried about you all,' he said defensively.

She sat next to him on the bed. 'I know,' she said quietly. Because she understood that was where his anger was coming from. He had always worried about them all, and since Paul had died, it had only confirmed that he had good reason to.

'I would never put our children in danger. Any of them,' she said.

Her turned and looked at her. 'I know.'

'And I have never regretted coming back to Liverpool. You and the kids mean more to me...' She wasn't sure she could finish the sentence. But she didn't have to. Michael leaned towards her and sealed her mouth with a kiss. Then his warm hands were removing her towel before he pushed her back onto the bed.

'I love you,' he whispered.

'I love you too,' Grace replied. She smiled as he trailed kisses down her collarbone, over her breasts and onto her stomach. Curling her fingers in his hair, she arched her back and concentrated on the feel of his soft lips and rough hands on her skin, trying to forget how the hell she was going to tell him her plans for later in the evening.

Michael lay on top of the covers with Grace's body pressed against his. He stroked her long dark hair as he waited for his heart to stop hammering in his chest. When she'd arrived home just over an hour earlier, he'd still been annoyed with her, but he couldn't stay angry at her for very long. He never could and he doubted he ever would. There was something about her that made it impossible for him – especially when she was sitting next to him in nothing but a towel.

Michael knew that his wife thought she was invincible. He supposed he couldn't blame her – she had survived things that most wouldn't – and yet she remained a woman capable of incredible compassion and warmth. If anything ever happened to her, or their kids, he didn't know what he would do. She was the glue that held their family together. But he couldn't shift an uneasy feeling that she was getting in over her head helping Leigh Moss.

'That lasagne will be burned to a crisp by now,' Grace said, snapping him from his thoughts.

'It's okay, it's only on low. I wasn't expecting you back so early,' he said as he kissed the top of her head.

'I love that you still made me dinner even when you weren't speaking to me.'

'Of course I was speaking to you,' he insisted.

She started to laugh and it made him smile. He loved the sound of her laughing. It had been one of the first things he'd noticed about her when he'd walked into her pub, The Rose and Crown. 'No, you weren't.' She nudged him. 'You came to bed last night and you didn't even touch me.'

'It was late and I thought you were asleep.'

'That doesn't usually stop you.' She looked up at him and smiled, and he laughed because it was true.

'I suppose I was a little bit pissed off with you,' he said, running his hand up her arm and up to her face, resting it on her cheek, where he rubbed his thumb across her flushed skin. 'But only a bit.'

'Well, I suppose I kind of blindsided you with the whole Jazz-speaking-to-Leigh thing,' she said with a shrug.

'You think?'

'Well, let me make it up to you,' she offered.

'I thought you just did?' He flashed his eyebrows at her.

'I mean, I'll sort dinner while you relax.'

'Okay. Sounds like a deal.'

At that minute, Bruce started howling from the bottom of the stairs. 'I'll see to the dog, you sort dinner,' Michael said as he jumped off the bed and started to pull some clothes on.

'I do love you, Carter,' Grace said as she propped herself on one elbow. She smiled at him and he felt his heart constrict in his chest. This woman had him by the balls – but he wouldn't have it any other way.

Grace had plied Michael with wine and lasagne and he was sitting opposite her at their dining table when she decided to tell him about her earlier conversation with Leigh.

He stared at her open-mouthed. 'Are you fucking serious?' he snapped.

She swirled her wine around her glass. 'Well, I was. But now that I'm home, and the kids are out, I can think of a much better way to spend my evening.'

That caught him off guard and she knew he didn't know whether to smile or frown at her, so he did a combination of the two that made her laugh.

'This isn't funny, Grace,' he said, the smile still playing on his lips.

'Oh, give over. I've been in much worse places than strip clubs and you know it. But anyway, I've just told you I'm not going. In hindsight, I think two women going into there might look a bit odd, do you think?'

'That's the only reason you're not going?' he snapped.

'Mostly, but also because I know you don't want me to, and I understand why.'

'So you're actually listening to me?' He raised an eyebrow at her. 'Well, wonders will never cease.'

'I always listen to you,' she said, feigning her indignation. 'Sometimes.'

'Always sometimes?' he said with a grin. 'So, what are you going to tell Leigh?' he said as he looked at his watch. 'You're supposed to meet her in half an hour.'

'Don't worry about that. I have a plan.'

Michael smiled at her and she felt her stomach flutter. She was glad they were on speaking terms again. Not that they ever fell out for very long. Michael was hot-headed at times, but he was never stubborn.

A few moments later, Michael was loading the dishwasher and Grace picked up her mobile phone. She dialled the number and it was answered after a few rings.

'Hi, Boss.' John Brennan's deep voice filled her ear.

'John,' she said sweetly. 'I have a favour to ask you.'

L eigh Moss shifted from one foot to the other and wrapped her coat tighter around herself as she stood in the biting cold. Glancing at her watch, she saw it was past 9 p.m., which meant that Grace Carter was late. Maybe that was a good thing? Was Leigh being completely reckless asking Grace Carter for help? On paper, Grace was a woman that Leigh shouldn't even be speaking to, never mind arranging off-the-books recon missions with. But there was something about Grace Carter that made Leigh drop her guard. It was more than just their shared history, or the fact that Grace had once saved Leigh's life, it was that they were so in tune. If circumstances were different, Leigh wondered if she and Grace could have been good friends. But circumstances weren't different, and no matter how alike they were, Leigh could not allow herself to forget who Grace Carter really was.

As she contemplated driving home Leigh saw the headlights of a car approaching. It took a few seconds for her eyes to adjust enough to the darkness to see that it wasn't Grace's Mercedes, or even Michael's Aston Martin, which she occasionally drove. It was a large BMW X5. Leigh's heart started to pound in her chest. Had she been set up? If not, why had Grace felt the need to bring back-up?

The car rolled to a stop next to Leigh and the driver switched off the engine. Leigh swallowed and willed her heart rate to slow. There was only one occupant in the car. It was John Brennan. What the hell was he doing here? The car engine was switched off and she watched as John opened the driver's door and stepped out onto the tarmac.

'Evening, Detective,' he said with a huge grin on his face.

Leigh felt her breath catch in her throat. The last time she had seen him had been almost twenty years earlier when he had been Nathan Conlon's right-hand man and she had been a deluded girl, in love with a psychopath. Now John worked for Grace, Nathan's ex-wife and the woman who had eventually killed him.

'John,' she snapped, not bothering to hide her annoyance. 'What are you doing here?'

'Grace has been unexpectedly detained. So, she sent me to look after you,' he said with a chuckle.

'What?' she started.

'Oh, calm down, Candy.' He laughed again. 'Or is it Leigh now? I'm just here to help, that's all. Boss's orders.' He held his hands up in mock surrender.

'It's Leigh. And if she wasn't coming, she should have let me know. Instead of...'

'Instead of what?'

'Instead of sending one of her Rottweilers to babysit me.'

If John took offence, he didn't show it. 'You should count yourself lucky that Grace Carter considers you important enough to warrant the protection of one of her Rottweilers. Especially her best one.'

Leigh was about to speak but John went on. 'So, are we going in your car or mine, Detective?'

She looked at his giant black beast of a car and thought about how her feet were aching from a long day. She was starting to regret the six-inch stilettos and short black cocktail dress she'd chosen to wear now. 'Yours,' she said with a resigned sigh.

John grinned again and she was reminded that Nathan always referred to him as The Smiling Assassin. 'Your carriage awaits, m'lady,' he said as he pressed a button on his key fob and the X5 beeped to life.

John parked his car in a side street a short walk from Jezebel's. He had made a few phone calls, on their drive from Liverpool to Manchester, to some connections he had in Manchester. By the time they'd arrived, he had managed to find out that one of the bouncers, Jordan, was the best person to speak to for possible information about any girls who had worked there three years earlier, when Melanie had. He also had the name of a stripper, Hazel, who'd had a run-in with Melanie herself. Leigh had listened to him as he chatted amiably to his associates, managing to glean the information he needed without revealing anything as to the reason why. Despite who he was, she found herself feeling impressed, and could see why Grace Carter valued his services so highly. John Brennan might look like hired muscle, but he had brains and personality to back it up too.

When they reached the club, John held the door open for her. As she walked through, he placed his hand on the small of her back and she flinched slightly. He bent his head low, his lips pressed against her ear. 'Relax, Leigh,' he said softly. 'Aren't we supposed to be incognito? A man doesn't bring a woman to a place like this unless they're fucking.'

Leigh took a deep breath. Of course he was right. She relaxed and forced her a smile onto her face as John guided her towards a table in a dark corner. She sat down.

'What do you fancy to drink?' he asked her.

'Just a Coke,' she said.

He leaned down and spoke in her ear again and she suddenly realised that he smelled incredible. What the hell was that aftershave he was wearing? 'I'm driving, and one of us has to drink,' he whispered.

She blushed. He was making her feel like an amateur. 'I'll have a brandy and Coke then,' she said with a smile.

'Coming right up,' he said, grinning at her.

She watched as he walked over to the bar. He drew the eye of the blonde waitress as she sashayed past him. Leigh continued to watch him with interest as he chatted to the barmaid, who was laughing at whatever it was he was saying. Leigh looked around the club. There was a long stage near the middle, where two women gyrated and danced to the music. There was a look in their eyes that she recognised all too well and it made her want to rush outside and vomit. But she didn't, forcing herself to breathe deeply and focus on the task at hand. She was suddenly glad she'd ordered a proper drink and was wondering what the hell was keeping John. She could see their drinks on the bar in front of him, but he continued chatting to the young barmaid.

A man in a suit staggered past her table and bumped into the chair beside her.

'Sorry,' he slurred, then he turned to look at her. 'Oh, hello,' he leered, his eyes glassy. 'Are you here on your own?'

'No, she's fucking not,' John barked as he walked up behind him. 'So fuck off!'

The drunk turned with an angry look on his face, but on seeing the mountain of a man standing behind him, he shrank back. 'Sorry, mate,' he mumbled.

John placed the two glasses on the table and sat down. 'I leave you on your own for two minutes and you're already in trouble?' he said with a grin.

'Two minutes? More like ten. Were you making plans with her behind the bar or something?' she asked sarcastically.

'Would you care if I was?'

'No,' she replied with a frown and he started to laugh.

'She told me that Hazel will be in in half an hour, but Jordan isn't working tonight. So we might as well relax and enjoy each other's company for a while?' John suggested with a wink as he picked up his glass.

Leigh rolled her eyes and took a swig of her drink. It

was going to be a long night. She was going to kill Grace Carter!

If Leigh had been worried that she and John would have nothing to talk about, then she soon realised she needn't have been. He was easy to talk to and they discovered they liked the same music, films and food. Given the establishment they were sitting in, she'd been sure that he wouldn't be able to stop himself making jokes at her expense about her time as a stripper, but he didn't mention it once. In fact, he was a perfect gentleman and before she knew it, forty-five minutes had passed and they were being approached by a young petite woman wearing lacy black underwear, with short dark hair and a body that only served to remind Leigh she should really get herself back to the gym. She was stunning, and Leigh felt a pang of jealousy as she ran a perfectly manicured fingernail down John's chest.

'Sylvie told me you were asking for me,' she purred as she indicated the barmaid. 'Do you want a dance?' She looked at Leigh too then and licked her lips suggestively.

'Hazel? Can you talk and dance at the same time?' John asked her.

'Depends how much you're paying me.' She grinned.

Leigh looked at John. She only had about twenty pounds in cash with her and thought it unlikely Hazel accepted Visa. She hadn't been expecting to have to pay for a lap dance.

John narrowed his eyes at Leigh as though to warn her off speaking. 'How does £150 sound?' he asked as he pulled the crisp notes from inside his coat.

Hazel took them from his hand and tucked the notes into her bra.

'Who wants to go first?' Hazel asked.

'Ladies first. Always,' John said with a wicked grin.

Leigh sat back in her chair while Hazel gyrated on her lap. She looked across at John, who could barely contain his amusement. But Leigh had been in more uncomfortable situations than this one and she grinned back at him. 'I'll get you back,' she mouthed.

During their lap dance, Hazel told them all about her spat with Melanie. It seemed that Hazel took her profession very seriously and she objected to people like Melanie who thought it was simply easy money and all she had to do was turn up and look pretty. According to Hazel, Melanie was often too out of it to perform properly and Hazel and the other girls had to pick up the slack. Melanie had no other links to Jezebel's and she hadn't stayed in touch with anyone. And that was pretty much the extent of Hazel's information. She had known Sol Shepherd and he had always been generous when she'd danced for him but she offered nothing further about him.

Hazel had finished her dance and moved on to her next customer. Leigh finished the last of her third brandy and Coke. 'Shall we go?' she said to John despondently. They hadn't learned much at all.

'Just give me a few minutes,' John said before he disappeared to the bar. Leigh watched him as he stood chatting to Sylvie the barmaid for the next ten minutes. The two of them were obviously having a good time and Sylvie kept grabbing hold of John's arm when she laughed. Leigh frowned. She was tired, grumpy and she wanted to go home. Surely there were plenty of women in Liverpool for John to hook up with?

She put on her coat and started to walk towards the door, deciding she would wait outside for John in the fresh air. She was passing by a table near the exit when an arm shot out and grabbed her around the waist. She looked down to see the drunken man from earlier, who now looked even more inebriated than before.

'Take your hands off me,' she snapped as she tried to wriggle free.

'Looks like your boyfriend has other plans tonight, love,' he slurred as he nodded towards the bar. 'Don't worry though, I'll take care of you.'

'Piss off,' Leigh spat as she pulled at his arm.

'Ow, you fucking scratched me, you bitch!' he snarled, then he pulled her roughly to him until she was sitting on his lap. They were in a dark corner of the bar and she suddenly realised it would be difficult for anyone to see anything other than a woman sitting on a man's lap. The music was thumping loudly and she wondered if John or any of the bouncers would hear her if she screamed. 'You're fucking asking for this,' he hissed in her ear as he started to push his hand up inside her dress. She was about to elbow him in the lip when the hulking figure of John Brennan loomed into view. He pulled Leigh up with one hand and, grabbing the back of the drunk man's head with the other, he slammed it down onto the wooden table in one swift move. The drunk man lay slumped on the table and no one around seemed to have noticed a thing – or if they did, they didn't let on.

'Come on. Let's go,' John said, pulling her by the hand.

Leigh followed him outside and he waited until they were a few metres away from the club before he stopped and turned to her. 'What the hell where you doing, Leigh?' he asked. 'I told you to wait for me. You can't go walking around a place like that on your own, especially dressed like that.' He nodded at her dress and she instinctively tugged at the hem. He shook his head. 'I'm sorry. There's nothing wrong with your dress. But men who go to those places … they don't like to take no for an answer.'

'Well, how long did you expect me to sit there and wait while you flirted with the barmaid?' she snapped.

He frowned at her. 'What?'

'You heard me.'

'I wasn't flirting with her. Well … I was, but I was getting you information!' he snapped.

'Oh?' she said. 'I thought…'

'You think Sylvie is my type?' He started to laugh.

'Why not? She was gorgeous.'

'Yeah?' He shrugged. 'And she was young enough to be my daughter.'

He started to walk towards the car and Leigh fell into step beside him. 'Are you okay?' he asked her.

'Yes. And thank you, John. I have a good mind to go back there and arrest the filthy pervert!' she spat.

'Your call, Detective,' he grinned at her. 'That prick got blood on my best shirt,' he said as he held up his arm. She saw the spatters of bright red blood as his white shirt cuff protruded from his jacket. 'But how about I drive you home and get you a nice glass of some decent brandy instead?'

Leigh looked at him. There was no way she could make an arrest and John knew it. There would be far too many questions asked, which would not only jeopardise the investigation but also quite likely earn Leigh a suspension. Nevertheless, his offer was tempting. 'Sounds good to me,' she replied with a smile. She wondered if the butterflies in her stomach were a result of the alcohol and lack of food – or something else entirely.

Leigh watched as John pulled up outside his house and turned off the engine.

'Come in and I'll get you that drink,' he said.

Leigh wondered whether to change her mind about the drink and ask him to take her to her car, which was still in the car park of The Rocket, instead. But after the evening they'd had, she needed one. She figured he did too. Unclipping her seatbelt, she smiled. 'Just the one though. I need to be up early in the morning.'

'Whatever you say, Detective,' John said.

Leigh was standing in John's tastefully decorated kitchen with a glass of cognac in her hand, watching him as he removed his bloodstained shirt and stuffed it in the washing machine before putting it on a cycle.

'Most people don't realise that the best way to remove bloodstains is to start with a cold wash,' he said.

'Well, I imagine bloodstained clothes aren't a hazard of the job for most people,' Leigh snorted.

John didn't respond to her comment. He stood up and stretched his arms above his head and she had to draw her eyes away from his muscular torso. She already knew where this night was leading but she couldn't, or didn't want to, stop it from happening.

'Like what you see, Detective?' he said with a wink.

'Can we drop the sarcasm now, John? I'm standing in your kitchen with a glass of brandy and you're half naked.'

He laughed. 'Fair point, Leigh.'

He crossed the kitchen until he was standing in front of her. Reaching behind her, he picked up his bottle of beer from the counter.

'You okay?' he asked, his tone serious for a change.

She was caught off-guard by his concern for her. 'Yes,' she replied a little too quickly, feeling the flush creep up her neck.

'You sure?' he asked, a frown on his face as he moved even closer, until there was only an inch of space between them.

'Yes, I'm fine,' she whispered as she looked up at him. She stared at him for a few seconds, aware of the heat from his body and his slow, steady breathing. 'I'm tough, you know?' she added.

'I have no doubt about that,' he said before he bent his head low and kissed her.

Leigh wrapped her arms around his neck and kissed

him back. Then his hands were on her waist. Her back. Unzipping her dress. His rough fingertips running over her flesh. Leigh concentrated on how good it felt to have his hands and his lips on her skin, rather than how wrong it was that she was standing in the kitchen of one of the biggest villains in Liverpool – and what they were about to do.

Leigh pulled the duvet over herself as she laid her head on John's broad chest, both of them breathing heavily from their exertions.

'That wasn't exactly how I expected this night to end,' John said as he wrapped one of his huge arms around her.

'Me neither,' Leigh agreed.

'If I had known, I wouldn't have given Grace such a hard time about having to babysit you,' he said as he started to laugh.

Leigh looked up at him. 'You were not—' she started until she realised he was trying to wind her up. 'Will you pack it in?' She gave him a nudge in the ribs.

'But you're so fucking easy,' he replied.

'Please don't tell Grace about this, will you?' she said to him, in all seriousness.

'Why? Are you ashamed of me or something?'

'It's not that. But you and me? It's not exactly a match made in heaven, is it? I'd just rather people didn't know.'

'Don't worry. I'm not about to go shouting from the

rooftops that I've copped off with a copper. Even one as fit as you,' he said as he kissed the top of her head.

Leigh didn't respond. Everything about the situation she was in should have felt awkward and wrong. She was a DI and he was the top henchman of the biggest crime family in the North West, never mind Liverpool. If that wasn't enough, John had known her a long time ago when she had been a different person, when she had been at her absolute worst. She would have thought that would have made her feel vulnerable around him, but she felt the exact opposite. It was a relief to be able to be herself without worrying that she would slip up and reveal some part of her past that she was unable to explain. She had never really thought about how the secrets of her past had weighed so heavily upon her. Not until she was free of that burden. She had loved Nick, but she had never been her true self around him, and he had never known the real Leigh, only the parts of herself that she had allowed him to see. Only those parts that she deemed worthy. How ironic that she felt more at ease in John Brennan's bed than she had felt anywhere else in the past twenty years.

Leigh had worked hard to erase any trace of her past. Nathan Conlon had ensured he'd had plenty of police officers in his pockets, but fortunately none of them had ever been stupid enough to frequent his club, The Blue Rooms, where she had worked as an exotic dancer. Leigh had changed her appearance, gone back to her real name, and had become an entirely different person to Candy Malone the stripper. She had thought that shedding her past would mean freedom, but over the past few years it had become increasingly difficult to maintain the constant façade. Sometimes, she wondered who was the real her. Occasionally, she felt more like Candy than she did Leigh, and it was on those days that she realised she was both. Her past had made her the woman she was today and it was exhausting to have to hide that part of herself around almost everyone she knew. But she didn't have to do that with John.

Leigh closed her eyes and listened to the steady thumping of his heartbeat against her ear as she drifted off to sleep.

Chapter Twenty

Grace was sitting in her office in Sophia's Kitchen when John Brennan walked through the door.

'Morning, Boss,' he said with his trademark grin.

'Morning John,' she replied as he sat opposite her. 'Thank you for last night. I really appreciate it.' Grace had told John about agreeing to help Leigh with the investigation and her reasons why. She'd sensed he wasn't entirely happy with her request, but he was loyal and he trusted her. She had never given him reason not to.

'No problem,' he replied. 'Always happy to help.'

'That's not what you said last night,' she said with a laugh.

'Well, I was just about to eat my tea, Boss. But it was fine.'

'I would have asked someone else, but I needed someone I could trust.'

'I know that,' he replied sincerely.

'So, did you find out anything worthwhile?' Grace

asked. She would speak to Leigh later but she wanted John's take on events first.

'We didn't find out much about Sol Shepherd, or that woman who was murdered. But I got chatting to the barmaid and I did find out something interesting about a mutual acquaintance of ours.'

'Oh? Who?'

'Joey Parnell.'

Grace sat forward in her seat. 'The guy who's been causing problems for Cartel Securities?'

John nodded. 'Apparently, he was a regular of Jezebel's a few years back. None of the girls could stand him. He was a bit too rough, if you know what I mean? Usually the bouncers wouldn't have that sort of thing, but Parnell seemed to be untouchable and he got away with whatever he liked. He even split one of the girls' lips open one night but he was allowed to walk out without a scratch. The bouncers would just ignore him, as though they were under orders to leave him alone.'

'How did his name come up?'

'When I was asking about Sol and about Melanie. The girls assumed Parnell was a buddy of Sol's because of the special treatment he got. And then when I asked if anyone stuck out as having a thing for Melanie, apparently the few times she was there at Jezebel's, Joey acted like he already knew her. He stopped going to the place after Melanie left though.'

'That all sounds a bit dodgy,' Grace said.

'It could be,' John replied with a shrug. 'But everything about Joey Parnell, Sol Shepherd and Jezebel's is dodgy.

From what me and Leigh were told, Melanie had her fair share of enemies. She had a raging crack habit and was barely able to perform on the nights she worked. Maybe it was just a dissatisfied punter? Or her pimp had enough of her?'

'Does Leigh know about Joey Parnell?' Grace asked.

'No. I got that from the barmaid. I thought I'd tell you and then if you decide to tell the plod, that's your call, Boss.'

'Thank you, John,' she said. 'I'm sorry if I put you in a difficult position last night.'

'You didn't,' he said and then he coughed. Grace could have sworn she saw him blush slightly.

'Anything else I need to know about last night?' she asked.

'No, Boss,' he said. 'That's all I found out.'

Grace studied his face. She knew John well, and she knew he was hiding something from her.

Grace was at home with Michael and their youngest children when Leigh phoned to ask if she could drop by. Michael had glared at her when she'd asked him if he objected but he'd reluctantly agreed. Grace reminded him that Leigh was in their debt and they'd had police visiting their house before. It was no different with Leigh. It would look much worse for her if word ever got out that she was visiting them at home.

'I hope she's not planning on staying long, Grace,' he

said as the doorbell rang.

Grace walked past him towards the door. 'You're really sexy when you're angry, you know?'

He grinned at her. 'Just make it quick. You promised the kids we'd build a den,' he said as he picked Oscar up and hoisted him over his shoulder.

'Den, Mummy!' Oscar squealed.

'Soon, baby,' she said as she kissed the top of his head. 'Mummy just needs to do a little work first.'

'Oh Muuum!' Belle whined from behind her. 'You were supposed to be on my team.'

'And I will be, angel. I'll be really quick. Promise.'

'Come on, monsters,' Michael said as he shepherded their five-year-old daughter down the hallway. 'Let's go and find our den-building gear, eh? Mummy will join us soon.'

Grace walked to the door as her family disappeared out of sight.

'So, do you think Parnell has anything to do with all of this?' Grace asked after she had told Leigh what John had discovered.

Leigh stared at her for a few moments, as though digesting the information. 'Why didn't he tell me last night?' she asked. 'John? Why didn't he tell me about Parnell?'

'Well, to be fair, he works for me, not you. He was just doing his job.'

Leigh nodded absent-mindedly. 'I suppose.'

'So, Parnell?' Grace asked again.

'Well, it looks like he was definitely connected to something to do with Sol and Melanie, doesn't it?'

'Seems so. So what happens now then?'

'I'll look into Parnell. See if he has any history of similar offending. Where is the link to Sunnymeade though?' Leigh shook her head. 'We're still missing something.'

'Did you look into Nerys's friend, Stuart? Or Steven?'

'Yes. I went through the interviews and one of my detectives interviewed a Stuart Halligan a few days after our second victim was found dead. He was at Sunnymeade at the same time as our victims and he did know them but he claimed he was never friends with them. Nothing else of note though and he had a cast-iron alibi. But given this recent information, I wouldn't mind speaking to him myself too.'

Grace wondered if police officers often felt constrained by process and procedure. Every single thing they did had to be done by the book or a conviction could be jeopardised, especially if the perpetrator had a good lawyer. Grace thought how infuriating it must be when they knew who the perpetrator was but couldn't prove it. She wasn't used to having to operate within such parameters herself.

'I hope you didn't mind too much when I asked John to go with you last night?' Grace said. 'But something came up.'

'Not at all,' Leigh said. 'He came in very handy actually. I can see why you like having him around.'

Grace watched as Leigh Moss sipped her tea. Slowly all of the pieces of the puzzle were starting to fall into place.

Chapter Twenty-One

G race sat down beside Michael on the sofa and he handed her a glass of Barolo.

'Tell me about Joey Parnell,' she said to him as she took a sip of her wine.

Michael frowned. 'He's a prick.'

'Well, I gathered that, but I was hoping for a little more,' she said with a smile.

'What do you want to know?' he asked as he lifted her fingers to his lips and kissed them gently.

'Who is he? What's his back story?'

Michael leaned forward and put his glass down on the coffee table before sitting back with a sigh. 'He ran one of the biggest door firms back in the Nineties. He did security for The Blue Rooms back when Tommy McNulty owned the place. At one time, he ran a good little operation, but he started to get greedy and began stepping on toes that he shouldn't have. Eventually, he ended up pissing off the wrong people one too many times and his firm was taken over. He was lucky he didn't end up in the Mersey in a pair of concrete wellies.'

'Whose toes did he step on?' she asked.

Michael ran a hand over his beard and leaned towards her before he answered. 'Tommy,' he said. 'Parnell started believing his own hype that he was as hard as nails. Then he and some of his bouncers started selling coke on the side, which Tommy got wind of and wasn't happy about. It got sorted but Joey kept on pushing the boundaries until...'

'Until what?'

Michael closed his eyes and shook his head. 'Are you sure you want to know all this?'

Grace assumed this was going to have something to do with her ex-husband Nathan, as most things from back in those days did. 'Yes,' she replied.

'He was caught banging some stripper, but she also happened to be a certain person's favourite bit on the side.'

'A certain person being Nathan?' she said with a roll of her eyes.

He nodded.

'So Nathan caught him with his bit on the side?'

Michael swallowed. 'Not exactly. Me and Sean did. Joey was supposed to be working but we caught him banging this girl and doing coke off her tits in Nathan's office. But we worked with Nathan then, and ... well, we didn't know you, obviously.'

'Oh, I don't care about any of that now,' she assured him, suddenly realising why he had been looking so uncomfortable. She supposed the fact that he had once defended the honour of her then husband's mistress might make him feel like he had somehow betrayed her – but he was right, she hadn't known either him or Sean back then.

'We gave him a good kicking and took him to Nathan and Tommy to deal with. The stripper incident was the last straw really. Tommy was prepared to be a bit more lenient, but Nathan had been looking for an excuse to get rid of Joey, and that was the perfect one. Tommy backed Joey's biggest rivals to take over and together they orchestrated a massive takeover. Joey put up a bit of a fight but half of his own bouncers had even had enough of him and defected to the rival firm, so he didn't stand a chance. If I recall, Joey ended up being put in intensive care after one particular nasty fight at The Blue Rooms – which me and Sean might have been involved in. Then he just seemed to disappear.'

'Until about eight months ago?' Grace asked.

'Seems so.'

'Any idea why he's come back?'

'Revenge?'

'Twenty-odd years is a long time to wait for revenge. Besides, Nathan and Tommy are both dead now. Who would he go after for revenge?'

Michael raised an eyebrow at her.

'What?' she asked. 'Not you and Sean?'

'Maybe,' he replied with a shrug. 'And John? As far as he was concerned we were all working with, or for, Tommy and Nathan, and maybe he holds us equally responsible.'

Grace leaned back and took a sip of her wine. 'Revenge, though? I'm not sure I buy it. I don't doubt he probably hates your guts, but there must be more to it than that. To come back after all this time? What's changed for him?'

'I don't know. He's in league with some of our competitors, I know that much. That prick Karl Morgan has got into bed with him, as well as some small firms who wouldn't usually bother us. But they could cause us some headaches if they all got their act together.'

Grace frowned. She had fired Karl Morgan, the owner of Trident Securities, from The Blue Rooms a couple of years earlier because he was unreliable and much like Michael had described Joey Parnell, was more interested in getting his leg over than doing his job.

'Eight months ago is around the time we started negotiating the merger with Luke and Danny, isn't it?' Grace said.

'Yes. They already told us they had some problems with Parnell though. But do you think either of them have anything more to do with him coming back?' Michael asked.

'I don't know. Maybe?'

'Really?' Michael asked with a flash of his eyebrows. 'I thought you rated the pair of them. You and Luke seem to get on particularly well,' he said as he took a swig of his wine.

'I do rate them. I don't think they're up to anything, but maybe there's a connection is all I'm saying. And I do get on with Luke. I like the way he thinks.'

'I'd noticed.'

'What's that supposed to mean?'

He put his glass of wine down and held his hands up in surrender. 'Nothing,' he insisted. 'I just noticed how well you get on with him, that's all.'

'Oh, don't start with him now,' she said as she rolled her eyes. 'It is possible for me to have a close relationship with a man without there being anything going on, you know,' she snapped. 'Besides, he's almost young enough to be my son.'

Michael pulled her into his arms as he started to laugh. 'Calm down. I'm just playing with you,' he said as he kissed her. Grace kissed him back but she knew that he wasn't entirely joking. His first wife, Cheryl, had cheated on him with almost every villain in Liverpool and he hadn't found out about it until he'd gone to prison. Grace knew than an experience like that left a mark – even if you tried your best to fight against it.

She pulled away from him. 'You do know you can trust me, don't you?' she said.

'Of course I do, Grace,' he said before he pulled her back to him and kissed her so hard she didn't have a chance to speak any further.

Chapter Twenty-Two

Stacey had just finished her shift in Sophia's Kitchen and was putting on her coat when her mobile phone started ringing. She saw the withheld number and her heart sank. She had six missed calls too. If she didn't answer, he would keep calling until she did. She slipped into Grace's empty office to answer it.

'Hello,' she answered.

'Stace,' Simon said.

She took a deep breath. 'Simon! I thought I told you not to—'

'Stace,' he interrupted her. 'I need your help, babe.'

'I'm not your babe,' she hissed. 'And why the hell would I help you?'

'I'm in deep shit, Stace. There are some people after me.' He sniffed and she wondered if he was crying.

'And why are you telling me?'

'Because they're going to kill me, Stace. I really need your help.' He did start to cry then. 'Please?' he pleaded.

Stacey leaned back against the wall. Simon Jones had been a part of her life for six years, since she was eighteen. She had met him on her first day of college and he had seemed so sophisticated and charming, he'd swept her off her feet. For the first two years, despite him persuading her to drop out of college and cutting her off from her friends, things had seemed perfect. Then she'd started to see the real Simon. He was jealous, cruel, petty and a typical narcissist. He cared about nobody and nothing but himself. But by then she was so deep in his clutches, she felt she had no means of escape. She couldn't go back to Liverpool to Danny and Luke and prove that they had been right all along. Prove that she really did need them. Prove that she couldn't look after herself. By the time she had discovered who Simon really was, she was too far gone. She was completely under his control and she could see no way out. The more she started to dislike him, the more of his true self he revealed. Until she found out the awful truth that he bought and sold women like a used-car salesman did cars. He would hold it over her constantly – that he could do the same to her if he chose to. When Danny and Luke had finally found out what was going on, they had driven up to Manchester and forcibly removed her from Simon's house, with a threat to Simon that they would kill him if he ever came near her again. For all his presentation, Simon was a coward, and he would never have challenged her brother or Luke. He was too focused on his own self-preservation to ever take on anyone who might give him a fair fight.

Now here he was asking for her help. God, he really was a narcissistic prick.

'Why on earth would I help you?' she snapped.

'Because you love me, Stace. You're my girl. There was only ever you. You know that,' he said, suddenly all charm again.

Her curiosity was piqued. 'How exactly do you think I could help you?'

'Come and meet me. We can run away somewhere together? We always talked about living somewhere hot and sunny. We could go to Spain?'

She laughed. 'With what? I don't have a pot to piss in, do you?'

'No, but your brother does,' he said.

So that was his game. 'Go to hell, Simon,' she spat. 'If you ever contact me again, I'll be telling my brother all about what you did to me. I'll tell the police too. You disgusting piece of shit!' she screeched and then she threw the phone onto the floor.

She leaned against the wall and held her hand to her mouth as she started to sob. She wiped her eyes as she saw the door open. It was Luke and she wasn't sure if she felt more relieved or mortified that he of all people was here to witness her at her most vulnerable.

'Stacey. What's wrong?' he said, his face full of concern as he walked into the room and closed the door behind him.

'It's okay. I'm fine,' she said as she wiped her eyes.

He placed a hand under her chin and tilted her face to look at him. 'You don't look fine,' he said softly as his dark eyes burned into hers. She felt her stomach contract. Her head was a swirl of emotions, stirred up firstly by Simon and now by Luke looking into her eyes. He was igniting something in her that she had tried to suppress since she was thirteen years old and he had first visited her in that children's home and taken her out for the day. It was all too much. She would only ever be like a little sister to him, and that hurt her almost as much as reliving her past with Simon.

'I'm fine, honestly,' she said as she brushed past him. 'Just heard some news about someone I used to know, that's all.'

Luke looked at her and she knew he could tell she was lying, but thankfully he didn't press her on the matter.

'I only called in to see if Grace was here, but it looks like she's gone for the day. Let me give you a lift home?'

'No. It's fine. I can get the bus,' she said.

'Stacey, I'm not letting you get the bus home on your own, especially when you're upset. Now, grab your things, and let's go. Please?' he said as he held out a hand to her.

She nodded but didn't take his outstretched hand. 'Okay.'

He picked her phone up from the floor and handed it to her. Then he pulled her into one of his infamous bear hugs and kissed the top of her head. God, why did he have to be so bloody lovely?

Chapter Twenty-Three

L eigh Moss turned off her computer and leaned back in her chair with a sigh. She had spent most of the afternoon looking into Joey Parnell. What she'd found out only served to increase her suspicion. Eleven years earlier he'd been sentenced to two years in prison for an assault on his seventeen-year-old girlfriend that had left her with a broken jaw. Joey had been forty-one at the time. There had been an allegation of rape too but the CPS hadn't proceeded with a charge due to a perceived poor chance of securing a conviction. Joey had been living in Manchester at the time and had done his time in Strangeways.

Three years after he got out, he'd done another twelve months for assault – this time against a male. Parnell broke two of the victim's ribs by stamping on him. On the surface, his second conviction didn't appear to form a pattern of violence against women. But when Leigh had dug a little deeper, she'd learned the circumstances of the offence involved a fight in a bar over a woman which had stemmed from Parnell's jealousy about her allegedly flirting with the victim. Probably most telling of all was that the probation service managed him under multi agency public protection arrangements (MAPPA) when he was on licence, which they reserved for only the most serious of offenders. Leigh had requested the notes of those meetings from the MAPPA chair and was awaiting a response. The intel on police systems also suggested that Joey was involved in the sex trade, but it wasn't from a reliable source. In all, Leigh had uncovered plenty to suspect Parnell of being involved in the murders, but not enough tangible evidence to apply for a warrant. Not yet anyway.

Leigh was just about to pack up and leave when she saw a shadow fall over her desk. She looked up to see Chief Superintendent Barrow standing in the doorway to her office.

'Evening, Sir,' she said.

'Evening, Leigh. I just thought I'd drop by and see how you're getting on with this investigation. You know the press are referring to our perp as the Liverpool Ripper?' He shook his head in frustration.

'I know, Sir, and it seems to have stuck.'

'This case is attracting enough attention without those sharks using it to shift papers.'

'Well, we do have three dead women in the space of a month, Sir. The press were always going to be all over it.'

'Hmm.' He rubbed his chin as he walked towards her and perched on the edge of her desk. 'How is it going then? Any suspects yet?'

Leigh leaned back in her chair. 'No one we can arrest

yet, Sir. The crime scenes are completely clean, as you know. I do have a lead but nothing of any substance on him yet. Certainly not enough for a warrant.'

Barrow frowned at her. 'Who is your suspect?'

'Joey Parnell. He used to be a bit of a name in Liverpool back in the Nineties. He came back to Liverpool about six months ago. He has form for violence against women. There was also an alleged rape and intel suggests he was involved in the sex work trade when he lived in Manchester. I've asked for further intel reports and I'm waiting on some MAPPA notes from probation too.'

Barrow frowned at her. 'Seems like a tenuous link at best, Leigh. Previous form? What else do you have to tie him to the murders? Any connection to Sunnymeade?'

'No. Nothing like that,' she admitted with a sigh. 'Just a gut feeling?'

'Well, a good detective always trusts their gut. But we cannot afford to make any mistakes with this one. We need a watertight case. My gut tells me there's a link to that children's home we're missing. I'd be concentrating my efforts there while you wait for this information on Parnell.'

Leigh wondered if he was right. Was she barking up the completely wrong tree?

'Thanks, Sir. I appreciate your input.'

'Happy to help,' he said with a smile. 'Keep me informed of your progress, won't you?'

'Of course, Sir,' she replied.

Then Chief Superintendent Barrow walked out of her office, leaving her sitting alone and contemplating her next move.

Chapter Twenty-Four

Joey Parnell walked along the path in Stanley Park until he reached his employer sitting on the bench. JB picked up the tennis ball and threw it for his dog Archie, a brown spaniel who chased after it furiously.

Joey sat down on the opposite end of the wooden seat.

'Your face is looking a little better at least,' JB said as he gave a cursory glance in Joey's direction. 'Have you had any luck in locating Simon yet?'

'Not yet, but I have my sources looking for him. He must be running out of friends and hiding places by now and I think it's only a matter of time before we find him. He doesn't have the resources to stay on the run for much longer.'

His employer sighed wearily. 'I told you I wanted this dealing with quickly. You're beginning to make me regret trusting you with this, Joey. We have three dead women and nothing to show for it.'

'At least they won't talk,' Joey said.

JB snorted. 'What did you want to see me about?' he snapped.

'Grace Carter,' Joey said.

'Not the Carters again. I've told you to leave it alone until this is over with. Then I don't care how you deal with your petty feud with them, but until then, concentrate on the job at hand.'

'That's just it, I think Grace Carter is onto something.'

'What?' JB's head turned as though on a swivel and he finally gave Joey his undivided attention.

'She's been asking questions about the three women we took, and about Melanie Simmonds.'

His employer's face started to turn that dangerous shade of red which meant that Joey was about to get an earful.

'How the hell does she know about any connection to that whore from Manchester?' he spat. 'You told me this job would be clean and there would no ties to anyone except that fucking godforsaken kids' home. She had nothing to do with that place. Nothing at all. So, tell me how the fuck Grace Carter knows about it, and why on earth is she even sniffing around this? What the fuck have a few dead whores got to do with her?'

'I don't know, Boss,' Joey added. 'But I can take care of them for you. All of them.'

His employer started to laugh out loud just as Archie came bounding back over to them with his ball. He dropped it on the ground before lying dutifully at his master's feet.

'You honestly think you're capable of taking care of

Grace and Michael Carter?' he snorted, not caring to hide his obvious derision. 'You can barely handle a few whores.'

'I think you underestimate me, Boss,' Joey said, feeling annoyed and hurt that his employer seemed to think so little of him after he had only ever done exactly as he'd asked.

'Okay. Prove it. Warn Grace Carter off. Get her to back away from the whole mess. I don't care what you tell her as long as it throws her off the scent.'

'And if that doesn't work?'

He tilted his head back, stretching his neck before he answered. 'Then you can make sure her and her husband are too distracted to come anywhere near us.'

'How?'

'By hitting them where it really hurts and disposing of their two trigger-happy sons,' he said as though the answer was completely obvious. 'It's too messy to go after Grace and Michael, and it would cause too much instability and that's all I need right now. But dealing with their errant offspring would keep the pair of them out of my hair.'

Joey smiled. He liked that idea much better than warning Grace off. He hated Jake Conlon and Connor Carter almost as much as he hated Sean and Michael.

Noting the smile on his face, his employer shook his head. 'Warn her off first,' he snapped. 'Only proceed with the next step if that doesn't work. Understood?'

'Understood.' Joey knew there was no way Grace Carter would listen to a warning, least of all from him. In fact, if he provoked her enough, maybe it would fuel her efforts even further, and then he would have permission to take out his competition once and for all.

Joey watched as his employer walked away with his loyal spaniel by his side and wondered what would be the best way to provoke Grace and Michael Carter. He smiled to himself as he walked through the park and back towards his car.

Chapter Twenty-Five

G race had just turned off her computer and was about to head home for the day when, in her peripheral vision, she saw the figure walking into her office. She looked up to see a tall, stocky man with silver hair, wearing a leather jacket, standing before her. He closed the door behind him and then turned back to her with a smile on his face.

She frowned at him. 'Who are you?' she snapped. She'd already stayed later than she'd planned and was eager to get home to Michael and their children.

'That's right, I don't think we've ever been formally introduced,' he said as he extended his hand. 'Joey Parnell.'

Grace felt her breath catch in her throat. This man had obviously made his way unnoticed through the back of their restaurant and to her office. The place was busy, as was usual for a Thursday evening. There was music playing as well as the constant background noise of a busy restaurant full of diners. She couldn't call for help as no-one was likely to hear her unless they were standing directly outside. If she screamed loud enough, perhaps she'd be heard, but she wasn't about to give Joey that satisfaction. Not until she knew what he was doing there, at least. He hated her husband and her brother-in-law, that much she knew, but what was he doing in her office? Standing there grinning at her like he knew something she didn't.

Grace ignored his hand. 'As you can see, I'm on my way out,' she said as she stood and shrugged on her coat. 'So, what can I do for you?'

Joey let his hand fall to his side and she noticed his grin turn to a scowl. She doubted he was used to people, particularly women, being so impolite to him. From the limited information she'd been able to glean about him, he considered himself a ladies' man and had the arrogance of a man who believed he was God's gift to women.

'You're not at all what I expected,' he said with a snarl. 'I remember how Nathan used to talk about you. He made out you were some sweet, naïve little girl who was scared of her own shadow. But, you're actually a bit of a bitch really, aren't you?'

Grace started to laugh. 'You think you know anything about me because of what my psychopathic ex-husband might have said to you over twenty years ago? Are you for real? Or are you really as stupid as my husband tells me you are, Joey?'

That obviously provoked something in him and he lunged over the desk towards her. Grace stepped back instinctively, but he had a long reach and he grabbed the lapel of her coat with his left hand. Then he dragged her around the desk towards him, wrapping his right hand around her throat when he got close enough.

He glared at her and she glared back. She had been threatened by tougher men than him before. He wouldn't dare do something so stupid in her restaurant. Would he?

'You think you're a fucking cut above the likes of me, don't you?' he snarled in her face. 'But you're just a weak, cock-teasing little bitch like the rest of them.'

Grace spat at him and watched as her spittle dribbled down his forehead and over his left eye. He wiped his face with his free hand and squeezed her throat harder until she started to struggle to breathe.

He brought his face closer to hers. 'What is it about you that has all these men following you around, obeying your orders?' he snarled at her. 'Let's face it, you're nothing special, are you? You certainly couldn't keep your husband happy. He fucked everything in a skirt.'

Grace pulled at his arm but he maintained his vice-like grip on her throat. Lashing out, she managed to scratch his face before he dodged out of her reach again. 'You fucking cunt,' he shouted before pushing her up against the wall. She gasped as the weight of his large frame crushed hers. He pushed his groin into her abdomen and she could feel his erection digging into her. Bile rose in her throat and she swallowed it down and closed her eyes. He shoved his free hand beneath her coat and squeezed her breast painfully until she cried out. But his movement had given her some wriggle room and using all of her strength she raised her right leg and kneed him in the groin.

Joey doubled over, and as he pulled his hand free, his

watch caught on her blouse, tearing some of the buttons away from the fabric and sending them skittering across the floor. Joey groaned in pain.

'Get the fuck out of here before I scream for my bouncers and they throw you in the fucking river,' she rasped as she rubbed her throat. The truth was her throat was so raw and tender that she couldn't have screamed if she'd tried.

Joey threw her one last look of disgust before he started to hobble out of her office. As he reached the door, he turned to her, and pointed a finger in her direction. 'I actually came here to give you a friendly warning,' he snarled. 'Stay out of things that don't concern you. Or you'll end up just like them girls they've been picking up out of back alleyways.'

Grace's blood ran cold. His visit could only mean that she and Leigh were onto something. She'd been wondering whether they had been barking up the wrong tree, but Joey's visit had now convinced her otherwise. How stupid of him to incriminate himself by trying to warn her off. Rather than doing that, now she was more determined than ever to bring the lot of them down. But how would she stop Michael from tearing Joey's head off and using it as a toilet brush once he found out what had happened to her tonight?

Grace buttoned her coat to cover her now gaping blouse and picked up her handbag. Still rubbing her throat, she left her office and wondered how she was going to convince her husband to let her deal with Parnell herself – at least until she had got to the bottom of what was going on. Once she had that, Michael could do whatever he liked with the arrogant little prick.

Grace walked through the restaurant and approached their head bouncer, Nick Walker. 'You been busy tonight?' she asked, wondering how Parnell had been allowed to walk into her office unchallenged.

'Yeah, Boss. It's been mental. I've never had to deal with so many kick-offs in this place on one night. Ten minutes ago, I had to throw a whole table of lads out,' he said as he shook his head in disbelief.

That went some way to explaining Parnell's presence in her office. Grace wondered if any of the trouble had been orchestrated by Parnell in order to create a diversion. 'Must be something in the air,' she said with a half-smile. 'Do you mind walking me to my car?'

'Of course, Grace. Not a problem. Let's go.'

Grace linked her arm through Nick's as they headed along the waterfront. He had worked for them for a few years and she trusted him. Her encounter with Parnell had her rattled and it was nice to have his solid presence for company on the short walk to her car. Who knew whether Parnell or any of his minions were still hanging around.

Chapter Twenty-Six

Grace walked quietly along the hallway of her house and up the stairs, hoping that Michael hadn't heard her, or, if he had, he'd be too busy cooking or tidying up after the kids to follow her. She looked in on Oscar and Belle quickly before walking into her own bedroom. She had taken off her shoes and was about to remove her blouse when she heard Michael's heavy footfall on the hallway landing. She sighed inwardly, having been hoping that she could freshen up and hide her torn blouse before she saw him.

Turning around, Grace smiled as Michael walked through the door. 'Hi,' she said as she started to undo the remaining buttons on her top.

'Hey,' he said as he smiled back. 'You okay?'

'Yes. Of course. Why?'

'You came straight up here?'

'I missed the kids' bedtime. I wanted to see them,' she replied as he started to walk towards her.

As he reached her, he slipped his arms around her waist and pulled her towards him. Leaning down, he gave her a brief kiss. 'How was work?'

'Fine,' she lied.

She saw the frown flicker across his face. God, he knew her so well. His hands trailed up her body and to her blouse.

'Let me help you with that,' he said with a grin as he started to undo the remaining buttons.

She flinched instinctively and tried to step back from him, but in doing so, lifted her head and exposed her neck to him. In the lamp light of the room, he obviously hadn't noticed the red marks on her neck until now.

Suddenly his eyes were full of concern and anger. 'What the hell is this? Has somebody hurt you?' he asked as he brushed the red marks on her neck with his fingertips. Then his eyes dropped to her blouse and he noticed the fabric near the buttonhole was torn. 'And this? Grace, what's happened?' he asked, his voice filled with urgency and anxiety.

'It was nothing. I handled it,' she insisted.

'Well, it doesn't fucking look like nothing,' he growled. 'Who did this, Grace? Tell me because I'm going to fucking kill him.'

'Michael, please. I told you I dealt with it.'

'Did you break every bone in his body and bury him somewhere he'll never be found?' he asked.

'Of course not,' she replied.

'Then you didn't deal with it.'

Grace sat on the bed. 'Just because I didn't handle it

your way, doesn't mean I didn't handle it.' She looked up at him.

She watched as his face softened and he sat beside her. She could feel the tension in his body, but his face remained calm. 'Tell me what happened,' he said softly.

'Okay. But let me finish before you start threatening to shoot people and bury them in unmarked graves,' she replied.

'I would never shoot anyone who hurt you,' he answered with a half-smile. 'That would be far too lenient.'

Grace looked at him for a few seconds and wondered what was the best way to tell him that someone who'd been a massive pain in his arse for the past few weeks had pinned her up against the wall before strangling and sexually assaulting her? Probably best not to use any of those words.

'Joey Parnell came into the restaurant—'

'Parnell?' he shouted, interrupting her.

'You said you'd let me finish?'

He closed his eyes before taking a deep breath. 'Go on.'

'He came into my office. Made some smart-arse comments about me and I obviously told him to piss off. That's when he grabbed me. He had his hand around my throat. He pushed me against the wall and started calling me a bitch. The usual stuff pathetic little men like him do to try and intimidate women. But I kneed him in the groin and he backed off when I threatened to scream for the bouncers. Then he left. My throat's a bit sore, but I'm fine.'

'Speaking of the bouncers, where the fuck where they?

What the hell were they doing? Parnell shouldn't have been anywhere near your office or you.'

'They were dealing with stuff. Apparently, there were a few separate incidents tonight that required their attention. We both know that it's unusual for there to be any trouble at Sophia's, so it all seems a bit coincidental, doesn't it? No doubt Parnell was behind it.'

'Probably, but it's still a massive fuck-up that shouldn't have happened. I thought Nick was better than that,' he said with a shake of his head.

'Nick is good at his job. He was dealing with trouble in the bar, just like we pay him to. How was he to know what was going on in the back?'

'It's his job to know what's going on everywhere, especially in the back,' he reminded her. 'But what happened to your blouse?'

'Oh, that?' she said as she looked down and inspected the torn fabric. 'After I kneed Parnell, he pulled his hand away and his watch got caught on my buttons, that's all.'

'Where was his hand to have it catch on your clothes like that?'

Grace swallowed. 'It was inside my coat. He grabbed my boob. That was all.'

'That's all?' he snapped. 'I'm going to fucking kill him.'

She placed a hand on his arm. 'Michael, let me finish. As he was leaving he told me that he'd come to give me a friendly warning to stay out of things that didn't concern me. Then he said I'd end up dead like those girls if I didn't.'

Michael jumped up at this point. 'So he threatened to kill you too?'

She shook her head in annoyance. 'Don't you see that must mean Leigh and I are onto something?'

He blinked at her. 'What?'

'I told you I thought there was something fishy about Parnell coming back when he did, and I think it has something so do with the murdered women.'

Michael shook his head. 'Grace, I don't give a shit about that right now. I'm going to rip his fucking head off his shoulders and take a shit in his neck.'

'And ordinarily, I'd be more than happy to let you deal with Parnell, but let me just get to the bottom of this first. Please?'

'But why? Why do you need to help Leigh with this?'

'This isn't about Leigh now though, is it? For some reason, Joey Parnell has it in for our family. And I suspect he is involved with some very dodgy stuff with some very bad people. I want to know who they are and what their connection is to Parnell. I want to find out who killed those women, Michael, before they do it again.'

'So I'm supposed to let Parnell walk around thinking he can threaten my family. That he can attack my wife and I won't do anything about it?' he shouted.

'Is that what this is about really? Your ego?' she snapped. 'I am not your property.'

Michael looked at her and she saw the hurt in his eyes. 'Grace,' he said softly. 'You know that's not what this is about. We can't afford to let something like this slide in our line of business.'

Grace swallowed. 'I know. I'm sorry. I didn't mean that. I'm just on edge, that's all. But look, I told you I've dealt with him for now. Please just give me a couple of weeks to find out what his part in all this is—'

'And then what? You'll hand him over to the police?' he said sarcastically.

'Of course not. Leigh might think I'm working with her on this, but once I started to suspect there was a connection to Parnell, all bets were off. Once I find out what I need, you can do whatever you like with him. I promise.'

Michael ran his hand down her cheek and onto the red marks on her neck. 'I have never doubted that you know what you're doing, Grace, but I think you're wrong on this one. Parnell is more dangerous than we realised, and the sooner we take him out, the better.'

'But you'll give me a little more time?' she asked.

He looked at her, as though considering her request. 'Two weeks. Tops. And then that fucker is mine.'

'Thank you,' she whispered.

'How do you always get me to agree to anything you want?' he said with a frown.

'My irresistible charm?' she replied with a flash of her eyebrows.

He smiled at her. 'I love you.'

She wrapped her arms around his neck. 'I love you too, Carter.'

Chapter Twenty-Seven

Michael knocked on the door of the top-floor apartment on Linnet Lane and waited for the owner to answer. A few moments later, the door opened and he saw the face of Sophia's Kitchen's head bouncer, Nick Walker.

Nick opened his mouth to speak but was unable to get a word out before Michael put a hand on his chest and pushed him through the door so that Nick stumbled backwards into the room.

'Boss!' Nick shouted. 'What the fuck?'

Michael stepped towards him and punched him in the jaw, causing Nick to fall on his arse. Michael stood over him. 'What the fuck do I pay you for?' he snarled.

Nick blinked at him as he rubbed his jaw.

'I asked you a fucking question. What do I fucking pay you to do?' he shouted.

'To manage the doors,' Nick stammered.

'And to provide security?'

Nick nodded.

'So, can you tell me why the fuck my wife was assaulted in her own office last night? In the restaurant that *you* manage security for?'

Nick's face paled as he started to scrabble to his feet. Michael stalked towards him. 'How the fuck did Joey Parnell manage to slip past you and the rest of those cretins and walk straight into Grace's office without anyone challenging him?'

'Fuck!' Nick said as he shook his head. 'I had no idea, Michael—'

'I know you had no fucking idea, you tool. That's the whole fucking point, isn't it?' he snarled.

Nick jumped up and took a step backwards. 'I don't know Parnell. I wouldn't know him from Adam...'

Michael raised his fist again and Nick held his hands up in defence. 'I'm not excusing what happened. No one should be able to get to Grace like that,' he said as he rubbed at his jaw again. 'I'm sorry, Boss. It will never happen again though, I swear.'

Michael stepped towards him and Nick flinched, but Michael walked straight past him and sat on the sofa.

'So, what the fuck happened then, Nick? How did Joey make you and your boys look like complete amateurs last night? I thought you were the real thing, or I would never have given you responsibility for Sophia's.'

'I am, Boss,' Nick protested as he took a seat on the armchair opposite. 'I know I fucked up last night, and I'm really sorry, especially if Grace was hurt, but I've never let you down before. And I promise it will never happen again.

I'll have a man outside her office permanently from now on. Or I'll do it myself if you'd rather?'

Michael shook his head. 'Have you met Grace? There's no way she'd fucking have that and you know it. I'm getting a panic button installed today and it will go straight to the door and the bar. But last night? Tell me what happened and convince me why I shouldn't kick your arse and put you on The Dog?'

Nick shuddered. The Dog was their codename for Dodgson's – aptly named as it was the dodgiest club in Liverpool. It sold the cheapest ale and was a magnet for drunks, coke-heads and trouble. There were more kick-offs there every Saturday night than in all of their other places put together. It was the place they often put new recruits to prove themselves, or anyone who had fucked up and needed a reminder of how good they really had it. There were some lads who absolutely loved a good scrap and would rather work on The Dog than anywhere else, but Nick had only worked at their more exclusive places, and Sophia's Kitchen was the jewel in the crown. It was the hottest place to be in Merseyside. Their exclusive, award-winning restaurant catered for people with plenty of money to spend on a meal, and the large bar area accommodated those who just fancied a few beers, cocktails from their famous cocktail bar, or a bottle of champagne. Their clientele was largely affluent, respectable, and there was very rarely any trouble. Good-looking bouncers like Nick were liable to go home with a different woman on their arm every night if they so chose, and Michael was aware that Nick indulged more often than not.

'We had loads of trouble last night, Boss,' Nick replied. 'More than I've ever known in the place. It was unusual, especially for a Thursday. We thought maybe there was a massive stag do or something. We must have been dealing with that when this Parnell fella came in. No doubt he was behind some if it then. I thought Grace looked a bit shaken up. She asked me to walk her to her car, but I had no idea.' Nick finished speaking and shook his head in disbelief. 'Is she okay?' he added.

'He had her pinned to the wall by her throat,' Michael snapped.

'I'm sorry,' Nick said again.

'Well, she's as hard as nails. So, yes, she's okay, considering,' Michael added. 'But I'm not. When I think about what could have happened to her...'

Nick looked down at his feet. 'I suppose I deserve to work in The Dog after that.'

Michael stood up. 'Fortunately for you, my wife seems to rate you regardless of what happened last night. And I'd never hear the fucking end of it if I gave you the boot, so your job is safe – for now. But if *anything* ever happens to her on your watch again...'

'It won't, Boss. I guarantee it.'

'Get some ice on that jaw. You're working tonight,' Michael said. Then he walked out of Nick's apartment.

Chapter Twenty-Eight

Leigh stood on the doorstep of John Brennan's house, shuffling her feet in the cold. She had only rung the doorbell ten seconds ago but it had felt like a lifetime. She shouldn't have come here. He wasn't expecting her, but when she had driven past his house and seen the light on at midnight, she hadn't been able to stop herself from paying him a visit. She was suddenly feeling very foolish. What if he had a visitor? A female visitor? He wasn't known for being a ladies' man, but he was a good-looking guy, with plenty of money – why wouldn't he have a woman with him? Leigh cursed under her breath. What the hell was she thinking?

She turned around and was about to make a hasty retreat to her car when the front door opened, bathing the doorstep in a faint glow from the hallway light. John stood there in a pair of boxer shorts and nothing else and she was sure she must have disturbed him and a lady friend. She dragged her eyes away from his muscular torso and concentrated on his face.

He folded his arms across his chest. 'Well, good evening, Detective. What can I do for you?' he said with a grin as he leaned against the door frame.

'Nothing. I'm sorry. It's late. I should have called first. I'll go,' she started to babble and he laughed, that deep laugh of his that made her heart race. She wanted the ground to open up and swallow her whole. Then the doorway was opened wider and John stepped aside.

'Well, by all means you can go, but wouldn't you rather come in?' he asked.

She looked up at him again and he smiled. Not the smile he had when he was teasing her, but a genuine one that made her legs tremble slightly. God, what the hell was she doing?'

'I was just on my way to bed,' he said softly as he held out a hand to her. 'Care to join me? Or I could make you a cheese toastie?'

She smiled at him. She'd told him that cheese toasties were her favourite comfort food and how she often loved to make one when she'd been working late. She had only just recalled mentioning it, and was touched that he had remembered too.

She took his hand and stepped inside the doorway. The door had barely closed behind her when he pushed her up against it and kissed her. She ran her hands over his back and groaned when he moved his head to kiss her neck.

'What about my cheese toastie?' she whispered when she came up for air.

'I'll make you one in the morning,' he replied with a grin before taking her hand and leading her up the stairs.

———————

John Brennan woke to his mobile phone vibrating on his bedside table. He picked it up and read the message on the screen.

Leigh rolled over and placed a hand on his chest.

'Grace is outside,' he said. 'I forgot she was calling to pick up some papers this

morning.'

'Oh God.' Leigh put a hand over her eyes. 'Can you get rid of her?'

'Yeah,' he said as he jumped up and pulled on a pair of shorts. 'She'd usually call in for a coffee but I'll put her off.'

John ran down the stairs and opened the door to find Grace already standing there. 'Here you go, Boss,' he said as he handed an envelope to her.

'You're not inviting me in this morning?' she asked.

He grinned at her. 'I'd rather not.'

Grace smiled. 'Oh, I see. Company?'

He grinned at her. 'Something like that.'

'Okay. I get it. I'll be on my way then.' She turned and started to walk down the path.

'I'll give you a call later, Boss,' he shouted.

Grace turned on her heel and smiled at him. 'Okay, and tell Leigh if she wants to sneak around with you, she should get herself a less conspicuous car.'

John burst out laughing as he noticed Leigh's bright red

BMW parked across the road from his house. 'Will do, Boss.'

Leigh pulled back the covers as John climbed back into bed beside her.

'I hate to break this to you, but your cover's blown,' he said.

'What? How?'

'Your car is parked right over the road, Leigh.' John laughed. 'And it's not exactly discreet, is it?'

'I suppose not,' Leigh conceded. Her car was her one indulgence. 'God, do you think she'll tell anyone?'

'No,' he assured her. 'Except for Michael.'

Leigh pulled the cover over her head. 'Oh God,' she groaned.

John pulled the duvet back to reveal her face. 'Hey, you think this looks bad for you. My bosses are Grace and Michael Carter and now they know that I'm seeing a copper. My reputation is going to be in tatters,' he said with a grin. 'I'll barely be able to show my face in public ever again.'

She punched him lightly on the chest. 'Don't be so dramatic,' she said.

'Says the woman who's hiding beneath the duvet.' He flashed his eyebrows at her.

'Okay. Point taken,' she said. 'At least we know Grace can keep a secret. Now, didn't you promise me a cheese toastie?'

'Yes, but I seem to remember you promising me something too last night?' He grinned at her.

'But I already did that,' she said, grinning back.

He rolled his eyes. 'I can't get anything past you, can I, Detective?'

'If I do it again, will you stop calling me Detective?' She raised an eyebrow at him.

He looked at her for a few seconds, as though considering her request. 'Okay,' he agreed before disappearing beneath the covers.

Chapter Twenty-Nine

Grace looked up at Luke Sullivan as he walked into her office carrying two mugs of cappuccino.

She stood up and walked around the desk. 'Thanks,' she said as she took one from him. She watched him as he leaned against her desk and began to blow on the hot liquid before taking a sip. He looked over the rim of his mug and smiled at her, his brown eyes twinkling.

'You're looking very pleased with yourself,' Grace said, smiling back.

'I am. I think I've just helped to land us a multi-million pound contract. I think we can call that a good morning's work, don't you?'

Grace laughed. 'You're very sure of yourself, Luke. Some would say cocky.'

'And what about you, Grace? Do you think I'm cocky?'

She considered him. He was tall, good-looking and funny. He could charm the knickers off a nun. He had every right to be cocky, but actually he wasn't. He was also smart, funny and considerate. 'No,' she shook her head. 'Not cocky. Self-assured.'

He nodded appreciatively. 'I'll take that. Thank you.'

Grace took a sip of her coffee. 'You're welcome. You were very good today, by the way. The way you handled Chris Morris... I was impressed.' Chris Morris was the CEO of Morrison Property Management, which managed one of the biggest property portfolios in the North West. Luke had discovered that Chris wasn't entirely happy with the security company they employed and was thinking of ditching them for a new firm. As a result, Grace had set up an initial meeting earlier that morning to speak to Chris about what they could offer. She had planned on letting Luke do most of the talking, and stepping in if he got out of his depth. To her pleasant surprise, she hadn't needed to. Luke had proved to be a skilled negotiator and an astute businessman. He was prepared for any question Chris threw at him, business or personal, and he answered them all without breaking a sweat. It had taken Grace a long time to find someone she felt confident enough to hand the reins of Cartel Securities to, and she was beginning to think she might just have found that person in Luke Sullivan.

———

Patrick Carter walked into the back of Sophia's Kitchen towards the office, hoping to find his daughter-in-law Grace. He wanted to speak to her about some ideas to surprise his wife Sue for her sixtieth birthday.

Patrick heard the sound of muffled laughter as he

approached. The door was slightly ajar and he assumed one of his sons, Michael or Sean, was also in there. He smiled. It would be good to see whichever of them it was. He adored his sons. He adored all of his family, and now that he was retired, he liked to spend as much time with them all as possible.

Pushing open the door, Patrick cleared his throat to announce his presence just in case it was Grace and Michael. The door was open but he had made the mistake of walking in on them once before. He wasn't sure who had been more embarrassed by his intrusion, him or them. Not that they had reason to be. They were a happily married couple, and they were in their own office with the door closed. He remembered how they'd started apologising profusely as they scrambled to adjust their clothing, while he had put a hand over his eyes and assured them he hadn't seen a thing. Then he had apologised sincerely afterwards, for barging in without knocking. But today the door was open, and he was sure that meant it was safe to enter.

Patrick looked across the room and saw Grace standing there, but he didn't recognise the man who was with her. He was much younger than her. In his twenties. Nearer to her son Jake's age than hers. He realised it must be one of their new business associates, Luke or Danny. Michael had told him that Grace had taken a shine to them, particularly Luke. They all seemed to have. Grace and the younger man stood close together, so deep in a private conversation that they didn't even see him enter.

'Hi, Grace,' Patrick said as he cleared his throat for the second time.

They both looked up at him and his blood ran cold. It was their eyes that gave them away. He saw it immediately and wondered how nobody else had. It was obvious, wasn't it?

'Pat,' Grace said with a smile as she walked over to him and put her arms around him. He returned her hug, all the while looking over her shoulder at her companion. After a few seconds Grace stepped back. 'Pat, this is Luke Sullivan,' she said as she looked towards the younger man. 'He's our new business partner.'

Patrick eyed Luke suspiciously as he too made his way over before extending his hand. 'It's great to meet you, Pat,' he said with a grin. 'I've heard so much about you, I feel like I already know you.'

Patrick shook his hand politely. He was too shocked to say any more.

'Are you looking for Michael or Sean?' Grace asked. 'They're not in today.'

'No. I was looking for you. I need your help with Sue's birthday. But I can come back later if you're busy?' Patrick replied.

'I'm never too busy for you, Pat, you know that,' she said as she squeezed his arm. 'Luke was just going anyway.'

'Yep,' said Luke, as if sensing his cue, 'I've got things to take care of.' He got up to leave. 'Nice to meet you, Pat, and I'll speak to you later, Grace.'

'Bye, Luke,' Grace said with a smile.

'Bye, lad,' Patrick added. Then he watched Luke walk out of the door and frowned. If what he suspected was true, then what the hell was that kid playing at?

Patrick Carter's mind raced as he walked towards his car. He should probably go to Grace, or even Michael, with his suspicions, but he wanted to be sure first. His whole family had been through so much in the past few years and he didn't want to throw another hand grenade into the mix without absolute proof, especially not considering the potential implications. He would need some evidence. The trouble was, he'd been retired for a few years and he was well out of practice at digging up information on people. Besides, it might provoke too much suspicion if he started snooping around, trying to glean information about Luke Sullivan. And not forgetting the fact that Grace was not only his daughter-in-law but she was also Grace Carter and everyone in the city worked for her, owed her or was afraid of her. Patrick shook his head. He would have to call on an old ally to help him with this, and hope that he remained discreet.

Chapter Thirty

Jack Murphy sat at the desk in his office and ran his hands over his shaved head. What he'd just been asked to do didn't sit comfortably with him at all, but how could he turn down Pat Carter? The man had saved his arse more than once.

'I don't know, Pat. You realise that Luke is basically my boss now? And you want me to keep this quiet from Michael and Grace too? It's a big ask, mate.'

'I know that, Murf, but there's no one else I can ask to do this. How long have we known each other?'

Murf started to laugh. 'Too long, Pat. No need to start with the emotional blackmail.'

Patrick smiled. Murf was ten years his junior, but they had known each other for decades. Pat had first met him when he was a teenager trying to make a name for himself. They'd worked together on and off through the years, and Murf had always proven himself to be a man Pat could trust. They had always had each other's back. When

Michael had set up Cartel Securities a few years earlier, Murf had been an experienced bouncer, and he was the perfect choice to be Michael's second in command. Since Michael and Grace had merged with Luke and Danny's firm, the two younger men had taken over the day-to-day running of the security business and Murf had been given a cushy desk job. Patrick knew that it was Michael and Grace's way of looking out for him as he got older.

'It's just a bit of digging, I'm not asking for any more than that.'

'Why though?' Murf asked with a frown. 'Is there something I should know?'

'No. Not yet. But can I count on you?'

Murf sighed and shook his head. 'Of course you can, Pat.'

'Good man,' Pat said gruffly as he stretched out his bad leg, which was aching from driving. 'Any chance of a quick brew before I go?'

'Course there is,' Murf said. 'Let me go and make us a couple and then you can tell me what you have planned for Sue's big birthday. Might give me some ideas for my missus.'

—————————————

Patrick Carter leaned back in the chair and waited for Murf to return. He could already hear that his old friend had been accosted by Edna, the cleaner at Cartel Securities, and realised he'd have at least a ten-minute wait for his brew now. Edna was a talker – Michael used to joke that her tongue was afraid of the dark. Patrick smiled to himself. He didn't mind waiting and he enjoyed being in the office, surrounded by the bustle of people. Sue was out on a shopping trip with his other daughter-in-law, Sophia, and the grandkids were at school, so the house would be empty for a few more hours yet.

Patrick stretched out his legs and listened as his bad knee creaked in resistance. He had never been the same since his attack a few years earlier at the hands of Grace's ex-husband, Nathan. He had never fully recovered, physically or emotionally and it was shortly afterwards that he had taken the decision to retire from that life. He glanced down at his left hand and his two missing fingers. It was funny sometimes he forgot that they were missing, and it still felt like they were there – still a part of him. Much like people whom he'd lost, he supposed.

Patrick looked around the office and noticed the photograph on the wall of Murf with Grace and Michael. It had been taken at some business awards event they'd attended. The three of them were smiling proudly, Grace holding their trophy aloft and the two men either side of her. Patrick smiled too. Grace was a force of nature. She drew people to her as though she possessed some kind of magnetic field. He'd met few people like that in his life. Patrick had met her fifteen years ago when he'd visited her pub to pay his long overdue respects to her dead father. Back then, Grace had been a pub owner but she hadn't been the businesswoman she was today. It had taken some encouragement from him for her to see what she was capable of, and he smiled with pride as he thought about the part he had played in making her the woman she was today. He had seen something in her from their very first meeting. She had a way about her that made people want to spill their guts, and to trust her. She had integrity too, and despite the world she lived in, she had never lost that. People admired and respected her, and she never took it for granted. She was as smart as anyone he'd ever met, with a head for business and a unique way of seeing the world. She saw opportunities where other people couldn't and seemed to have an in-built bullshit detector.

The more he thought about it, the more Patrick realised that she was just like her father, Pete.

Pete Sumner had been a few years older than Patrick. He and his best mate, Tommy, had idolised him. They followed him around like a pair of puppy dogs and when he had finally relented and allowed them to join his burgeoning firm, the three of them had become firm friends and business partners. Pete had always treated people fairly and with respect. He was a natural leader – enigmatic and full of charisma, but he was humble with it. When his wife had fallen pregnant with Grace, she had given him an ultimatum. It was her and their child, or the life of a villain. Pete chose his wife and child and never looked back. He bought the Rose and Crown pub and left his considerable empire behind. Patrick had been gutted at the time. He had loved Pete like a brother, but he had always respected his decision, and admired him for sticking to his guns. Tommy McNulty had taken Pete's place and, not being a natural leader himself, Patrick had followed Tommy and worked for him. But Tommy had never quite had the same air about him that Pete had, and so he'd never engendered the same level of loyalty and respect. Patrick saw of lot of Pete in Grace and he adored his daughter-in-law. He hoped that Luke Sullivan wasn't going to try and ruin the life she had built with his son. Patrick would murder the bastard himself if he had to.

Chapter Thirty-One

Michael took off his suit jacket and hung it over the chair in the bedroom. He sat on the bed next to Grace.

'So, John and DI Moss, eh?' he said with a grin. 'Who would have thought it? Big John and a copper?'

'I know. I could hardly believe it. But I suppose it makes sense.'

'Oh? How?'

'Well, he knows all about her past. She doesn't have to pretend to be someone she's not with him. There's a lot to be said for that. And besides, John's quite the catch, isn't he? I mean, if I wasn't married to you...'

Michael frowned at her. 'What?'

Grace started to laugh as she placed a hand on his cheek. 'God, you're so easy, Carter.'

'Easy?' he said with a grin as he pushed her down onto the bed and rolled on top of her. 'Is that so?'

'Very.'

'Well, maybe I just don't like my wife talking about other men being a good catch,' he said, raising an eyebrow.

'Especially John?' She grinned at him.

'Especially John,' he said before kissing her.

'You know I only have eyes for you, Mr Carter,' she said as she began unbuttoning his shirt.

'Hmm, you better had,' he growled.

Grace lay in bed with Michael's arm draped over her stomach and his body pressed against hers.

'Now that John is Leigh's new sidekick, does this mean she no longer requires your services?' Michael asked.

'Not quite,' Grace replied.

'Oh, I see. Still needs your brains as well as your muscle, does she?'

She ran a fingertip over his bicep. 'Something like that. I could always offer your services. Brains and muscle in one package?'

'What, you're pimping me out now then?' He laughed.

She looked at him and bit her lower lip, as though giving his question serious thought. 'On second thoughts, I have much better uses for your muscle,' she purred.

'Well, you'll have to give me ten minutes to recover, babe. I'm not as young as I used to be,' he said with a flash of his eyebrows.

She kissed him on the lips. 'Actually, I was thinking you could come with me to my meeting with the contractors tomorrow. They want to go over the renovations for the new restaurant. I was going to ask Luke, but if you don't mind?'

'Of course I will. Are you expecting trouble?'

'Not trouble as such. But the foreman is a bit of a dick who thinks he can shaft me because I'm a woman. I can handle him, but it would still be nice to see his face when you walk in behind me.' She laughed as she imagined the smug grin being wiped from Jim the smarmy foreman's face.

'Then yes, of course I'll come with you. It will be nice to get to work with you for a change. Wasn't that the point of us working together – so we could actually spend more time together? I feel like I've hardly seen you lately, between you overseeing the new restaurant and you and Luke sorting out the new security contracts.'

'I know. We were supposed to be taking a step back, weren't we?' she said with a laugh. 'It feels like we're busier than ever. You can do the security contracts with Luke if you'd prefer?'

'It's not Luke I'm interested in spending more time with.' He laughed. 'Besides, he needs to learn the ropes from the best if we're going to be able to hand the contracts side of the business over to him and Danny too. Anyway, I'd rather be the one overseeing the boys' business dealings,' he said pointedly, referring to the fact that their family were the primary importers and suppliers for drugs across Merseyside and beyond. The idea was that Jake and Connor would eventually take over the business full time, but not until they had proved they were capable of doing so without getting themselves killed or arrested. 'You are the respectable face of our business, after all,' he went on. 'Can't have you tarnishing this new image you're creating, can we?' he teased.

'Do you regret the decisions we've made?' she asked. A few months ago, Michael had been ready to pack it all in and move to the suburbs. But after they had successfully prevented a takeover bid and managed to get the boys out of jail for murder, Grace had persuaded him that they needed to keep hold of the reins for a little longer. When they did eventually retire she wanted them to be able to do so safe in the knowledge that Jake and Connor would be capable of making good decisions that would benefit the whole family. And she also wanted to make sure she and Michael had made enough money to be comfortable for the rest of their lives.

'No,' he said softly. 'I don't want to leave this behind if you're not leaving with me. There's no point in any of it if I don't have you.'

'You will always have me.'

'I certainly hope so, Mrs Carter,' he said as he rolled on top of her and smothered her with a kiss.

Chapter Thirty-Two

Joey Parnell sat on the bench in Sefton Park and waited for his employer to arrive. Up until a couple of weeks ago, they had always met in the little wine bar which JB part owned, but since things had started to heat up, he insisted on meeting in the park with his dog Archie for cover. Joey supposed JB could explain away a chance meeting, but not so much the two of them sitting together in a wine bar. And now that Joey was attracting attention for lots of different reasons, his boss couldn't afford anyone learning about their connection.

Joey sat back and watched two teenage girls sitting under a nearby tree. Each of them was posing for selfies on their smartphones. Despite the cold weather, they wore midriff-revealing crop-tops beneath their open padded jackets, and jeans with more holes than a string vest. He felt his dick twitch as he watched them both and wondered whether they ever took photographs of themselves when they were alone in their bedrooms.

'Close your mouth, Joseph. You're drooling,' his boss snapped as he approached him.

Joey frowned and sat back on the bench.

His boss sat down and took a faded tennis ball from his pocket before throwing it for the excited spaniel, who had just been let off his lead.

'Yet again, you disappoint me,' his boss said with a shake of his head. 'Grace Carter has been asking questions about that bloody care home again,' he hissed. 'I swear I should have had that place shut down when I had the chance. I thought Collins and his wife going to prison would be the end of it, but I've had nothing but grief. I'm starting to wish I'd never got involved with the place. I'm sure we could have found girls some other way.'

Joey nodded. In his experience, there was always a way of identifying and exploiting vulnerable girls, particularly if you had a knack for doing so, like Joey did. He could have found plenty of girls for JB and his associates if they'd only come to him sooner, and not relied on Vince Collins, the warden of Sunnymeade, and his wife. Simon Jones had been the go-between. Vince and his wife would identify the most vulnerable girls as they were leaving care, and provide Simon with enough information about them that he could pounce. He'd spend a few weeks or months grooming them – however long it took – before introducing them to drugs and then a life on the game. It was the perfect set-up in a lot of ways, if only Vince and his wife hadn't been stupid enough to get caught abusing the girls themselves.

'What do you have to say for yourself?' JB snapped.

Joey shrugged. He sensed that JB was beginning to get

desperate now and that meant that the power balance was shifting ever so slightly in his favour. 'I warned her off, but she's a stubborn cunt. I half expected it not to work. Should I move on to Plan B?'

JB sighed and rubbed the bridge of his nose. 'I'd rather it not have come to this, but, yes. Deal with Jake Conlon and Connor Carter and make sure you do it properly.'

'And what about Grace and Michael?' Joey asked.

'I'll make sure they don't bother you for now. And then I'll take care of them when the time is right,' he said, in that tone that Joey knew meant he didn't want to discuss the matter further.

Joey disagreed but didn't say so. In his opinion, the entire Carter family should be taken out. He would rather make a pre-emptive strike than wait for them to make a move. They would know exactly who was behind Jake and Connor's disappearance and would come looking for him. But despite his newfound confidence, he was still terrified of the man sitting next to him, the power he wielded and the ease with which he could destroy his life.

'Any luck in finding Simon Jones, or the memory card?' JB asked.

'Not yet.'

'Shit!' JB hissed, in a rare display of frustration. He often appeared angry, but this was something else and Joey wondered whether he felt the net was closing in. 'You know if that falls into the wrong hands, you are implicated too?'

'I'll find it. Just give me time.'

'Time is something we don't have the luxury of,' he

snapped. 'Speaking of which, it's time to dump the last one.'

'Are you sure?' Joey asked. 'It's not quite been two weeks yet.'

'I think it's time to put an end to this. The press have got a right hard-on for this so-called Liverpool Ripper. Besides, I don't think she's going to talk, do you?'

'No,' Joey said solemnly. 'I've tried every tactic I know of, and she hasn't said anything about the memory card. She talked a lot about Melanie, and Simon Jones, but nothing about the card. I don't think she knows where it is. I think Jones has played us like a fiddle, Boss. If you want my opinion, he's got it.'

JB turned to him and scowled. 'No, Joseph! He's played *you* like a fucking fiddle! So, you'd better bloody find him then, hadn't you?' He stood up then and called Archie, who came bounding over with his ball in his mouth. 'Don't forget to leave the evidence with her. I think it's about time The Liverpool Ripper was brought to justice.'

'I'll dump her later. It's a shame though. I was having fun with her.'

JB's eyes lit up then. He couldn't help himself. 'Is she a screamer?'

'No, not this one. She's quiet. She cries a lot and asks me to let her go. I can't stand the screamers myself. Give me a headache.'

'Well, there are always ways of shutting them up when they become too annoying.' JB chuckled to himself. 'I'm sorry I've missed all the fun,' he said wistfully.

'I'll tell you all about it some time,' Joey said.

As though he suddenly remembered where he was and who he was talking to, JB stiffened. He bent to put Archie's lead on and walked away without another word.

Joey sat back against the bench. He was disappointed to see that the two teenage girls had left while he'd been talking to JB, especially now that he was being forced to give up his latest plaything. He had thought he'd be keeping Anna, the fourth Ripper victim, for another week in the basement of the old farmhouse in Scarisbrick. He did enjoy playing with her. But now he would have to refrain from doing anything that might leave his DNA on or inside her. Instead, she would be cleaned up and then killed quickly. He couldn't even take any enjoyment in prolonging her death. If JB wanted her dumped tonight, then that's what needed to happen. He sighed. Life was a bitch!

This time the body wouldn't be entirely clean though. He would plant the DNA of their chosen fall guy on her body and sit back and watch as the police arrested the poor sod. Joey stood up and stretched his legs. At least he had the kidnap and murder of Jake and Connor to look forward to. He had a good group of hard lads together who were more than willing to do those two in, and his boss would make sure that Joey and his firm were untouchable. Joey smiled to himself. He had a very powerful friend in a very high place and he couldn't wait to take his rightful standing in the hierarchy of the Liverpool underworld again.

Chapter Thirty-Three

G race was walking to her car after finishing work for the day when she felt someone fall into step beside her. She turned to see Leigh Moss had joined her.

'Afternoon, Detective. To what do I owe this pleasure?' she asked. 'You do realise it's broad daylight and anyone could see us?'

'We're just two people walking next to each other.' Leigh shrugged. 'I wanted to ask you something.'

'Something about the case?' Grace said as she reached her car.

'Yes,' Leigh said.

Both women stopped and Grace opened the door to her car. 'Then get in, Leigh. I don't want to be seen talking to you in the middle of the city centre.'

Leigh rolled her eyes. 'Fine,' she said.

Grace hadn't even pulled away from the kerb when Leigh spoke.

'Is this better?' she asked.

'Much,' Grace replied. 'I'm not sure why you're suddenly so at ease with being seen with me, but I'd rather not be seen talking to you out in the open. No offence.'

'None taken. I was in town and I thought I'd swing by to see you in your office, but then I saw you leaving.'

'What did you want to talk to me about?' Grace asked. Leigh's growing familiarity was disconcerting. She liked Leigh, despite who she was, but they were from different worlds. It was one thing to have the odd drink in secret when necessary, but Leigh was becoming almost friendly. Grace wondered if it had anything to do with Leigh's blossoming relationship with John.

'I went along with one of my Detective Constables to speak to Stuart Halligan today.'

'How did that go?' Grace asked.

'He continued to deny being a friend of Nerys's even when I told him a source had told me otherwise. He claims they are mistaken.'

'Perhaps she was?' Grace replied, thinking back to her conversation with Stacey a few days earlier.

'The thing is, I didn't believe him,' Leigh said.

'Why?' Grace asked.

'I don't know. Call it intuition. He seemed scared...'

'Well, he was being interviewed by you and your colleague. Isn't that normal?'

'Nervous maybe, but not scared. Not like that. I think he was hiding something.'

'Do you think he's the killer?' Grace asked as she pulled the car over into a quiet car park. She turned in her seat.

Leigh shook her head. 'No. He's short. Very slender. Small hands,'

'Not capable of strangling someone to death then?' Grace said.

'I wouldn't think so. And he has a solid alibi. And while I was there I notice a framed photograph on his mantelpiece. It was the only photo on display. It was a picture of a couple in their thirties – and their little girl. I asked him who they were and he said it was his aunt and her husband and their daughter Daisy. When I asked how old Daisy was he turned as white as a sheet. She's five, by the way.'

'The same age that Nerys's daughter would be? You think Stuart has something to do with her child then?'

———————————

'Maybe? If she was still at Sunnymeade when she got pregnant, maybe Stuart helped her to cover it up? Maybe he is the father? We spoke to Vince Collins as soon as we identified the tooth as belonging to Nerys's child, and he denied any knowledge of her having one. Of course, he could be lying.'

'Perhaps the child was his?' Grace suggested.

'No. He couldn't have children of his own. The doctors confirmed that at the trial.'

'So you think the child in the photograph might actually be Nerys's daughter? That's some leap, Leigh.'

'You didn't see the look on his face. He is definitely hiding something, and his reaction when I asked about the child makes me think she has something to do with it.'

'But how would they ever cover something like that up? Nerys has a child and she's being raised by Stuart's aunt as her own?'

'Birth certificates are easy enough to forge if you know the right people. You know that.'

'Yes, certificates are, but not official records. This couple would have had to have the child from birth and passed her off as their own.'

'It's improbable, I know, but not impossible.'

'True,' Grace agreed. 'And it's certainly a much better explanation for Nerys's child than the alternatives that have been running through my brain,' she said with a shudder. 'But if that was the case, why not just make the couple the child's legal guardians? Surely there were easier ways than to pass the child off as their own?'

'There are…'

'So, if your theory is true, Nerys and Stuart have has gone to great lengths to cover this child up?' Grace added.

'Exactly, and I could be putting her in danger,' Leigh said as she leaned her head back and sighed.

'Can't you just check Daisy's DNA?' Grace asked, remembering how easy it had been to prove that Jake was Isla's father a year earlier.

'It's not that easy. I have no reason, other than a gut feeling, which could well be wrong, that Daisy might be Nerys's child. I can't just walk into a family and ask for a child's DNA without evidence to back up my theory. Stuart has an alibi. I have nothing other than the word of your source that he and Nerys were even friends. There is no reason to suspect him other than he happened to be at Sunnymeade at the same time as our victims – which is true of many people. I have no cause to request a DNA sample.'

Grace looked at Leigh. 'Your processes are so restrictive.'

'They're there for a reason though. And they have to be followed.'

'How annoying! If you just had the child's DNA.'

'Don't even think about it,' Leigh said. 'If we obtained it illegally then we couldn't use it at all and it would completely undermine the investigation.'

Grace held her hands up in defence and laughed. 'I wasn't suggesting anything.'

Leigh laughed too. 'Sorry,' she said as she rubbed the bridge of her nose.

'So, if your theory is right, why have Nerys and Stuart gone to such lengths to hide Daisy's identity? If Stuart is her father and Nerys her mother, there would be no reason to, surely?'

'I know. It wouldn't make sense,' Leigh agreed.

'So, if Stuart isn't her father, and Collins isn't, who is?' Grace asked as her head started to throb. It seemed like the more they found out about this case, the less they knew.

'Someone that Nerys and Stuart were afraid of? Someone they never wanted to find out he had a daughter?'

'Joey Parnell?' Grace asked. 'He likes young girls, doesn't he?'

'It crossed my mind, but we ran the DNA from the tooth

through our database and it doesn't match Joey's DNA, or anyone else's on there.'

'This case gets stranger every day, Leigh,' Grace said.

'Tell me about it,' Leigh said with a sigh.

Grace started the engine of her car and pulled out of the car park. She wanted to get home to her own children.

Chapter Thirty-Four

J ake sat in the back of the transit van and looked across at Connor sitting on the wooden bench opposite. Connor was looking down at the crowbar he was turning over in his hands. Jake felt a pang of sadness as he wondered if Connor was thinking about the same thing he was. The anniversary of the death of Connor's twin, Paul, was approaching and his absence was even more noticeable than usual, especially on nights such as these when Paul would have been right up for it and in the thick of the action.

'He'd love this, wouldn't he?' Jake said.

Connor looked up and smiled. 'Yeah, he would.'

As well as Jake, Connor and the driver, there were another three of their best men in the vehicle. Two more vans followed behind them, containing another twelve of their toughest bouncers. A similar convoy led by Luke and Danny was also on the road, heading out of the city towards Southport. It was finally time to take down Parnell and his new firm, and to do that they would take out his two most lucrative contracts – a nightclub in Southport and a pub on the outskirts of the city centre. Jake and Connor didn't usually get overly involved in the operational side of Cartel Securities, since they had plenty of other business to keep them occupied, but Danny and Luke had told them about their plan and they had been happy to help. Danny and Luke were determined to prove themselves capable of running Cartel Securities and taking out any potential competition.

The strikes would be co-ordinated so they would both happen at midnight. That would ensure that no warning could be given about an impending attack from one venue to the other.

'We're nearly there, Boss,' Timmo, the driver, shouted.

Jake looked at his watch. It was five to midnight. 'Drive around for a few minutes and pull up outside at twelve.'

'Will do,' Timmo shouted back.

Jake looked around the van at the other lads, all tooled up and sitting quietly.

'Remember the plan. Take the bouncers out. No one else gets hurt. The last thing we need is the bizzies on our case.'

The men all nodded and he heard mumbles of assent.

'You ready for this, Con?' Jake asked Connor as he patted his knee.

Connor looked up and him and grinned. 'Fuck, yes! I've been feeling like knocking someone out all week.'

When the three vans pulled up outside Singleton's pub a few minutes later, Jake, Connor and the rest of the lads were primed and ready. The three van doors were slid open almost simultaneously and eighteen men dressed in black and armed with a variety of weapons jumped out. The bouncers at Singleton's barely knew what had hit them. They were outmanned two to one and the whole thing was over in less than ten minutes. Parnell's men knew they were beaten and the ones who could still do so walked out of there. The two men who had been knocked unconscious were carried by their mates. While their own men held the door, Jake and Connor walked through the club, reassuring the customers who were sober enough to realise something was going on that everything was under control. 'Where is the manager?' Jake asked one of the bar staff.

'In the back,' he said as he eyed them warily.

They walked into the back stock room and found the manager with his hand up a woman's skirt and his tongue down her throat.

'Are you responsible for this place?' Connor barked.

'Who the fuck are you?' the man snapped as he looked up and saw them walking towards him.

'There's been a change of personnel,' Jake said with a smile.

'We'll be handling your security from now on,' Connor added as he took a Cartel Securities business card from his pocket and handed it to the man, who stood there staring at the pair of them.

'What happened to our usual security?' he asked.

'We've relieved them of their duties. And let's face it,

they weren't very good, were they, if they let us walk back here to find you feeling up one of your customers?' Jake said.

He shrugged and turned to face them, pulling up his zipper as he did. 'You'll have to square it with the owner.'

Jake shook his head and looked at Connor who rolled his eyes.

Jake walked over to him and jabbed his finger into the man's chest. 'No, *you* will square this with the owner, because you were too busy trying to get your end away while sixteen of my men walked in here and took over this place. And you didn't have a fucking clue about any of it until we walked in here. If I was the owner, I'd be letting you go and all. But you can tell him he's getting a better service for the same price, so it's a win-win for him. We don't even mind if you want to tell him you approached us and did him a favour.'

The manager nodded, as though he'd suddenly realised who he was dealing with.

'Nice doing business with you,' Jake said and then he and Connor turned around and left Singleton's manager standing with his mouth hanging open.

Chapter Thirty-Five

'I think we can call that a huge success, lads?' Jake said with a grin on his face as he poured four large measures of Johnny Walker Black Label. Danny and Luke's takeover of the nightclub in Southport had been as successful as Jake and Connor's enterprise at Singleton's.

'Indeed we can,' Danny said as Luke and Connor nodded their agreement.

The four men each took a glass of whisky and toasted their victory.

Connor downed his whisky in one gulp and set his glass on the table with a satisfied sigh. 'It's been epic, lads, but I need to get home to the missus and the baby.'

Luke placed his now empty glass on the table too and patted Connor on the back. 'I'll come with you.'

'You and all?' Jake said with a shake of his head. 'Just where do you need to be that's better than here with your best mates?'

Luke flashed his eyebrows. 'Hot date,' he said.

'It's almost 2 a.m.,' Danny said as he glanced at his new Breitling.

'What can I say,' Luke said as he held out his hands. 'I'm worth waiting up for.'

'See you clowns tomorrow then,' Jake replied as he downed the last remnants of his own drink.

Jake watched as Connor and Luke left his office, closing the door behind them.

'You're not buggering off as well, are you?' he asked Danny.

'Nope. I can go all night,' he said with a grin.

'Fancy another?' Jake indicated the open bottle of Scotch on his desk.

'Yeah, thanks,' Danny replied as he walked over and sat on the edge of the desk.

Jake poured each of them another generous measure of whisky and handed the glass to Danny, who took it with a nod of thanks.

'The night's still young, mate. You up for going somewhere a bit more interesting?' Jake asked, thinking he would introduce Danny to the private Xcalibur club – the place he and Connor frequented when they wanted to have a drink without being disturbed.

'Yeah.' Danny took a sip of his Scotch. 'Or we could just go to your place? I'm up for anything you want,' he said, his voice low and gravelly. He downed the rest of his drink and stared at Jake over the rim of his whisky glass.

Jake looked at Danny, his brows knitted into a frown as he wondered what had just passed between them. Was there any meaning to it, or was Jake simply desperate to find one? Danny continued to stare back at him as he placed his empty glass on the desk, not breaking eye contact even when Jake rose from his chair and took a step so he was standing directly in front of him.

Jake placed his hands on Danny's shoulders, then ran them down the lapels of his finely tailored jacket before taking hold of them in his fists. Danny didn't flinch as Jake pulled him towards him.

'Are you flirting with me?' Jake asked.

'I hope so,' Danny whispered.

'Well, you're fucking shit at it, you know that, right?'

Danny was about to speak, but before he could, Jake kissed him, pushing his tongue into Danny's mouth and pulling him closer, until their bodies were pressed together.

'Anything?' Jake whispered when they came up for air.

'Anything,' Danny breathed.

Danny Alexander blinked in the bright sunlight as he woke. Stretching his arms above his head he was aware of a dull ache in his muscles and smiled as he remembered the cause. He turned and saw Jake Conlon lying next to him, his lower half covered by the expensive cotton sheets but his magnificent torso on full display. Danny looked at him as he lay there, all abs and tattoos, and he felt a familiar stirring in his groin. Jake Conlon wouldn't look out of place advertising the latest expensive aftershave on a fifty-foot billboard and here was Danny lying in bed beside him after the most incredible night of his life.

Danny had never experienced anything like what he was feeling right now, and as he looked at Jake he wondered what the hell he had let himself in for. The truth was he'd been having feelings for Jake for a while but he'd tried to bury them – for many reasons, including the facts that Jake was his boss, he went through men even quicker than Danny did women, and Danny was straight. At least he'd thought he was. He'd never so much as kissed a man before. Sure, he'd admired them from afar at times, but that was just an appreciation of the male form, wasn't it? Nothing like this. What happened with Jake had completely blown his mind.

Jake stirred and opened one eye. 'What time is it?' he asked gruffly.

Danny glanced at the digital clock beside the bed. 'Half past eleven.'

'Fucking hell! I haven't slept that well in about a year,' Jake said as he rubbed his eyes.

'Really?' Danny asked in surprise. They'd gone to bed around 3 a.m. but hadn't fallen asleep until six.

'Yeah,' Jake replied before rolling over and onto Danny, pinning him to the mattress with the weight of his muscular body. 'You got anything to do today?' he asked.

Danny shook his head. 'I don't think so. Unless there's something you need me to do?' he replied, wondering whether he was about to be unceremoniously dismissed. He knew that most of Jake's conquests didn't even make it to the next morning, and certainly weren't invited to stay for breakfast. Maybe Jake had some business for him to take care of today? He was still technically his boss after all.

'There is something actually,' Jake growled. 'I need you to stay here for the rest of the day and let me fuck you senseless.'

Danny swallowed as he looked into Jake's bright blue eyes. He felt his whole abdomen area contract involuntarily. This man was going to turn his whole world upside down, but at that exact moment, Danny didn't care. 'Sounds good to me,' he answered with a smile.

Jake glanced at his watch and saw it was after five, before picking up his belt from the floor. He smiled as he remembered discarding it the previous night. As he looped it through the waistband of his trousers, Danny walked out of the en-suite, freshly showered and with a towel wrapped around his waist. Jake looked at him appreciatively and contemplated whether they had any time to spare. They had stayed in bed for most of the day and would still be there if Jake wasn't needed at the club.

Jake turned away as Danny started to get dressed. If he didn't, he wasn't sure they would make it out of the apartment. To say he'd been shocked by how last night had panned out would be an understatement. If he thought about it, he'd had probably had some suspicion that Danny was interested in him, but he'd dismissed it, worried that his intuition was off. The men he usually fucked about with practically threw themselves at him and he'd never had to make an effort to determine their sexuality. His skills in that department were sadly lacking. Paul Carter had always had a finely tuned gaydar and Jake had always envied him that. Jake felt a pang of guilt as he thought about Paul. It had been a year since his death and Jake still thought about him every day. No one had ever been able to get to him the way Paul had. He looked up again at Danny, who was pulling on his shirt, and swallowed. No one until now.

Chapter Thirty-Six

DI Moss walked away from the crime scene with her DS, Mark Whitney, following close behind.

'Good news, Ma'am?' he said.

She frowned at him. 'A woman is dead, Mark.'

'Sorry, Boss,' he said apologetically. 'I meant no disrespect to young Anna. But it looks like our killer has fucked up this time. We're going to nail this bastard soon. I can feel it.'

Leigh nodded absent-mindedly, but she didn't share Mark's enthusiasm. Something just wasn't right. They would still need the forensics results to confirm, but it seemed like the perpetrator had left vital clues on Anna's body.

'Why has he fucked up this time though, Mark? It doesn't make sense.'

He shrugged. 'Maybe he got too cocky? Maybe he was disturbed? There are lots of reasons.'

'But it's just so sloppy, and it doesn't fit with what we

know about him so far. Up until now, he has been meticulous. So meticulous that we've been wondering if he has forensic knowledge of a crime scene. And now he just happens to leave footprints, a weapon and semen-stained underwear behind? It's all a little convenient, isn't it?'

'Let's see what the forensics come back with,' Mark suggested as they reached Leigh's car.

'Yes. Let's.'

Leigh was in her office poring over forensics reports when Chief Superintendent Barrow walked into the room. He had a huge grin on his face.

'Well done, Leigh. You got the bastard,' he said. 'The Chief Con is over the bloody moon!'

'Thank you, Sir,' she said as she stood up and felt her cheeks flush pink. She and DS Whitney had arrested Stuart Halligan earlier that morning after the forensics had confirmed his fingerprints were on the knife found at the scene. And whilst that hadn't been the murder weapon, it had been used to slice wounds into the victim's skin a few hours prior to her death. If that wasn't enough, his DNA was also found in the victim's underwear. Leigh didn't mention that she felt the whole thing was a little too easy, and that her gut still told her that Stuart Halligan was not the perpetrator. He was barely five foot four for a start, with small feminine hands. It took considerable strength and pressure to strangle someone to death, and she wasn't sure Stuart had it in him.

Then there was the underwear. Anna was a size 8-10, but the underwear she was wearing was a size 6. It not only had her DNA in, but that of one of the other victims, Nerys Sheehan, who had been a size 6. Why was Anna wearing Nerys's underwear, and soiled underwear at that?

Chief Superintendent Barrow crossed the room and put an arm around Leigh's shoulder. 'You did good,' he said as he gave her a squeeze.

She smiled awkwardly. Barrow didn't usually go in for hugs or praise, but she supposed the Liverpool Ripper case was one of the most high-profile and notorious cases they had ever worked on, and she had no doubt her superiors had been under considerable pressure from the Police Crime Commissioner and the public to bring the killer to justice.

'It's not over yet, Sir,' she said. 'He's denying everything.'

'Well, he's hardly likely to admit to anything, is he?' Barrow scoffed. 'But the forensic evidence is undeniable. He's bang to rights, and sooner or later that legal aid brief of his is going to convince him to plead. If he drags this through a trial...' He sucked in air through his teeth. 'Who's interviewing him?'

'DS Whitney, Sir. But Halligan is sleeping now. PACE rules and all that?' she said with a shrug.

'I'm sure you'll have it all sewn up in no time, a smart girl like you,' he said.

Leigh bristled at the term 'girl' and the patronising tone, but wondered if she had overreacted. She was on edge. This whole case was driving her crazy. She was missing something big and she knew it.

Just as she thought he was about to leave, Barrow perched himself on the edge of her desk.

'You used to run the OCG task force?' Barrow asked.

'Yes, Sir.'

'Any particular reason you left?'

Leigh took a second to regulate her breathing as her heart started to pound in her chest. Why the hell was he asking her this? He knew the reason why. He'd rubber-stamped her transfer.

'Like I said in my transfer request, Sir, I didn't want to work there any longer after what happened to DS Bryce.'

'You were worried for your own safety?' he asked with a raised eyebrow. 'Because you don't seem the type, Leigh.'

'Not so much that, Sir. But DS Bryce and I were good friends. There was a sense that we could become more than that and I felt it was better to move on before anything developed.'

'It wasn't because of what happened to him then? It was because you and he were in a relationship? So you lied?'

Leigh shook her head as she felt the flush creep up her neck. Shit! 'No, Sir. What happened to him made me realise that I had feelings for him and I thought it was best to make a fresh start elsewhere.'

He seemed satisfied with her response. 'Are the two of you still in a relationship?'

'No, Sir. It didn't pan out.'

'So there's nothing stopping you going back to the OCG task force if you wanted to?'

She frowned at him. 'Aren't you happy with the work I'm doing here?'

He started to laugh, his eyes crinkling at the sides. 'Yes. Very. But you seemed to have a –' he paused as though searching for the right word '– determination that your successor is lacking.'

'Oh. Well, I enjoyed my time there, but I understand DI King is doing well, Sir.'

He leaned in closer to her. 'Not as well as you though, eh? I mean you had Conlon and Carter in the nick within a few months of you taking over the team.'

'But they walked,' she reminded him.

He shrugged. 'No one else has been able to manage it though, have they?'

'What's this about, Sir?' she asked him, sensing there was something he wasn't telling her.

'I want Liverpool to be a safer city, Leigh. And to do that I want Grace Carter and all her little minions put away for a very long time.'

Leigh was taken aback. This was the first she'd heard of the Chief Super's mission to tackle the Carters. In fact, when she had been DI of the OCG task force, there were rumours that the Chief Super liked Grace in charge as it kept the rest of the factions in line. Clearly those rumours were unfounded – or something had happened to change his mind.

'If you think you're up to the task, then just say the word. I'll even give you extra resources. We have that violence reduction money to spend and I can argue the case for it to be spent on your task force if you make Grace and

Michael Carter your priority.'

'But they haven't come to police attention for years. You know as well as I do that they don't get their hands dirty any more, Sir. Respectable business people, according to anyone you'd care to ask.'

'Well, I'm sure a smart girl like you could find something on them,' he said with a wink. 'It might keep Grace Carter from sticking her nose where it doesn't belong,' he added quietly, almost as an afterthought.

'Pardon, Sir?' Leigh asked as she felt the hairs on the back of her neck stand on end.

'Just let me know if you think you're up to the job, Leigh,' he said as he stood up and walked out of her office.

Leigh's legs felt weak and her head began to spin. What the hell had that been about? And what had he meant about Grace sticking her nose in where it didn't belong? Did he know about her helping out with the case? And if so, how? And why hadn't he bollocked her for it? It was gross misconduct, pure and simple.

Leigh swallowed as all of the pieces of the puzzle that had been scattered in the wind started to slowly fall into place. And the picture that was forming made her want to gouge her own eyes out. It was unthinkable, but it all made sense somehow.

She stood on shaky legs and made her way across the office, down the stairwell and to her car. Only once she was inside did she take her phone out of her pocket and dial Grace's number.

Chapter Thirty-Seven

G race watched as Leigh Moss walked into her office in Sophia's Kitchen and took a seat opposite. It had been less than thirty minutes since she'd phoned in something of a panic. Grace had been about to head home but had agreed to stay behind to discuss whatever it was that Leigh seemed so agitated about.

'I heard you arrested Stuart Halligan this morning,' Grace said. 'So it was him after all? Who'd have thought it?'

Leigh frowned. 'That information isn't public yet...' she started to say and then she shook her head. 'Of course, you're not exactly the public, are you? Did Webster tell you?'

'No,' Grace replied with a smile.

Leigh flinched. 'I don't suppose you'd tell me who did?'

'Of course not. Why would you even ask?'

'It might be important,' Leigh said but Grace wasn't going to provide the name of her contact. Leigh stared at her for a few seconds before sitting back in her chair. 'I don't know who to trust any more, Grace,' she said with a sigh.

'You can trust me. You know that already,' Grace offered. 'Despite our differences, I have always kept my word.'

'I still don't think it was Halligan,' Leigh blurted out.

'I was told it was an open-and shut-case. Irrefutable DNA evidence?'

'God, you really do do your homework, don't you?' Leigh said with a look that Grace could only describe as admiration.

Grace held her hands up. 'What can I say? I'm thorough.'

'The thing is, DNA is conclusive evidence. Stuart Halligan definitely used the knife we found at the crime scene at some point, even his own blood was on it, and his semen was found in the underwear the victim was wearing, but that doesn't mean it wasn't planted.'

'You think he was set up?' Grace sat forward in her seat.

'I told you, Stuart was shorter than I am. Really thin with small hands too. Do you honestly think he'd have the strength to strangle a woman to death?'

'Perhaps he had an accomplice? Don't forget Parnell could still be linked to this.'

'I haven't discounted Parnell. And it's possible he and Stuart worked together, but there's no connection between them that I'm aware of. And this crime scene was completely different to the others. The first three were professional – impeccable, not a trace of evidence anywhere—'

'Except for the tooth?' Grace reminded her.

'Yes, except for that, but I believe the killer wasn't aware that Nerys had it on her person. That's why he never took it with him.'

'Okay.'

'This recent crime scene was either the work of a complete amateur—'

'Or someone who wanted the evidence to be found?' Grace interjected.

'Exactly.'

'What about the underwear though? How did Stuart's semen end up on the victim's underwear?'

'I think it was Nerys's underwear. It was her size. Perhaps she and Stuart occasionally had sex.'

'So the killer is still out there and they have somehow framed Stuart? But why him?'

'Think about it. He's perfect. The weird kid from the children's home who most of the other boys bullied, but who befriended some of the girls and used to sit in the attic listening to jazz records with them? Then Nerys reveals, quite probably under torture, that she and he have a child together and he becomes the perfect patsy. All it takes to establish motive is for the prosecution to produce some witnesses to tell the jury how he was rejected by some of the girls, which we know to be true. Then this becomes all about his revenge.'

'So do you think you're any closer to finding the real killer then?'

Leigh visibly blanched at this and Grace frowned. 'What is it?'

'It's almost too awful to contemplate,' she said.

'Well, tell me anyway.'

Grace sat back in her chair as she digested the information Leigh had just given her. It was a hell of a leap, but the way Leigh laid it out, it all made sense. It would certainly explain why the killer was able to leave such a clean crime scene.

'So it could be Parnell then?' Grace said. 'We'd wondered how he was able to pull this off, but if he's working for who you think he is, then he wouldn't need to use his brains.'

Leigh nodded. 'So, we have two suspects, but one huge problem. How the hell do we prove any of it?'

Chapter Thirty-Eight

J ake and Connor were walking down the Dock Road
towards Jake's car when the white transit van pulled
up alongside them. The door slid open and six masked
men jumped out armed with baseball bats and tried to force
them into the van. Jake threw a punch at one of them and it
connected with bone, but before he could throw another, a
second man was on his back with a baseball bat across his
throat. 'Just get in the fucking van, you prick. Or I'll snap
your neck.'

Jake bristled. He looked across at Connor, who was in a
similar position, and realised that fighting back at this point
was futile and would expend too much valuable energy. He
and Connor were boxers and trained with some of the best
street fighters in the North West; they could take on most
men one on one, or even two on one. But three to one was a
bit of an ask. Jake tried to shrug the man off his back, but he
held the bat firmly in place.

'All right. I'm getting in,' he snarled as he allowed

himself to be frogmarched into the back of the van. Connor was mumbling obscenities beside him, but he too stopped resisting and stepped into the vehicle. As the door to the van was being pulled closed, Jake saw Luke and Danny opening the door of the café they'd only just left themselves, and when he caught their eye, he breathed a sigh of relief.

Jake and Connor were sitting on the dusty wooden floor surrounded by the six masked men when the van pulled away from the kerb. Jake hoped that Danny and Luke had got to Luke's car in time and were in pursuit. Luke drove an Audi S3 and there was no way the van would be able to lose him, even if the driver did notice he was being followed, although he seemed more preoccupied with congratulating himself and his associates for a job well done than paying much attention to his surroundings.

Jake and Connor weren't tied up, which Jake considered a rookie mistake. It was as though their kidnappers assumed that sheer numbers were enough to keep Jake and Connor in their place.

'You too scared to show your faces?' Connor snarled. 'Shithouses!'

One of the masked men started to laugh. 'I think you should take stock of your surroundings, Carter. You sure you want to be insulting the men who quite literally hold your life in their hands?'

'What? It took six of you to take us on, and you still won't take your masks off?' Connor snorted. 'You seem like a bunch of brainless fuckwits to me. What do you think, Jake?'

'Couldn't agree more, Con,' Jake said as he glared at their attackers.

'Is that so?' the one who had been talking shouted before he kicked Jake in the jaw and the other men seemed to take it as a signal they could join in as heavy boots rained down on Jake and Connor. They lashed out to protect themselves until a voice shouted, 'Enough for now. The boss wants them in one piece.'

The kicking stopped and Jake sat up against the side of the van. He looked at Connor, who was bleeding from a cut on his eye. He put his hand to his lip as he tasted blood in his mouth and realised that he was bleeding too.

'Still got your fucking masks on though, haven't you? Shithouses!' Connor spat blood onto the wooden floor.

Suddenly one of the men pulled off his balaclava. 'There!' he shouted. 'Fucking happy now?'

Jake recognised him as Karl Morgan, the owner of Trident Securities. Trident had been a decent firm a couple of years ago and had even ran the doors at The Blue Rooms for a short time, but then Cartel had taken over most of their business, and Trident, and Morgan along with them, had faded into obscurity.

Jake started to laugh. 'Jesus, Karl, you look like shit!'

'Fuck off, you arrogant little prick!' Karl shot back. 'I look like shit? You'll be fucking unrecognisable when we're through with you. Even your fucking mother won't be able to identify your body when it's pulled out of some ditch in the middle of nowhere.'

'I think you have a thing for my mum, don't you? I

remember how you were always perving at her when you worked in my club.'

Karl started to laugh. 'I wouldn't touch her with a fucking bargepole. Stuck-up bitch!' he spat. 'You're just fucking like her. Pair of arrogant cunts who think you're better than the rest of us. It's like my old nan used to say – what's in the cat is in the kitten.'

Jake glared at Karl. 'Yeah? You'd better fucking believe it.'

Connor and Jake were bundled out of the van and across the forecourt of the disused warehouse until they reached a large steel door. One of the masked men banged on it with his fist and they were pushed inside. Jake took in his surroundings as soon as he stepped inside. He and Connor were still untied – a massive mistake! Joey Parnell stood in the middle of the large empty room beside two chairs, and a large shaven-headed man stood beside him, grinning maniacally.

'Joey fucking Parnell, I might have known,' Jake spat. 'What the fuck is this all about?'

Parnell laughed as he indicated the two chairs. 'Sit 'em down,' he snarled.

'I asked you a question,' Jake said.

One of the men pushed Jake into the middle of the room towards Parnell and the grinning man.

'This,' Parnell spat, as he reached out and took Jake's face in his hand, 'is about finally showing your family that they are not quite as untouchable as you fucking think.'

Jake snarled as he tried to shrug off the giant goon who was holding onto him but the grip on his arms was too tight. Jake spat in Parnell's face and Joey responded by punching Jake in the jaw.

'I've always wanted to do that,' Parnell said with a grin as Jake spat the blood from his mouth onto the floor.

'You're going to fucking regret this,' Connor snarled.

'Oh, I don't think so, boys. In fact, I think it's you two who are going to regret ever fucking with me and my firm.'

Connor was marched across the room and pushed onto a chair, and Jake likewise. 'Tie them up,' Parnell barked.

Jake looked across at Connor, who nodded at him. Jake launched himself off the chair and into the legs of the man standing in front of him, pushing him to the floor, as Connor jumped up and punched one of the men in the face. Using the element of surprise, they managed to overpower half of the men. The room was filled with shouting and Jake could hear Parnell barking orders and hurling insults. Jake was straddling one of Parnell's men and punching him in the face when he was pulled backwards by two men. 'Fucking do him in first,' Parnell snarled.

'Whatever you say, Boss,' one of them answered. Jake turned to see the glint of metal as his attacker waved a machete in front of his face. He glanced across the room to see Connor fighting with three men, but he was losing too. Jake's heart started to pound in his chest. Where the fuck were Danny and Luke?

Jake saw the metal of the blade coming closer to his face

as it was pressed against the side of his throat. 'Still think we're a bunch of amateurs now?' he said with a grin, revealing he had a missing front tooth.

'Eight of you against two of us? Yes, I fucking do,' Jake spat. There was no way he was going to show any weakness in front of this shower of cunts.

The sound of the heavy metal door banging open made everyone look up in surprise. Jake felt the relief wash over him in a huge wave as he saw Danny and Luke charging into the place armed with hammers. The distraction was enough for Jake to break free and he kicked his machete-wielding attacker in the side of the knee, causing him to drop to the floor like a sack of spanners. Jake stood on his wrist, pressing into the flesh with the heel of his boot and causing the machete to fall free. Jake picked it up and turned quickly, swinging the blade as he did, right across the chest of the man bearing down on him. Luke and Danny meanwhile had run straight into the melée and were swinging hammers indiscriminately over heads, arms and backs.

'Let's get out of here,' Connor shouted.

Jake, Luke and Danny nodded in agreement and made a run for the door. Luke's car was parked right outside and the four of them dived into it.

'Get us the fuck out of here, mate,' Danny said to Luke.

Luke started the engine and sped out of the car park. As they drove away, Jake sat back against the leather seat in the back of the car. His head and jaw were throbbing and he could taste blood in his mouth. He looked across at Connor. 'You okay, mate?'

Connor touched his eye, which was bleeding. 'Yeah. Are you though?'

Danny turned in the passenger seat. 'Fucking hell, Jake, your neck is bleeding.'

Jake put his hand against his neck and felt the warm wet liquid trickling from underneath his right ear.

'That prick with the machete,' he snarled. 'If you hadn't turned up when you did, lads…' He shook his head; he couldn't bring himself to say the words.

Connor leaned over and put his hands on either side of Jake's face, pulling him closer and examining the wound.

'Does he need go to hospital?' Luke asked.

Connor held onto Jake and pushed his head up so he could take a closer look at the cut. 'No, it's not deep. Some steri-strips and a bandage will sort him out,' he said as he sat back. 'It looks worse than it is.'

'Easy for you to fucking say,' Jake said, wincing as he held a hand up to his neck, which had now begun to throb along with his head and face.

'We should probably get Timmo to check you over though, just in case,' Connor added.

'I'll ring him now and get him to meet us at the club,' Danny said.

Jake nodded. Timmo was not only one of their bouncers but had served as a combat medic in the army for years and knew his way around knife and bullet wounds – a skill that came in very handy in their line of work.

'There's a towel in my gym bag, there, Con,' Luke said as Danny spoke to Timmo.

Connor picked up Luke's gym bag from the floor and

took out the towel. He folded it and held it against Jake's neck with his right hand as he put his left arm around his shoulder. 'You'll be all right, mate,' Connor said quietly.

Jake nodded again. He'd been through worse.

Danny finished speaking to Timmo and put his phone back into his pocket. He looked down at the knuckles of his right hand and rubbed his thumb across the red skin. He had almost shit a brick when he'd seen Jake and Connor being bundled into the back of a van earlier. He would have happily murdered every fucker who had laid a hand on them, given half the chance. Danny glanced at the back seat and felt a sharp pain in his chest as he saw Jake sitting there bleeding all over the towel Connor was holding to his neck. Connor had told them the cut wasn't deep, but maybe he was just saying that for Jake's sake?

Danny frowned and turned back to look out of the window. Connor wouldn't risk Jake's life. If he needed to go to hospital then they would be on their way there – simple as. Danny needed to stop letting his emotions cloud his judgement. It wasn't like him to be emotional under pressure, but then it wasn't like him to think about other men the way he thought about Jake Conlon.

An hour later, Jake's wound had been cleaned and dressed by Timmo, who had been waiting for them when they'd arrived.

'Thanks, Timmo,' Jake said as he looked at the small square of white medical plaster on his neck in his reflection in the mirror.

'No problem,' Timmo said. 'Happy to help.'

'Sorry to drag you out of the house so early in the day,' Danny said as he patted Timmo on the shoulder.

'Oh, you didn't, I was in the office. I had to see Murf about changing my nights.'

Jake and Connor sighed in unison.

'So Murf knows you're here?' Connor asked.

'Yeah,' Timmo said with a frown.

'Does he know why?' Jake asked.

'I mentioned you'd been hurt and needed a wound looking at. I didn't know it was a secret. Should I not have said anything?'

'Don't worry about it,' Jake said.

'It's just Murf will have been on the phone to my dad—' Connor said.

'And my mum,' Jake added.

Suddenly the penny dropped. 'Of course. Sorry, lads,' Timmo said. 'I expect half of Liverpool have been brought in and interrogated already,' he said with a chuckle.

'It's not fucking funny,' Connor said. 'We'd rather handle this ourselves.'

Timmo shrugged. 'You should have said to keep it quiet.'

'I thought he was in the house with his missus,' Danny said apologetically.

'Look, it's done now,' Jake said. 'Thanks, Timmo, you can get off. You'll be starting your shift in a few hours.'

'Yeah. Make sure you change that dressing tomorrow,' he said to Jake. 'Keep it clean and let me know if you have any problems. If it turns green and your head falls off, probably best to get to A and E,' he said with a grin before he walked out of the room.

Jake had just suggested a round of Scotch when his stepfather Michael bounded into the room.

'Connor? Jake?' he said as he crossed the office. 'Are you okay?'

'We're fine,' Connor replied but that didn't stop him examining their faces and the wound on Jake's neck. 'What the fuck happened?' he shouted. 'Who did this?'

Connor picked up a bottle of brandy from the minibar in Jake's office and poured a glass. He handed it to Michael. 'You might want to sit down, Dad,' he said.

Chapter Thirty-Nine

Grace stared at Michael and tried to digest what he'd just told her. She could hardly believe Joey Parnell had been so reckless, and so bloody stupid. She wondered why Murf hadn't called her earlier and told her about what happened. Or why Michael hadn't told her as soon as he'd found out the boys had been hurt. She supposed the main thing was that Connor and Jake were okay, but from what Michael had told her, things could have easily been so different. He stared back at her and she could feel the anger radiating from him. Rubbing her temple, she wondered if she had made the wrong decision when she'd allowed Parnell to go unchallenged after he'd assaulted her.

'He's not getting away with this,' Michael snarled.

Grace stepped towards him and placed a hand on his cheek. 'I know,' she said. 'Do what you need to do. But please be careful.'

'I will,' he replied as he wrapped his arms around her waist. 'I always am.'

Jake stood in his kitchen holding the cold bottle of Budweiser to his bruised eye. His head and jaw still throbbed and his ribs felt bruised, but he considered himself lucky to be standing in his apartment. The way Michael had rushed out of his office earlier, almost foaming at the mouth, surely meant that Joey Parnell's days were numbered.

'You sure you're okay?' Danny asked as he crossed the kitchen and stood in front of him.

'Yeah.'

'When I saw them driving away with you and Connor in that van...' Danny shook his head. 'I don't think me and Luke have ever moved so fucking fast trying to get to his car in time so we didn't lose you.'

'Well, I'm just glad you saw us, mate, or God knows what would have happened,' Jake replied as he put the bottle on the kitchen counter.

'That looks painful,' Danny said, pointing at his bruised eye.

'Just a bit. Does it ruin my good looks though?' he asked.

'I think it would take more than a black eye and a split lip to do that, mate. Don't worry.'

Jake smiled and then they stood there in awkward silence. It had been two days since the two of them had spent the night together and they had barely spent a minute with each other since. Jake and Connor had gone to sort some business in Scotland and Luke and Danny had been busy dealing with the fallout from their takeover of Parnell's firm. The first time they'd had a chance to get together had been earlier that afternoon in Maria's café, before Parnell's goons had jumped him and Connor. When Danny had offered to drive Jake home, he'd agreed, wondering whether there would be a repeat performance.

'You fancy another beer?' Jake asked.

Danny smiled then. 'Yeah, go on.'

Jake took another bottle from the fridge and handed it to him. As Danny reached out and took the bottle from Jake's hand, their fingers brushed.

'You staying the night?' Jake asked.

Danny swallowed. 'Yeah,' he said, the word sounding like it caught in his throat.

'Good,' Jake growled. Putting his hands on the back of Danny's neck, he pulled him closer. 'I liked waking up next to you.'

Danny smiled. 'I liked waking up next to you too.'

Michael pulled up outside Eric's gym and watched as his older brother Sean jogged across the dark road towards him. Michael had told Sean about Parnell's attack on Grace when it happened the previous week, and earlier that evening he had also told him about Parnell's attempt on Connor and Jake's lives. Sean was supposed to be retired from the game, although lately he had been allowing himself to get sucked back in, and Michael could tell that getting involved in the whole McGrath incident a few months earlier, and taking the Essex gangster down, had given Sean a taste of the life again. And as much as he protested otherwise, Michael knew that Sean missed it. Even if that weren't the case, when it came to family, Sean was always happy to help out and Michael knew that there was no favour in this world that he couldn't ask of his big brother. They had always had each other's back, and they always would.

Sean opened the passenger door and climbed into the car. He glanced into the back seat and, noting it was empty, raised an eyebrow at his younger brother. 'Just you and me?'

'Just you and me.'

'Oh?' Sean said as he sat back in his seat. 'We're going old school then?'

'Yeah. You okay with that?' Michael asked.

'If that's what you need from me. I just assumed you weren't into that stuff any more? I mean, after So l...'

'What about Sol?' Michael snapped as he pulled the car away from the kerb.

'You just shot him.'

'I know. I thought it was for the best. But maybe it sent the wrong message?'

'What? That you're not the sadistic fucker that you used to be?'

'Exactly.'

'But you're not,' Sean said. 'And there's nothing wrong

with that,' Sean added before Michael could respond. 'Neither of us are those people anymore.'

Michael stared at the road ahead. 'I know that. But this is too personal. Maybe I should have dealt with Sol differently? Maybe just shooting him in the head was too good for that cunt. And I won't make the same mistake with Parnell. This fucker has attacked my wife, and now my sons. A message needs to be sent, Sean. I can't have people thinking that coming after my family is in any way acceptable.'

'Well, on that score, I couldn't agree more, Bro,' Sean said as he turned to his brother and grinned. 'Let's go make this fucker beg for death.'

Joey Parnell lived alone in a two-bedroomed apartment on Crosby's seafront. Unfortunately for him, the CCTV and maintenance for the complex, like many in the area, were provided by Taktik Secs – a subsidiary of Cartel Securities. The CCTV was suffering from a temporary failure and a copy had been made of the master key to get through the external door. It was almost 2 a.m. and the car park was deserted, as were the dimly lit interior corridors.

Parnell's apartment was on the top floor. There was an access code needed for the lift, and each landing had a keypad entry system via the stairwell. All in all, it was considered a secure building, and Michael imagined that Parnell thought he was pretty safe tucked away in his penthouse suite with his glorious views of the sea. He was about to realise how very wrong he was.

Michael keyed in the access code for the lift and he and Sean stepped quietly inside. They were both dressed all in black, with the hoods of their sweatshirts pulled over their heads – just in case they did happen to run into another resident in the early hours. When they reached the top floor, they walked quietly along the hallway, their trainers not making any sound on the thick carpet. Reaching Parnell's apartment, Michael signalled Sean to stop as he pulled out the small toolkit from his trouser pocket. It had been put together for him eight months earlier by Murf, who had once been an expert burglar, when he had needed to break into Sol Shepherd's house. Michael worked quietly, picking the lock. The only noise he could hear was the sound of Sean's steady breathing as he stood behind him keeping a watchful eye.

In a few seconds the lock was open and Michael pushed the door inwards slowly. He expected Parnell would have weapons at the apartment, and probably a gun, if he knew what was good for him. It was important that he didn't hear them and they maintained the element of surprise if they were going to get him out of the place with minimum noise and fuss. Michael crept inside with Sean close on his heels. Sean closed the door, the soft click of the latch amplified in the quiet apartment. Michael scanned the dark room quickly, his eyes taking a few moments to adjust to the darkness. It was empty. He knew the layout of the place and started to walk towards the bedroom. There was no sound in the room except for the ticking of a clock and Sean's soft, steady breathing.

Michael concentrated on his heartbeat, which thrummed in his ears as he reached the bedroom door. He glanced back at Sean and nodded at him. They had already agreed the plan in the car. Once they confirmed Parnell was in there, they would act quickly and Michael would grab Parnell and put him in a choke hold until he was unconscious. Then he would inject him with enough morphine to knock him out for at least an hour before binding his wrists and ankles with cable ties. Following that, Parnell would be carried to Michael's car and thrown into the boot before being driven to Nudge Richards' scrapyard, where Parnell's nightmare would really begin.

Michael pushed open the bedroom door. It made no sound except for a quiet whoosh of the wood against the bedroom carpet. He saw the figure of Parnell under the covers. Thankfully, he was alone. A few seconds later Michael had Parnell in a choke hold. Parnell struggled, his arms flailing wildly behind him as he tried to grab his attacker. He tried to shout but the pressure on his windpipe made the sound a muffled cry that no one was likely to hear, let alone take any notice of.

As the oxygen and blood supply to his brain was cut off, Parnell's body fell limp. Michael held out his hand to Sean, who passed him the hypodermic needle from his jacket pocket. Michael found a vein in Parnell's arm and pressed the needle into his skin, injecting the morphine into his bloodstream.

'Well, you still do that like a pro,' Sean said appreciatively.

'Let's get this fucker out of here,' Michael grunted as he hoisted Parnell from the bed. 'Before anyone sees us.'

One hour later, a naked Joey Parnell had his ankles strapped to a wooden chair with gaffer tape and his wrists tied behind his back with cable ties in an old container at the back of Nudge Richards' scrapyard. A single electric light hung from the ceiling, illuminating the steel workbench in the corner, and the array of tools spread out upon it including a wrench, a pair of pliers, a bone saw, a blowtorch and a selection of knives. Michael and Sean Carter stood in the open doorway and chatted casually to each other as they waited for Parnell to fully regain consciousness.

A few moments later, a loud groan alerted them to the fact that their charge was awake.

'Hello, Sleeping Beauty,' Sean said as they stepped into the container.

'Fuck off,' Parnell spat.

Michael laughed and turned to his brother. 'I think Joey has forgotten what we're capable of, Sean?'

'Seems like, doesn't it?'

Michael picked up the wrench. 'Shall we remind him?'

He didn't wait for an answer before swinging the wrench and bringing it down onto Joey's left knee smashing his kneecap into pieces. Joey screamed in pain, spittle flying from his mouth as he swore at the brothers.

'Have you heard the urban legends about us, Joey?' Sean asked. 'You must have.'

Joey glared at them both and Sean went on. 'We like to play them down, to be honest. Even deny some of the horror stories that we've heard about ourselves. But you have reminded us how important it is to remind people that they're true.'

Michael brought the wrench down on Joey's other kneecap and heard the satisfying crunch of bone.

'Fuck!' Joey screamed. 'You fucking cunts!'

Michael leaned down into Joey's face. 'I haven't even started yet,' he snarled. 'Did you think I wouldn't react when you attacked my wife? My fucking sons?' He punched Joey in the jaw to emphasise his point.

'I never touched your son,' Joey said as he spat blood onto the floor. 'I might have given that fag Jake a good slap, but I left your boy alone.'

Michael saw red and he raised his foot and kicked Joey in the groin with the solid heel of his Timberland boot. 'Jake is my son,' Michael spat. 'And you've just had the nerve to call him a fag? You must really fucking enjoy pain, Joey.'

Joey winced, the tears springing from his eyes. Then he shook his head. 'Just fucking get this over with,' he shouted, but the desperation was clearly audible in his voice.

'I already told you. We haven't even started,' Michael said as the sound of the blowtorch being lit behind Joey's head made him piss himself.

'You heard the rumours about what my brother likes to

do with that thing?' Michael asked as he indicated the weapon that Sean was now holding near Joey's face.

Joey started writhing in his chair and shaking his head furiously. 'No. No!' he screamed. 'Please! Not that.'

'You should have thought about how much your cock meant to you before you went anywhere near my family, you piece of shit!' Michael snarled and then he turned away and walked towards the door. A few seconds later, the smell of burning flesh and Joey Parnell's screams filled the small container. When he could stand the noise no longer, Michael turned back to the room. 'Enough,' he said to Sean as he walked over to stand beside him. Joey looked up at him, tears streaming down his face and the veins bulging in his temple. 'We don't want his heart packing in before we've shown him what I can do with a surgeon's knife, do we?'

Sean took a step back and admired his handiwork as Joey started to scream. Michael closed the container doors. Nudge's scrapyard was fairly secluded but Joey's screaming was becoming louder and they couldn't chance being heard.

'Shut the fuck up and have a bit of dignity, you crying cunt,' Michael snarled.

Joey started to cry then, big bawling tears and snot running from his nose. 'Please?' he begged. 'Let me go.'

'Is he fucking serious?' Sean said.

'Did my wife ask you to let her go when you had her pinned to the wall by her throat, Joey?' Michael asked him as he brought his face closer to Joey's. Joey looked up at him, his eyes wide as he stared into Michael's face. Then Michael saw it – that look a man has when he knows he is about to die.

'I know things. Let me speak to Grace,' he pleaded. 'I can help—'

Michael grabbed hold of Joey's face with his hand and squeezed his cheeks until he stopped talking. 'Is this about those girls that were murdered? It was you, wasn't it?' he snarled.

Joey snivelled and shook his head. 'He made me. I didn't want to.'

'I tell you what, Joey, you tell me what you know, and I'll decide if we should let you live to tell Grace. How about that?' Michael asked.

Joey's eyes started to roll in his head as the morphine they had given him earlier started to wear off and the pain started to kick in. 'This goes up higher than you can imagine. She needs to find Simon... He's got the card... It will bring down JB,' he mumbled before he passed out. None of which meant much at all to Michael.

Two hours later, Michael and Sean Carter had changed into a fresh set of clothes and were placing Joey's body, and the parts of him that they had removed, in the back of the old Fiesta they had driven him there in. On the seat beside him, they placed their clothes and the now bloodstained rags they had soaked in a solution of hydrogen peroxide and water and used to clean their skin. Sean emptied a full jerry can of petrol over the seats and stepped back as Michael lit the match and tossed it into the car. They both stood for a few moments and watched as the flames engulfed the vehicle. Michael turned to his brother, the glow of the fire making his face appear an unnatural shade of orange.

'This is the last time we do this?' Michael said. A question rather than a statement.

Sean shrugged in response as he started to walk away from the burning car and towards the parked car a few metres away where John Brennan was waiting for them. 'We only do what we have to, Michael,' he replied over his shoulder.

Chapter Forty

Grace had been lying awake for hours waiting for Michael to come home. Every time she heard a car pass by, she wondered if it would be him. It reminded her of all those nights she had lain awake waiting for Nathan, except that, for the most part, she had prayed that he wouldn't come home. She would always wonder about what kind of mood he would arrive home in, and whether he would feel the need to start an argument, or drag her out of bed by her hair because of some imagined insult. Waiting for Michael was completely different. She couldn't wait for him to come home to her, and all that she prayed for was that he was safe.

Grace must have drifted off because she was woken by a cool hand slipping over the warm skin on her waist and onto her stomach. She woke with a start, at first unsure of her surroundings. For an awful moment, she wondered if she was in the little flat above her pub, The Rose and Crown, and it was Nathan crawling into bed beside her. But then she felt Michael's body press against hers and his soft lips against her shoulder blade. He smelled of fresh air and soap. She placed her hand over his, her fingertips brushing over his wedding ring, and felt the relief wash over her. He was home.

She turned onto her back so she could look at him in the dim light of the room. Placing a hand on his cheek, she smiled at him. 'Are you okay?' she asked.

'I'm fine.'

'Did you do what you needed to?'

'Yes,' he said.

'Is everything taken care of?' she asked pointedly, although she already knew the answer.

'Of course it is.'

'Did Sean go with you?'

'Yeah,' he said with a soft sigh.

'Sophia will kill the pair of you if she finds out,' Grace warned.

'She won't find out,' he replied and then he bent his head and started to plant soft kisses along her collarbone.

'Are you sure you're okay?' she asked him again.

'Yes,' he replied sharply. 'I don't want to talk about it, Grace.' He rolled onto his back and lay with his hands behind his head.

Grace rolled onto her side and rested her head on her elbow. With her fingertips she traced the tattoo of her name on his abdomen, smiling as she remembered how he had surprised her with it the day after they had returned from their honeymoon in France.

She studied his face as he stared at the ceiling – his jaw

clenched shut as he wrestled with his thoughts. She understood that sometimes, to protect his family, he had to do things that he'd rather not tell her about. She had a good idea what he'd done tonight, and he knew that she did. The rumours about Michael and Sean and what they used to do, and occasionally still did, to people had been around for years. Grace knew they were more than just rumour and she was well aware of the violence that her husband was capable of. But she also knew how much it cost him and how he worried that one day he would go so far that he would never be able to come back. But that would never happen. He loved his family too much to ever let it. Besides, she would never let it happen. She would always bring him back to her, and to do that, she would be whatever he needed.

She placed a hand on his cheek. 'Okay,' she said softly. 'Then what do you want?'

He tilted his head to look at her, his eyes searching hers. 'Just you,' he whispered.

'Well, I'm right here,' she replied with a smile.

Michael rolled on top of her, pinning her to the mattress with the weight of his large frame.

'I love you, Grace,' he said before his head disappeared and he started to trail kisses down her stomach.

'I love you too,' she breathed as she enjoyed the feeling of his hands and lips on her skin.

'Coffee?' she asked.

Chapter Forty-One

Grace walked into the kitchen to see Michael putting dishes away. He had treated her and Belle and Oscar to a breakfast of freshly made pancakes with strawberries and Nutella. To say that the kids, and their dog Bruce, had enjoyed themselves would be an understatement. When Grace had left to drop the kids off at school and nursery, the kitchen had looked like a bomb site. But now there was no trace of chocolate spread or pancake batter to be found.

'You've been busy,' Grace said with a smile as she placed her phone on the countertop and sat down.'

'Coffee?' he asked her.

'Yeah,' she said and watched as he silently moved around the kitchen and made two coffees in the new-fangled machine he'd bought. He was so at ease in the kitchen. Like his brother Sean, he was a great cook and he used it as a stress reliever. She supposed that he needed that today.

When he'd made their drinks, he placed them on the breakfast bar and sat opposite her.

'You okay?' she asked.

He nodded at her and raised his mug to his lips, blowing on the hot liquid.

Grace watched him and sat in silence. He would talk to her when he was ready.

'Parnell told me to give you a message last night,' Michael said.

'Oh?'

'Hmm. He seemed to think that he'd be able to use it as a bargaining chip.'

'What was it?'

'It didn't all make sense. He was pretty incoherent by that point,' Michael said and looked at her, as though he was waiting for her to press him for more details, but she sat back and allowed him to talk.

'He'd lost most of his teeth and his jaw was probably broken,' he said and then looked down at his coffee.

Grace remained silent.

'Listening to his dying confession wasn't exactly my top priority. Men sometimes want to tell you all kinds of shite before they die. But from what I could understand, he said that the girls were killed to cover something up and it went higher than you knew. Then he wasn't really making sense, but he said that you needed to find Simon because he had the card and that the card would give you JB.' He looked up at her then. 'See, I told you it didn't make much sense,' he said with a shrug.

'It does to me,' Grace replied.

He didn't respond and she thought that now wasn't the time to tell him about what she'd learned from Leigh the previous day. He looked like he had the weight of the world on his shoulders. She would speak to Leigh as soon as she could.

She got up and walked around to the other side of the counter where Michael was sitting. Placing her arms around his neck, she rested her head on his shoulder. 'I love you, you know?' she said quietly in his ear. 'You are the best man I know.'

He turned his head to look at her and offered a faint smile. 'Then you must know some pretty shit ones.'

'Actually, I do,' she said with a laugh. 'But I know plenty of good ones too, and you stand head and shoulders above all of them. You are a better father and a better husband than I could have ever imagined was possible. You do what you have to so you can protect me and our family and I love you for it.'

He moved his arm and put it around her waist, pulling her towards him. He looked into her eyes and she saw the emotion in them. 'What did I ever do to deserve you?' he said.

She placed a hand on his cheek. 'Well, you do make excellent pancakes.'

He laughed then and she was relieved to hear the sound filling the quiet kitchen.

'I love you too, Grace.'

Grace had phoned Leigh from the car and arranged to meet in the back room at Stefano's where they could have some privacy. Grace was just getting out of her own car when she saw John Brennan's BMW X5 pulling up alongside her. She was surprised to see Leigh stepping out of it and Grace flashed her eyebrows at her.

'You're being very indiscreet, Detective,' Grace said with a grin.

'My car got a flat this morning—'

'And John just happened to be driving past, did he?' she asked as she waved to John before he sped off.

'You know that's not what happened,' Leigh said with a roll of her eyes.

Grace laughed and held the door open and Leigh stepped inside.

'I just didn't expect to see the two of you out in public together, that's all.'

'Well, given what we discussed yesterday, I'm rethinking my position on the whole situation,' Leigh joked.

'That's exactly what I wanted to talk to you about,' Grace said as they walked through to the back room.

Ten minutes later, the two women had a fresh pot of tea. Leigh sat back in her chair and waited for Grace to speak.

'I can't tell you how I know this, but I think you're right about who is orchestrating all of this.'

Leigh sat forward, her mouth a ring of surprise. 'Okay. Why?'

On the drive over, Grace had thought about what information she could impart that wouldn't implicate Michael in Parnell's murder the night before. Soon enough, his disappearance would be noted. The body and the car had been burned and crushed at Nudge Richards' scrap yard, and would remain there for as long as Nudge was alive. They had no concerns that his body would be found, or, even if it was, that there would be any evidence to tie Michael or Sean to the crime. Grace was sure that Leigh would suspect Michael had a hand in Parnell's disappearance, but that didn't mean she was going to confirm it for her. At the end of the day, Leigh was still a DI.

'I have come by some information that Simon Jones is the key to it all. He has something in his possession that could blow the whole case wide open.'

'Simon Jones, the missing pimp from Manchester?'

Grace nodded.

'Okay. How is that linked to my theory?'

'My source said this went high up and then the name JB was mentioned.'

Leigh sat back and let out a low whistle. Grace supposed it was one thing to suspect your boss of being involved in a heinous crime, but when it was starting to look like it might be true, well, that was an entirely different story. 'We can't find Jones though. His landlord reported him missing two months ago and my colleagues have him as a registered missing person. Maybe he's dead too?'

Grace shook her head. 'He's not.'

'How do you know that?' Leigh frowned.

'His ex-girlfriend works for us, and Simon has been in

touch with her. It was a week or so ago. But he's in hiding, he's not dead.'

'Where?' Leigh sat up straighter, like a hunting dog who'd caught a sniff of its prey.

'She doesn't know, but she might be willing to talk to you and you can see if there's some clue we're missing. But it would be off the record.'

'Of course. Everything is off the record now that I'm investigating my own Chief Super.' She shook her head. 'This is all crazy. John Barrow has been a copper for over twenty-five years. He oversaw the operation that eventually shut down Sunnymeade and the drug-trafficking ring.' Leigh visibly shuddered at the realisation. 'God, he's been covering his tracks for years. I wonder if he and Sol Shepherd were in on it together?'

'Looks like, doesn't it? That must have been how Sol got away with it. He always bragged about having a very powerful friend. Plus, it would make sense after what Jazz said about Sol's mood changing when he was on holiday. Barrow must have had Melanie killed while Sol was away.'

'I wonder if he killed her himself? I mean his DNA was never going to show up on the police database, was it? It was the perfect crime.'

'Well, almost. But if they hadn't moved on to the girls in Liverpool, the connection would probably have never been made. I wonder how the girls from Sunnymeade fit in with the whole thing.' Grace said.

'Well, let's hope Simon Jones can tell us. But how the hell do we find him? As far as my superiors are concerned, we have our man in custody. I can't use valuable resources on tracking down a missing person.'

'Don't worry. I have just the men for the job,' Grace said with a smile.

Chapter Forty-Two

Grace walked into her office at Sophia's Kitchen to see Michael and Sean sitting at opposite sides of the desk.

'I was hoping to catch you two,' she said as she walked over to Michael and gave him a kiss on the cheek before sitting on the small leather sofa.

'Oh no, what have we done?' Sean asked.

'Or what are we about to do?' Michael said with a smile.

'Well, I know how much you two enjoy working together. And I know you enjoy using your very unique and particular skill set. So, how about using it in a way that won't have me, or Sophia, worried sick about the pair of you?'

'Sounds intriguing,' Michael said. 'What?'

'I need you to find someone for me. His name is Simon Jones. He is Stacey's ex-boyfriend.'

'Danny's sister Stacey?' Michael asked.

'Yes. So, she might be a good person to speak to first.

And I'm sure Danny and Luke would be more than happy to help you out if you need it.'

'I'm sure we can handle it on our own,' Sean said.

'Why do you want him found?' Michael asked. 'Is it something to do with Stacey?'

Grace smiled and proceeded to tell them about the latest developments in the Liverpool Ripper case. As expected, they were both happy to help track down Simon Jones. She knew that having the chance to help bring down the corrupt Chief Superintendent of Merseyside police would be hard for them to resist.

———————

Michael sat back in the Land Rover and watched Sean flicking through a brochure on commercial kitchen fittings. It had been two days since Grace had asked them to find Simon Jones, and, using their considerable contacts across the North West and beyond, they had tracked him down to a derelict outbuilding in Burnley. It hadn't been too difficult to find the elusive Mr Jones and Michael wondered if Parnell had been searching for him too. He imagined so, if he really had been working for Barrow. The pair of them would have wanted whatever it was that Jones had on them. For all Barrow's power and authority, he still hadn't been able to find Simon Jones. Whilst he had a wealth of police intelligence data at his fingertips, it didn't always help when people with as many connections as Simon decided they didn't want to be found. Barrow could hardly send a team of his finest officers after him. Jones didn't have a warrant out for his arrest, and he hadn't been a suspect in the Ripper murders, although given what they knew now, he probably should have been.

Sometimes it took good old-fashioned arm twisting and threats to find a person who didn't want to be found, and Michael and Sean were very good at that, which is how they came to be sitting on the edge of a field in Murf's old Land Rover, waiting for Simon Jones to emerge for his daily trip to the local shop. They could have gone into the building and dragged him out, but there were too many exits and if he'd been quick enough, he might have got away and into the nearby woods. From their vantage point, they could see the building and would see him leave, but he would be travelling towards the road and would be unlikely to spot them.

Half an hour had passed and Michael was starting to get fed up. Sean was still engrossed in stainless-steel worktops and ovens. Every now and then he would turn to Michael and show him a picture of one he thought would be good for the new restaurant and Michael simply smiled – they all looked the same to him. Grace was responsible for most of the design and furnishings of the restaurants they opened, but she allowed Sean free rein when it came to the kitchen, and he took his role very seriously. Michael was about to suggest to Sean that they take their chances and go in there and get Jones when he saw a figure appear in the doorway. He had his hood pulled up over his head and a large backpack on his back. He glanced left and right but didn't notice the old khaki Land Rover sitting beneath the trees fifty metres away.

'Here he is,' Michael nudged Sean. 'We going on foot, or in the car?'

'If we start this beast up, he might scarper. You up for a run, Bro?' Sean asked. 'You could do the hundred metres in under twelve seconds when you were a kid. You'll be there in six.'

Michael turned and stared at him. 'Yeah, thirty years ago, mate. I'm an old man now.'

'Fuck off!' Sean laughed. 'You're two years younger than me, and I am not fucking old! Now come on,' he said as he unclipped his seatbelt and jumped out of the car.

Michael followed suit and they both closed the doors quietly.

'You know the plan?' Michael murmured. Sean nodded and they jogged quietly through the soft grass towards Simon Jones. Michael was only a few metres away from Simon when he finally heard him. He spun around, shouted 'Fuck!' then ran off like a whippet. Fortunately, he ran straight into the path of Sean, who had run behind the house and ahead along the treeline. Sean grabbed him, restraining him easily with one arm across his throat and the other pinning Simon's left arm behind his back. Simon lashed out with his right arm but Michael caught him by the wrist. He took the syringe from his pocket and then held it between his teeth as he rolled Simon's sleeve up above his elbow.

'What are you doing?' Simon stammered as he tried to wriggle his arm free. Michael squeezed Simon's wrist hard and he stopped wriggling. 'Please, don't,' he wailed.

Michael tapped the inside of Simon's elbow and felt for

the vein. Then he looked into Simon's eyes and saw the genuine fear in them before taking the syringe from his mouth. He pierced the skin, injecting the liquid into Simon's arm. 'Night, night,' he said with a smile.

'You really are too good at that,' Sean said as Simon slumped in his arms. 'Hardly a drop of blood. You should have been a nurse, Bro,' he added with a grin.

'Fuck off,' Michael said good-naturedly. 'Come on, let's get him in the back of the Lanny before someone sees us.'

'We're in the middle of nowhere, Michael. Who's gonna see us?' Sean said as they wrestled Simon's backpack from his back. When it was free, Michael carried it by the handle and Sean hoisted Simon onto his shoulder before carrying him to the Land Rover.

Once they were on the drive home, Michael phoned Grace and told her where to meet them.

'Is she going to be nice Grace or frightening Grace today then?' Sean asked as he glanced over into the back seat, no doubt to make sure that Simon was still out for the count.

'Don't worry about him. I gave him enough to knock a rhino out. And what do you mean?'

'I mean is she going to get him to give her whatever information he has by pretending she's his mate, or by making him shit his pants? Both effective, I was just wondering what kind of mood she's in.'

Michael started to laugh. He'd never quite thought of it like that, but she did tend to get people to do what she wanted via one of those two extremes. There was no middle ground. 'I imagine, given what Stacey has told her about our friend Simon, she will be employing the latter. But who knows? I expect it will also depend on how respectful Mr Jones is when he wakes up.'

'Well, let's hope he tells her to go fuck herself or something.' Sean started to laugh.

'Excuse me?' Michael turned and stared at him. 'That's my fucking wife you're talking about.'

Sean continued laughing. 'Sorry, mate. But it would make our evening more interesting, wouldn't it? And from what you've told me about this horrible prick, he deserves to have the shit kicked out of him.'

Michael smiled. He knew exactly what Sean meant and if Mr Jones happened to piss Grace off later, then it would be he and Sean who would happily teach him some manners.

———

Grace walked into the empty warehouse with John Brennan close behind her to see the man she assumed to be Simon Jones, tied to a chair, with Michael and Sean sitting nearby. They appeared deep in conversation. The sound of her heels echoed around the building, making Michael and Sean look up. Michael smiled and Sean gave a quick nod of greeting as she approached them.

'Did you check his bag?' Grace asked.

'Yes. I think this is probably what you're looking for,' Michael replied as he held up a small 10MB memory card. It was the kind that was used in cameras before the widespread use of smartphones. 'But the rest of his shit is on there.' He indicated the wooden table behind him.

Grace walked over to it and noted the empty backpack, with its contents spread out across one side of the table. Some items of clothing. A penknife. A roll of twenty-pound notes. A near-empty pack of tobacco. Some Rizlas. A lighter and an old-style Nokia phone. On the other side of the table was an array of weapons and tools, which Grace knew were probably there only for effect. Probably. She didn't approve of torture as a method of getting information. Not as a rule anyway. But she was prepared to bend that rule for scumbags who abused women and children. So everything would depend on how willing Mr Jones was to talk.

Grace walked over to Simon and looked at him. He was unconscious and his head was resting on his chest. His dark hair was curling over his ears and the collar of his shirt and she suspected he usually kept it short, but getting a haircut wasn't a top priority for someone in hiding. He was lean but muscular and, from what she could see, fairly good-looking. She supposed that had helped when he'd been grooming young girls to pimp them out.

'Time to wake him up then,' Grace said as she looked across at Michael.

'I've asked Luke and Danny to find us a camera that we can watch this thing on,' Michael said. 'They should be here shortly.'

'Good. Let's see if he tells us the truth about what's really on there.'

He walked over to her, taking a syringe filled with

adrenalin from his pocket. He was about to put the needle into Simon's arm when Grace suddenly had an idea. 'Stop,' she said, taking hold of Michael's arm. 'I want him to give Barrow up, and to do that, he has to be more scared of us than he is of him.'

'Well, we can make sure of that,' Michael said.

'I know that, but your methods aren't exactly scientific, are they? What if his heart packs in or something?'

'Then we'll still have the card,' Sean said as he walked over.

'But we don't know what's on it yet,' Grace reminded them. 'If the police have the card and him, then maybe they stand a better chance of sending Barrow away for life?'

'You plan on handing him over to Leigh then?' Michael asked.

'I think we have to, or she may not be able to prove that Barrow had anything to do with any of it.'

Michael and Sean nodded. 'So what are you thinking?' Sean asked.

'I'm thinking, he's been knocked out and kidnapped. What would be the most terrifying sight he could wake up to?'

———

Ten minutes later, Grace gave the nod to Michael and he injected the adrenalin into Simon's vein. Michael stepped back as Simon blinked, a bright light from overhead shining in in his face. The rest of the warehouse was dark, making him squint to see what was in front of him. He looked down then, noting no doubt that he was stark bollock naked. His clothes had been cut from his body about five minutes earlier while he was still strapped to the chair. He looked up again.

'Who's there?' he shouted, still squinting as his eyes adjusted to the light. Then he saw him. The giant of a man that was John Brennan, standing bare-chested on a sheet of plastic sheeting and holding a rusty bone saw in his hands. On the floor beside him was a blowtorch and a pair of jump cables – the kind that you used to attach to a car battery. It didn't really matter that they weren't actually connected to anything. It would be hard to see given the light.

'What the fuck?' Simon said and then he started to scream, thrashing around on the chair so much that it almost toppled over. Michael came up behind him and steadied the chair. He bent down and growled into Simon's ear. 'He's just for starters. You haven't seen my toys yet.'

Simon stopped screaming, his eyes wide with fear as he tried to turn to see who was behind him. But Michael had disappeared. He turned back to John, who took a few steps towards him. Simon started to cry before he pissed himself.

Grace had seen enough and thought if that hadn't been enough to convince Simon he was better off in the hands of the police, then she didn't know what would be. She pulled a wooden chair over and placed it a few feet in front of him. Then she placed a hand on John's arm. 'Let's see if he wants to talk first, eh? Big fella? If he doesn't, I promise you'll all get your turn.' She looked around the room and the banging of tools being placed on a table could be heard.

Simon tried to turn his head to see what was behind him, but the warehouse was too dark.

John stepped back and waited patiently with the saw resting against his leg.

'We found your little memory card, Simon,' Grace said. 'Some of our associates will be here shortly with a camera so we can view the images. But if you can tell me what's on it first, I might be persuaded to call off my men and hand you over to the police,' Grace said.

He looked at her, his lower lip trembling. 'I can't go to the police. They'll put me in jail. And he'll make sure everyone knows what I did,' he snivelled.

'Who?' she asked.

He shook his head. 'I can't,' he mumbled.

'You mean to tell me you are more afraid of whoever this man is than of all my men in here? Men who know exactly what you do to young women and girls and who wouldn't mind doing the same to you?' She tilted her head and looked at him. 'You're scared of going to prison? Because of what you are and what they might do to you in there? The men in this room will do things to you that will make you beg for the safety of a prison cell. Did you know that Danny Alexander and Luke Sullivan work for me now too? In fact, they're on their way here with that camera,' Grace said and she watched as Simon retched and vomited bile onto the floor.

'We're going to see what's on the card anyway. Are you on there, Simon?' she asked.

'No.' He shook his head furiously.

'Then who is?'

'I'm no safer with the police,' he sniffed.

'Perhaps? But I happen to know a DI who will take you in and make sure that you are protected. Once you're in police custody, they have a duty to protect you.'

He looked up at her and then across at John, who was still holding the saw.

'It's your call, Simon. You have five seconds before I leave you to this lot.'

'If I tell you, you'll hand me over to this DI? And you won't let them touch me?' He nodded towards John.

'It depends what information you have, I suppose. I mean, I already have the card, don't I?'

'The card on its own isn't enough,' he said. 'It needs someone who was there.'

'And let me guess, you are the only person left alive who was there? Is that right?'

Simon nodded.

'You gave up those poor women to save your own skin, didn't you?'

He started to cry again and Grace sighed.

'Tell me what I need to know, Simon, or you will spend the next twenty-four hours of your life in pain you can't even imagine.'

He looked up at her again and sniffed. 'There's a video of a party on there. It was a sex party. I was recording it. There were six women and three men. It was taken six years ago and some of the girls were underage.' He continued to cry and Grace rolled her eyes.

'So they were girls, not women?' Grace snapped. 'Children?'

'Some were fifteen. Some sixteen.'

'So children! Who were they?'

'The four girls from the kids' home who've been murdered. Melanie Simmonds and Samia Munro.'

'Samia Munro?' Grace asked.

'Yes. She was a kid we found on the streets. A runaway.'

'She was? Other than the girls being underage, what else happens on that video? People have died for this video and you went into hiding?'

'Things got out of hand. Someone went a bit too far, and she…'

'She what?' Grace snarled.

'She died. It was an accident. All of the girls knew that these particular customers liked it rough. They knew what they were getting into.'

Grace resisted urge to crush Simon's balls with the heel of her stiletto. She looked up and saw Michael and Sean stepping out of the shadows. She held up her hand to them to indicate she wasn't done with him yet.

'Who else was on the video?'

'Joey Parnell, Sol Shepherd…'

'And?'

'Chief Superintendent Barrow.'

Grace sat back in her chair and rubbed her temples. 'You can get dressed, John,' she said quietly and he slipped away to retrieve his T-shirt.

'If this happened six years ago, why wasn't this memory card destroyed then? Why is it surfacing now and why have the women been murdered for it?'

'Barrow and the others didn't know that I'd filmed the party. I always filmed them – secretly.'

'God, you're fucking disgusting,' Grace couldn't help snapping.

'Sol and Barrow had Samia's body disposed of and the other five girls were warned to never speak of the incident. They were too terrified of all of us not to agree, so Barrow, Parnell and Sol assumed that would be the end of it. Then Melanie Simmonds got clean and she started talking to people about what had happened.'

'So she was disposed of too?'

'I had no part in that. I thought Barrow was just going to warn her off. Slap her around a bit, you know?' Simon said, as though that would have been entirely acceptable. 'But he went too far, and…'

'Seems he had a habit of going too far.' Grace snapped. 'What about the women from Sunnymeade?'

Simon started to cry again and looked down at his feet. Grace looked over at Michael and nodded at him. He walked across the warehouse, grabbed hold of Simon's head by the hair and pulled it back sharply. 'Tell her what she wants to know, because if I have to listen to you much longer, I will cut out your fucking tongue.'

Simon howled in pain as Michael let his head snap back. He sniffed loudly before he carried on talking. 'After I got out of prison, I needed some cash, so I contacted Parnell about the video. I thought that we could blackmail Barrow and make a bit of easy money.'

'But you hadn't counted on Barrow and Parnell being such good buddies?'

'I didn't realise they'd worked together so closely and Barrow had made sure that Parnell was looked after in prison. So, instead of blackmailing him with me, Parnell told Barrow about the video and the next thing I know someone is trying to kill me. Barrow and Parnell contacted me and tried to get me on side. They wanted to know who'd taken the video and who had it, so I told them it was one of the girls,' he snivelled. 'That's why they went after them.'

'You're a piece of shit!' Grace spat at him. 'I'm going to hand over that memory card to the police. If what you say is true, I don't want to see it. I'll hand you over too, you waste of oxygen, but only because you'll be needed to put Barrow away.'

Simon's shoulders slumped, possibly out of relief, and he sobbed quietly.

Grace stood up and Michael, Sean and John walked over to her.

'I'm going to contact DI Moss and let her know we have Mr Jones and the memory card. I'll give her the heads up about what's on it. John, can you contact Danny and Luke and tell them to stand down? We won't be needing that camera after all.'

'Yes, Boss,' John said. 'I'll go and call them from the car.'

As John walked away, Grace turned back to Michael and Sean. 'Can you cut him free and make sure he's dressed and presentable? Because we're going to drop him at the police station ourselves. And do you think you can do that without killing or maiming him?'

Michael and Sean nodded and Simon looked up in fear.

'We'll be leaving here in ten minutes. He needs to be in one piece if we're handing him over,' she said to them.

'We'll behave ourselves,' Michael replied.

Grace smiled at him. She knew that he and Sean would like nothing more than to give Simon Jones a taste of the pain and torment he had caused the six women who had died at the hands of his associates. 'Thank you,' she said. Then she looked at Simon again. 'If I find out you've lied about what is on that video, or if you suddenly change your story about what happened and end up for some reason walking out of that police station, these men will track you down again and they will make sure that you suffer the same fate as those poor women you allowed to be tortured and murdered just to save your own skin. Do you understand me?'

Simon nodded furiously.

Satisfied with his response, Grace kissed Michael on the cheek. 'I'll wait outside.'

Then she walked out of the warehouse to phone Leigh and tell her they had the evidence to bring down her boss.

Chapter Forty-Three

G race walked into the kitchen and inhaled the aroma of the lamb rogan josh Michael was preparing.

'That smells delicious,' she said as she selected a bottle of wine from the rack. 'Red or white?'

'Hmm, red. What about the new Rioja?'

'Perfect,' Grace said as she selected the wine from the rack. The doorbell ringing signalled the sound of their guests arriving. 'I'll get it,' she said as Michael poured boiling water into a pan for the rice.

Grace poured out four glasses of wine as Michael dished out the curry.

'I've been looking forward to this all day. I believe your lamb curry is something to behold, Michael?' Leigh Moss said as she took a seat at the dining table.

'Well, you should count yourself lucky. I only usually

make it for people I like,' Michael said with a half-smile as he handed her a plate.

Leigh grinned at him and Grace laughed. She knew her husband was only half-joking but she appreciated that he was willing to try and get to know Leigh a little better.

'Pile my plate high,' John Brennan said as he rubbed his hands together.

'I bought a whole extra lamb shoulder once I heard you were coming, mate, don't worry,' Michael said with a laugh.

John grinned and picked up his knife and fork.

'So, I saw they charged your dodgy boss today, Leigh?' Michael asked as they started eating.

'Yes. The Chief Constable is doing his best to minimise the fallout, but the press are having a field day. As you can imagine.'

'Well, it's not every day a Chief Superintendent is charged with murder and kidnap, is it?' Grace said. 'I bet your bosses are all having their arses handed to them over this?'

'On a daily basis! Things are not good, let's just say that. But we've got a strategy. Barrow is going to have the book thrown at him and that should assure the public that we're taking the whole thing very seriously.'

'So, he's been charged with killing Melanie and the girls from the children's home?' Grace asked.

'He denies everything of course. But his DNA was all over Melanie Simmonds. His semen was found in her vagina, but obviously there was no way to tell it was his at the time or during the investigation.'

'Do we have to talk about this when we're eating?' John said with a grimace.

'Oh, shut up and finish your curry, John,' Grace said good-naturedly. 'Enquiring minds need to know.'

Leigh swallowed her mouthful of food and went on. 'The evidence suggests that he raped and killed Melanie himself. Apart from the semen, she had his DNA under her fingernails.'

'What? How stupid could he be?' Michael asked. 'He's a copper and he left all of that evidence on the body?'

'Well, I expect he thought he would never be connected to the crime. At that time neither he or his associates knew that the memory card even existed. Barrow and Sol Shepherd thought that Melanie was the only loose end to tie up. They didn't know about Simon and the memory card until Simon contacted Joey about his plan to blackmail Barrow. I also suspect that Barrow hadn't intended to kill Melanie, and would have had Joey or one of Sol's men do it for him, but with an ego like he has, I imagine he wanted to teach her a lesson of some sort. A display of his power, maybe? But he went too far.'

Grace shook her head as she digested the information. 'So then when he was told that one of the girls from Sunnymeade had the video of him with Samia Munro and the underage girls, Barrow had Joey kidnap and kill them all?'

Leigh nodded. 'We knew the girls must have been held somewhere fairly remote because they were tortured for some time before they were killed. When we did some digging into Barrow, we found an old farmhouse in

Scarisbrick listed in his assets. He inherited the house from his father. Our forensics team have been through the place and found evidence of all four of our Sunnymeade victims being held in the basement, as well as Joey Parnell's DNA and some of his possessions all over the upstairs living area. There's no CCTV near the place as you can imagine, but we do have Parnell's car leaving the A road nearby on key dates, including the dates the victim's bodies were disposed of. It looks like some of the women were there at the same time, and also that he left them alone for days at a time. Can you imagine how terrified they must have been? Tied up? In the dark? With God knows what down there with them? Never knowing if their tormentor was coming back for them?'

'Wasn't that a bit dodgy though? Just leaving them alone? They could have escaped. Or someone could have heard them,' Grace said.

Leigh shook her head. 'The place was pretty isolated and the cellar was an old stone construction. It was completely underground. Those poor women could have screamed all day and night and no one would have heard them. They were tied up and kept in cages—'

'Cages?' Michael almost choked on his curry. 'What kind of cages?'

'Those big dog crates.'

Everyone at the table stopped eating and stared at Leigh in horror.

'Yes, I know,' she said. 'Besides that, the door to the cellar was a huge steel thing and it was bolted shut. There was no way anyone was escaping the place.'

'Wow,' Grace said. 'So we were right about Parnell all along?'

'Yes,' Leigh confirmed as she continued eating. 'He'd left everything as though he'd intended to go back and clean the place, but obviously he disappeared and never got the chance to.'

Grace continued looking at Leigh intently and was impressed by how Michael and John didn't even flicker at the mention of Parnell's disappearance.

'So, how are you intending to tie Barrow to the Sunnymeade murders? Surely everything you have so far could be explained away by his expensive brief?' Grace asked, partly to change the subject, but also because she was desperate to know that that horrible fucker was going to pay for what he'd done to those poor women.

'Well, we have him and Parnell on the video so we know they are connected. We know that he murdered Melanie, although we can't prove his part in the trafficking ring – yet! The crate that the girls were held in belonged to Barrow and we've tested some of the animal hair found in it, which belong to one of his dogs. The farmhouse belonged to him. And Simon Jones has agreed to testify against him for a plea deal. Jones was the one who provided him and Parnell with the four names of the Sunnymeade girls.'

'And that sick fuck gets a plea deal?' Michael snapped.

'Don't worry, he's still going away for a very long time.'

'Still?' Grace said, knowing all too well how a good barrister could make all of that appear circumstantial. 'It's still not concrete, is it?'

'How much more evidence do you think they need,

Grace?' John said as he stared at her. 'That fucker is banged to rights.'

'Well, we know he did it, but it's a jury that has to be convinced. I doubt he's going to plead guilty to any of it, is he?'

Leigh shook her head. 'Not a chance. And Grace is right, what I've told you is enough to charge and enough to persuade most people that he was probably involved, but a jury must believe beyond all reasonable doubt, and that's different.'

'So he might get away with it?' John snapped.

Leigh smiled triumphantly. 'I haven't told you about our trump card yet. We put this piece of evidence to him today and I wish I could have taken a photograph of his face when we did.'

'What is it?' Grace asked.

'It's something you were most helpful with, actually, Grace. I'm not sure we'd have made the connection if you hadn't gone speaking to the girls at Number 69 for me.'

Grace smiled. 'The tooth?'

'What tooth?' Michael asked.

'When Nerys Sheehan was found, she was carrying a child's tooth.'

'A child's tooth? But how, if she was strangled? She wouldn't have been able to hold onto anything,' Michael asked, revealing his intimate knowledge of the topic.

Leigh didn't flicker and Grace supposed she was well aware of what the three people she was sitting eating dinner with were capable of. 'She wasn't holding it. She had pressed it into the open ligature wound on her wrist,' Leigh said and John and Michael both shuddered at the thought. 'We took DNA from the tooth, and whilst initially we couldn't determine who or where the child was, because she wasn't in any database, we were able to match the DNA and prove that she was Nerys's daughter. Our database didn't have any DNA matches for her father—'

'Until recently?' Grace finished for her, as though as someone had flicked a switch in Grace's brain.

Leigh nodded.

'Barrow?' Grace said.

'Exactly. She had just turned sixteen when she had Daisy, so we have conclusive proof that Barrow had sex with her when she was underage. Additionally, now that we know what has really happened and have Barrow in custody, Stuart Halligan has confirmed that Nerys was pregnant when she left Sunnymeade. She'd managed to keep it a secret because she was terrified that Barrow would have Vince Collins kill her – and her baby. Stuart was a year younger and was one of her only friends. He'd left Sunnymeade just after Nerys had fallen pregnant. His aunt Beth had moved back from Australia with her new husband and when she found out where he was, she took him out of the place straight away. Stuart went to live with her, but he stayed in touch with Nerys and he was her vital link to the outside world. When Nerys left on her sixteenth birthday, she was six months pregnant. With nowhere else to go, she turned up at Stuart's and that was when Beth learned of what had been going on and the abuse Nerys and Stuart had suffered. When Nerys talked about giving the child up for adoption, Beth suggested a better option. She and her husband couldn't have children and had been through two unsuccessful cycles of IVF. As she had moved from Australia a few months before, her medical records weren't available. Nerys had the baby and Beth and her husband were able to convince medical professionals that Daisy was a complete shock and Beth hadn't even known she was pregnant. Then one afternoon, at home, she had arrived. Mother and baby were checked over by the attending midwife, and all was deemed to be above board.'

'Didn't the midwife notice she hadn't just given birth though?' Michael asked.

'No. Perhaps Beth refused to be examined? Or perhaps the midwife was in on it? Beth works at the hospital and is a well-respected paediatrician.'

'Wow!' Grace said as she took a sip of her wine. 'At least little Daisy is okay. What will happen now though? Have they committed a crime?'

'Technically, but Beth and her husband have a great legal team. Daisy is thriving. She is almost six and they are the only parents she has ever known. And they also have a sworn statement from Nerys handing over all legal guardianship of her daughter to the couple. Their solicitor drew it up in the event of anything ever coming out like this. It's not like Daisy's father is in a position to object, is it?'

'No,' Grace agreed. 'God, what a horrible bastard! So Stuart was a good guy all along then, just like Stacey said?'

'Exactly. When I started asking questions about Daisy, Stuart was terrified that Barrow was onto them. He also told me that Nerys visited his flat two nights before her death.'

'Two nights before? But wasn't she being held by Parnell then?'

'Yes. Perhaps it was Parnell's plan all along? Perhaps it was part of Nerys's plan to negotiate her freedom? I suppose we won't know unless Barrow talks, or we find Joey Parnell.'

'But why not tell Stuart and phone the police?' Grace asked. 'It was her chance to escape.'

'Fear. You and I both know that women in fear for their safety are often very compliant. It's a defence mechanism.'

'Of course,' Grace said. 'Or she was protecting her child?'

'Either way, she was used to collect evidence to incriminate Stuart. He said it wasn't unusual for her to turn up whenever she was in need. She had seemed hurt and was scared but she wouldn't tell him why. She told him she was going away for good and asked for a keepsake to remember Daisy by. He offered her a teddy bear or a doll, but she didn't want anything like that. He recalled her asking for a hairbrush, but he didn't have one. He picked Daisy up from school twice a week and never had cause to brush her hair as she is by all accounts a very neat and tidy little kid. When he mentioned that she had lost a tooth while playing at his house a few days earlier, Nerys asked for it. He said no at first. It was Daisy's first lost tooth and he was supposed to have given it to his aunt, but Nerys was insistent. He gave it to her, reasoning that there would be more lost teeth for his aunt but none for Nerys. Then he agreed to let Nerys spend the night and claims that he woke up to her masturbating him. He didn't stop her, although they had never had a sexual relationship before. She left shortly afterwards. I can only guess at this, but I suspect Nerys must have known she was going to die when she visited Stuart and she knew that something with Daisy's DNA would also hold the DNA of the man responsible for it all.'

'Clever girl, Nerys,' Grace said as she smiled in admiration. Then she raised her glass in a toast. 'To Nerys, Tracy, Ellie, Anna, Melanie and Samia,' she said quietly. 'May they never be forgotten.'

Her three dinner companions raised theirs too and toasted the victims.

Grace was clearing the dishes while Michael entertained their guests in the living room when she heard footsteps behind her.

'Need any help?' Leigh asked.

'Don't be silly. You're a guest,' Grace said. 'I'll be done in a minute anyway.'

'Thank you for inviting me,' Leigh said with a smile.

'You're welcome. And how else was I going to find out about Barrow's arrest? I hope they convict that bastard and throw away the key,' she said.

'Me too.'

'It sounds like you've got a pretty good case though, Leigh.'

'Yes. I couldn't have done it without you though. I really appreciate your help.'

'I'm happy I was able to. Don't go getting any ideas about me helping you out again though,' Grace said with a grin. 'I'm not coming over to the dark side.'

Leigh laughed and placed her wine glass on the counter. Grace looked at her and wondered if she had ever seen Leigh looking so relaxed and happy before.

'Don't worry. I won't ask again,' Leigh said as she raised her hands in surrender. 'I'm not even sure if I'm going to stay in the job, to be honest.'

'What?' Grace asked as she shook her head in surprise. 'But you love your job.'

'I used to. I guess I still do, but this whole thing with Barrow...'

'And John?' Grace added.

Leigh laughed. 'Is it that obvious?'

'You both seem very happy. That much is obvious,' she replied as she picked up the wine bottle and refilled their glasses.

'I've never met anyone like him before, Grace. I should despise him. I should hate everything he stands for...'

'But?'

'Well, obviously I don't, do I? So, what does that say about me and my principles? Do I actually have any if I'm willing to let myself fall for a man like John?'

'Just because he sometimes does bad things, doesn't mean he's not a good man, Leigh,' Grace said.

'I know that. But I can't have him *and* my job. So...' Leigh said and then shrugged.

'Have you spoken to John about it?'

'God, no. I don't even know if he wants anything

serious. I don't know if I do. If I did give up my job, it wouldn't be for him anyway, but because I'm not sure I can do it any more. The job used to be my life, Grace. But lately I've been wondering if the sacrifices I've made have been worth it. I've been feeling restless for a while, and all this shit with Barrow has made me question whether I want the job to be the only thing I have in my life. So, whether John is in the picture or not, I need to think about my future. And if John is going to be a part of it, I can't be a police officer, can I? Anyway, for now it's just a bit of fun. I mean, John is the typical eternal bachelor.'

Grace sipped her wine and took a step towards the door, signalling Leigh to follow. 'I have known John Brennan for many years and we have been good friends for about five of those. I have never once known him to bring a date to my house for dinner. In fact, I have never once met one of the women he was seeing. Read into that what you will,' she said with a flash of her eyebrows.

Chapter Forty-Four

Michael sat in the warm office of Morrison Property Management while the CEO's secretary poured him and Luke a coffee.

The new restaurant they were opening in Chester was Grace's latest pet project and the original plans had needed to be scrapped and redrawn because the place was a listed building. Despite her paying the surveyor to comply with regulations, there had been some significant oversights, which she had learned of that morning and which meant a further delay. She had dropped the kids off at school and nursery that morning and headed off through the Wallasey tunnel. She was not a happy woman. Michael smiled to himself as he thought about the poor bastard who was going to feel his wife's wrath today. Despite who she was, and the fact that ordinarily his wife could work miracles, even she had no sway over Chester Council's Listed Buildings office.

As a result, Michael had been drafted in to oversee the

last day of negotiations for a new contract with the biggest property management company in the North West, who were looking for new security contractors. From what Grace had told him, Luke had done an excellent job so far, and the only reason for her, and now his, presence was to reassure the CEO that his company was a priority. Grace had told Michael that all he would need to do was sit in the office, drink coffee and look good in a suit. But when Chris Morris had walked into the room, Michael had been caught off guard. He realised that Chris must be short for Christine. He supposed that was what he got for making assumptions, and now he understood better Grace's comment about looking good in a suit. Christine had held out her manicured hand and shaken his, holding onto it a few seconds longer than could be considered necessary. She smiled at him sweetly before walking around to her desk and taking a seat.

Michael sat and listened to the negotiations, and realised that beneath her sweet smile Christine was a ruthless negotiator. Luke handled himself well and Michael realised that Grace was right. He was suitably impressed. Luke Sullivan had just gone up significantly in Michael's estimation and he was beginning to see why Grace valued his input so much.

'You've been very quiet, Mr Carter,' Chris suddenly said, her blue eyes staring into his as though she was trying to see inside his soul. He imagined she was an intimidating opponent, or partner, to most people, But then, most people weren't married to Grace.

'I think Luke has covered everything, Ms Morris. You

have our terms. We out-perform our nearest competitor and your current supplier in both efficiency and service, and for minimal additional costs. We can send one of our associates back tomorrow if you'd like more time to think it over, or you can pick up your beautiful Mont Blanc pen and sign those papers,' he said with a smile.

Chris smiled at him. 'You know your pens?' she said with a raised eyebrow.

'My wife uses them. Apparently it's a thing?' he said with an exaggerated shrug.

Chris nodded and picked up the pen from her desk.

Ten minutes later, Michael and Luke were climbing into Luke's Audi S3 with a signed contract.

'Grace will be happy when you tell her Chris has finally caved,' Luke said. 'I was worried she was going to hold out for us to match her current provider for a minute.'

Michael smiled at him. 'Never give them more for less, mate. It makes us look amateur. We provide a premium service for a premium rate.'

'You were great with her. She scares the shit out of me.'

Michael laughed. Luke had done all of the hard work really. 'Well, I learned from the best. You did a good job. She was going to sign anyway, I just hurried her along.'

Luke smiled appreciatively. 'Thanks, Michael. It feels good to have closed the deal at last.'

'I'll let you tell the Boss,' Michael said with a wink. 'I won't steal your thunder.'

Luke laughed as he pulled the car away from the kerb. 'Thanks.'

Michael's phone started to ring and he took it from his inside pocket.

'Hiya, Murf,' he said as he answered, having seen his face flashing up on the screen. 'Everything okay?'

'Is it ever lately, Boss?' Murf asked with a chuckle. 'I swear I'm getting too old for this shit.'

Michael smiled. Both he and Murf had been saying they were too old for this game for the last five years. 'What is it, mate?'

'There's a woman here asking for Luke and Danny. Says her name is Glenda. She looks like she's just been dug up, but she's a persistent mare. She's refusing to leave until she speaks to one of them and has plonked herself on a stool at the bar. She's causing merry hell but I can't exactly cart out a little old lady, can I? Besides, I think she'd scratch my eyes out if I tried. I wouldn't mind, I only popped in to put some money in the safe for Jake.'

'For fuck's sake,' Michael snapped and then turned to Luke. 'Who is Glenda?'

Luke frowned at him. 'I only know one Glenda, why?'

'Because Glenda is at The Blue Rooms wanting to speak to you or Danny. Who is she?'

Luke's face paled. 'It can't be.'

'Can't be who?'

'Danny and Stacey's mum. She's the only Glenda I know of. But it can't be her.'

'Murf said she looks like she's been dug up.'

Luke gave a long sigh. 'It is her.'

'Then you need to get to the club and deal with her, because she's giving Murf aggro. Or phone Danny and ask him to go and have a word with her?'

'No. Danny doesn't need to know anything yet. Let me speak to her and see what the hell she wants. Although, knowing Glenda, it will be money. You mind coming with me?'

'We're on our way, Murf. See you in half an hour or so,' Michael said as he hung up the phone.

'Thanks,' Luke said to him. 'She's a right handful and I wouldn't mind some back-up.'

'How long has it been since Danny saw his mum then?'

'God, years. She left when he was thirteen and I don't think he's seen her since.'

'And she just turns up now after fifteen years? Fucking hell! The cheek of her.'

'She's fucking vile, mate. Vile.' He spat.

———

Grace sipped her glass of wine and looked at the other three women around the table in Stefano's. They were all so different, yet so alike. Even Leigh was looking relaxed as she laughed and chatted with Jazz and Stacey. But then, since she had started seeing John, she looked much more relaxed in general. And John seemed a lot happier too. She wondered if they would make it work, and how they would manage to, given their very different career choices.

Grace noticed her mobile phone ringing on the table and saw Michael's name and photograph appear on the screen.

'Hi, love,' she answered. 'How did the meeting go?'

'The meeting?'

'Your meeting with Chris?'

'Oh, Chris?' he said as though he had forgotten about it. 'It was good. I'll let Luke fill you in later.'

'Okay. Well, I'm glad it went well.'

'Hmm, you might have mentioned Chris was a woman though.'

'Well, you shouldn't have assumed the CEO was a man.'

'I did that because her name was Chris, not because she was the CEO.'

'Liar,' she said with a laugh.

'Can you meet me at The Blue Rooms? I haven't got my car and I thought we could drive home together. We could pick up a takeaway on the way. I can't be arsed cooking, can you?'

'Sounds like a good idea. Is everything okay?'

'Yeah. Why?'

'Well, you forgot about your meeting with Chris and you're on your way to the club?'

'Oh, it's nothing. Something Luke has to sort out. I'll tell you about it later.'

'Okay. What time do you want picking up?'

'About an hour. We're just on our way to the club now.'

'Okay, I'll see you in an hour,' Grace said.

'Bye, babe.'

Grace put her phone in her handbag and fixed her attention back on the group.

'Do you fancy another one, Grace?' Jazz asked as she held her empty wine glass aloft.

'No, thanks. I'm driving. I think I'll order a coffee though,' she said as she signalled the waiter for service.

'Oh, I could go for a coffee,' Leigh agreed. 'I'm driving too.'

'I'll have another wine, Jazz,' Stacey said. 'Shall we get a bottle?'

'Why not? I have no baby duties this evening. Connor, Jake and Danny are introducing Paul to his first football match,' she said with a roll of her eyes.

Grace laughed. 'Connor was so excited about it this morning.'

'Aw, that's so cute,' Stacey said.

'Oh, you wouldn't believe it, Stacey. You'd think they were going to Anfield, not sitting in our living room.' Jazz laughed. 'Paul even has his own little Liverpool kit. It is very cute actually.'

'What will Connor do if he turns out to be a blue like his grandad and uncle though?' Grace said.

'Oh, don't even joke about that, Grace. Can you imagine? I think it would break Connor's heart, honestly,' said Jazz. 'He can't wait to take him to the match when he's older. Him and Danny have even been talking about getting a box at Anfield.'

'Oh no. Really? That means Jake and Michael will want one at Goodison too,' Grace said with a groan.

'Apparently, it's good for business,' Jazz said. 'As if they won't just be there with their mates!' she snorted.

'I hope they do. I love the footy,' Stacey said.

'So do I. Although I'm a Man U girl myself,' Leigh added.

'Me too!' Jazz screeched. 'Nobody around here will ever admit to that. I knew I liked something about you, Leigh!'

The four women broke into laughter as the waiter approached their table to take drinks.

Ten minutes later, when Grace and Leigh had their coffees and Stacey and Jazz had topped up their wine glasses, Leigh proposed a toast. 'To the incredible women who cracked the Liverpool Ripper case,' she said as she raised her mug into the air.

'I'll toast to that,' Jazz said with a smile.

'Me too,' Stacey added.

Grace raised her mug too and looked around the table at the four unlikely friends. 'Cheers, ladies.'

Chapter Forty-Five

Michael leaned back on the leather headrest in Luke's car and closed his eyes. It had been a long day and he was looking forward to getting home. At least Grace was meeting him at The Blue Rooms and they could drive home together. He felt like he'd hardly seen her for the past few days, but the kids would be at their grandparents' for the night, and that always meant an early night and a sleep in. He smiled to himself at the thought.

The sound of Luke's mobile ringing interrupted the Bruce Springsteen song he was enjoying on the radio and Michael heard Luke answer before a woman's voice filled the car.

'Can I speak to Mr Sullivan?' she asked.

'Yeah, speaking,' he answered gruffly.

'Hello, Mr Sullivan, it's Helena from the hotel. I'm so sorry to bother you but there seems to have been an anomaly with your bill.'

'What?' he snapped.

Michael opened his eyes and looked across at his companion.

'There was a bottle of champagne on room service that wasn't paid for,' she said curtly.

'Shit!' he cursed under his breath. 'I'm just in the middle of something. Can I call you back?'

'I understand you're busy, but you persuaded me to allow you to not use a card for the room,' she said pointedly. 'I really need you to pay this bill today,' she added, an air of desperation creeping into her voice.

'I'm sorry, Helena,' he said, turning on the charm. 'I really appreciate you helping me out yesterday, but I'm in the middle of something right now. Can I call you back in an hour, and I'll pay over the phone?'

'I'll be here until seven,' she replied with a sigh. 'Please ring back before then or you'll get me into trouble.'

'I will. Thanks. Speak later,' Luke said as he ended the call.

'What was all that about then?' Michael asked Luke with a raised eyebrow.

'Nothing. Just a mix-up,' Luke said breezily but Michael noticed the skin on his neck turning pink.

'Why were you in a hotel yesterday? You were working with the lads last night and the night before.'

'I didn't stay overnight,' Luke replied as he kept his eyes fixed on the road ahead.

'Oh, I see. Just needed it for a few hours, did you?' Michael started to laugh. 'That explains the champagne.'

Luke continued to stare at the road.

'So, who is she then?'

'No one,' Luke snapped as he shifted in his seat.

Michael was starting to think Luke was hiding something bigger than an afternoon rendezvous. 'Why didn't you just use your place?'

'I just didn't want to,' Luke answered, still not making eye contact.

'Oh, for fuck's sake, she's not married, is she?' Michael asked with a sigh. 'We don't need any more drama right now without you pissing off someone's husband as well.'

Luke turned to him but he didn't meet his eyes. 'No, of course not. It was just a convenience thing,' he answered and then turned back to the road.

Michael continued to stare at him for a few moments, noting the flush on his neck deepening. Luke Sullivan was keeping something from him, of that he was one hundred per cent certain.

———————

Luke could feel the heat of Michael's gaze on his neck as he drove to The Blue Rooms, and he resisted the urge to pull at his collar to let some air at his flushed skin. He should never have answered the call but he often had calls from unknown numbers. The people he worked with were prone to changing their numbers as frequently as their bedding. But now Michael Carter knew he was lying to him and he could feel the tension in the car growing with each passing moment. Why hadn't he come up with a perfectly plausible explanation instead of trying to shrug it off and getting defensive? He could have just said that he'd met a woman and he took her to a hotel for a quick shag. He could have bragged about what a good time they'd had – even though that wasn't Luke's style. But it was perfectly legitimate, wasn't it? To take a woman he fancied to a hotel for the afternoon? In fact, that is what had happened. He had taken her to a hotel and he'd had the best afternoon and the best sex of his life. And now he couldn't stop thinking about her. Despite who she was, and the fact that he was going to go to hell, or quite possibly get his head ripped off his shoulders, he couldn't wait to see her again. And when he did, would he be able to keep the fact that he was completely besotted with her from everyone else in the room?

Despite the discomfort of Michael's suspicion, and the guilt of what he'd done weighing on him, Luke couldn't help but feel a thrill when he thought about her and he wondered if she felt the same as he did. She had seemed like she did. But then she had been wracked with guilt and had spent the drive back to Liverpool making him promise not to tell anyone about their fledgling affair. Not that he would, but she'd seemed even more anxious than he was. Yesterday had been the culmination of months of stolen glances and whispered conversations with hidden meanings. It had been intense and passionate and everything he had imagined it would be. They had both crossed a line yesterday. One that they really shouldn't have, albeit for different reasons. But there was no going back now. Whatever happened, Luke wasn't going to give her up without a fight.

Chapter Forty-Six

Patrick Carter sat back in his armchair with a smile on his face as he watched his wife Sue painting with their youngest grandchildren, Oscar and Belle. They picked the children up from school and nursery a few days a week and had them overnight every Wednesday and Saturday, and they loved it. Sue often joked that it kept them both young. Sue had never had any children of her own. Having nursed her ill parents into her late thirties, she didn't meet her first husband until she was forty-three and by then felt she'd left it too late. Their marriage had only lasted two years and then Sue had felt this had confirmed she'd made the right decision. She was almost sixty now and Patrick often wondered if she regretted her decision, especially as she was so close to Grace, who'd had Belle and Oscar later in life, and she was so good with the little ones, who all adored their nanny Sue.

Patrick had never thought he'd marry again after Marie, his first wife and the mother of his two sons, had died so young. He had been devastated by her death. He had considered her the love of his life and thought it would be somehow disrespectful to her memory to fall in love again. Sean and Michael had encouraged him to find someone else, but he had never wanted to. Then he had met Sue, when he was recovering from the assault that had nearly killed him. She was one of the nurses in the outpatient clinic and he had fallen for her hook, line and sinker. She was one of the warmest and most caring people he had ever met in his life. They had dated for a few months before he'd told her about his family and their business, fearing it would be the beginning of the end. But Sue had accepted that that was who he was. Then, when she had met Sean and Sophia and their daughters, and Michael and his sons, she had fallen in love with them all – and they with her.

But it was when Grace came back to Liverpool with little Belle in tow that Sue had really come into her own. She'd never experienced the other grandchildren as little ones, but now she had this little granddaughter, and Sue was the only nanny that Belle had ever known. Sue had been as delighted as Patrick was when Michael and Grace finally got their acts together and became a couple. It had been a long time coming, and then Oscar had arrived a year later and Sue had stepped up again. She told Patrick that he had finally given her the family she had always dreamed of, and that made him so happy he felt like his heart would burst.

Patrick's thoughts were interrupted by his mobile phone ringing. He picked it up from the coffee table beside him and saw Murf's name flashing on the screen.

'Hello, Murf,' he said.

'Hiya Pat,' Murf answered. 'How are you, mate?'

'Good. Belle and Oscar are here so they're keeping me and Sue busy.' He smiled at Sue as she looked up at him. 'How are you?'

'Can't complain, Pat. I got that information you wanted. Sorry it took me a while but we've been swamped these past couple of weeks.'

'I heard about Parnell and his firm giving you some grief. It's all sorted now though?' Patrick asked. He was retired now, as he liked to tell anyone who would listen, but he worried about Michael and his grandsons, who were still very much in the thick of it.

'Yeah. It's all quiet again on the western front – for now.' He heard Murf sigh quietly.

'What did you find out?' Patrick asked as he stood up and walked into the kitchen. He wasn't sure he wanted Sue to hear what he might or might not be about to discover just yet. At least not until he'd spoken to Michael.

'It's true,' Murf replied. 'Luke and Grace. You were right.'

Patrick shook his head. 'Wow. I mean, I suspected, but to have you say it's true…'

'I know. I can't believe it myself, Pat. If I hadn't seen the proof with my own eyes, I'd say you were having me on.'

'Did you look into Luke for me?' Patrick asked.

'Yeah. Everything he's told Grace and Michael so far checks out. He doesn't appear to have any skeletons in his closet. Not that I can say the same for his business partner, Danny.'

'Oh?'

'Nothing to do with this, Pat. At least I don't think so.'

'Okay, maybe tell me some other time. So, what do you think he's playing at then? Luke, I mean? What's his endgame?'

'I'd have thought it was obvious. Money? Power? He wants a slice of the Carter empire?'

'Maybe. Listen, I need to speak to Michael about this. Can you keep it to yourself, Murf? I don't want this getting out before I've spoken to Michael and Grace.'

'Of course, Pat. I have a lot of respect for you and your family, you know that. I would never betray your trust like that.'

'I know you wouldn't. Sorry, Murf. It's just that … when this gets out…'

'I know, mate,' Murf said with a sigh. 'I'll keep schtum though. I'll be seeing Michael and Luke shortly. They're on their way here.'

'Just act normal then. You don't know anything. It's probably safer for all concerned. I'll speak to Michael as soon as I can.'

'Okay, Pat. Make it sooner rather than later though, eh? I feel like I'm in the eye of a storm here.'

'I will, and thanks, Murf. I knew I could count on you.'

'No problem, Pat. Take care, mate.'

'Take care,' Patrick replied before hanging up the phone.

He leaned back against the wall and swallowed. He had known it was true, but it still didn't bother him any less now that he had confirmation. He trusted that if Murf had seen the proof, there was proof. What the hell was Luke Sullivan playing at trying to muscle in on his family?

Patrick picked up his coat. If Michael was on his way to The Blue Rooms, then Patrick would go there now and see him. The sooner this was out in the open the sooner Luke could be dealt with. He popped his head around the living-room door. 'I've just got to pop out, love,' he said to Sue. 'I need to see Michael. I'll be back in a few hours.'

'Everything okay?' she asked.

'Yeah,' he said, trying to sound nonchalant. 'I just need to talk to him about something. Bye, kids,' he shouted.

'Bye, Grandad,' Belle and Oscar shouted happily.

Chapter Forty-Seven

M ichael and Luke walked through the corridor of The Blue Rooms to Jake's office at the back, where Glenda had been escorted by Murf to keep her out of trouble. Luke's earlier conversation in the car still had Michael curious. What had that been about, and why hadn't Luke just been honest with him? Who had he been at that hotel room with? Why had the usually calm and collected Luke Sullivan suddenly appeared so flustered?

Whatever the reason, now wasn't the time to dwell on it. They had Glenda Alexander to sort out first because the last thing they needed was another ghost from the past causing any more problems.

Michael stepped through the open door of Jake's office to see one of his most trusted soldiers, Murf, sitting at Jake's desk staring at the woman sitting on the small sofa opposite him. Michael couldn't help but think of Zelda from the Terrahawks when he looked at her, and he was suddenly reminded of how he and Sean would lie in front of the TV watching it every Saturday morning. She had a cigarette in one hand and cradled an empty glass in the other. She looked up at him and Luke as they walked further into the room.

'Hello, Luke.' She almost spat his name, then looked past him and at Michael. 'And who's this?' she asked as she licked her lips and sat back against the sofa.

'This is my colleague, Michael Carter,' Luke replied.

'Oh, yes, I know your name, of course, although I've never had the pleasure,' she said as she beckoned him over to her and held out her hand.

'Hello, Glenda,' he said, still feeling the urge to call her Zelda and ignoring her outstretched hand.

'I'll leave you both to it, Boss,' Murf said as he stood up and straightened his jacket. He placed a hand on Michael's shoulder as he walked out. 'Good luck,' he said quietly and with a grin.

Michael perched on the edge of Jake's desk and Luke remained standing beside him.

Glenda sat back in the chair, a toothless smile stretched across her thin face as she stubbed out her cigarette in her empty glass.

'What do you want, Glenda?' Luke snarled at her.

'What do you think, Luke? I want to be a part of Stacey and Danny's lives. They're my children after all,' she cackled.

'You lost any right to call them that when you abandoned them to live with that nasty piece of shit you married,' he replied.

'I came back, didn't I? After Terry was gone, I came back

for them. Do they know what you did? Do they know you paid me to leave them alone?'

Michael looked at Luke. This information was new to him. Luke was certainly full of surprises today.

Luke laughed. 'No, they don't know that five grand was all it took to make you turn your back on them for a second time. Would you like to tell them about that, or should I?'

Glenda scowled at him. 'Don't you dare sit in judgement of me. You think you're some hotshot businessman, but I know where all your money came from. Does he know?' She nodded towards Michael.

'What?' Luke snapped, looking as surprised as Michael felt.

Michael frowned. What the hell did any of this have to do with him? Why would he know where Luke's money had come from? 'What's she on about?' he asked.

Luke turned to him and shrugged. 'I honestly don't know, mate. She's a fucking fruitcake, isn't she?'

Glenda started to cackle. 'So he doesn't know then, does he? About you and his wife?'

'Shut the fuck up now, Glenda!' Luke shouted.

Michael felt like he had been punched in the gut. He stood up, looking between Luke and Glenda. 'What about him and my wife?' Michael snarled, directing his question to Glenda.

'Take no fucking notice of her. I told you she's off her head,' Luke insisted.

'Tell me what is going on between him and my wife,' Michael shouted again.

'She's lying, Michael,' Luke interrupted.

'No, I'm not.' She blinked as though deeply offended. Then she stared directly at Michael and grinned. 'I have the proof.'

Michael took a step towards Luke. 'Tell me what the fuck she is talking about,' he snarled, feeling the anger surging in his chest like a geyser. He'd known there was something between the two of them. Luke and Grace had a connection that Michael had been prepared to overlook because he trusted his wife, but now here was this old hag claiming she had proof to tell him otherwise.

Luke stared at him, his hands held up in either surrender or feigned ignorance. 'I haven't got a clue, Michael. I swear there's nothing going on between me and Grace.'

Michael blinked. Of course it couldn't be that. He trusted Grace completely. She would never do that to him. But then he remembered his and Luke's earlier conversation in the car. Luke and the hotel room. The champagne. The married woman. Grace had been at a meeting with the contractors all afternoon yesterday. She hadn't replied to a text message he'd sent her and had said it was because she'd been so distracted by the pain-in-the-arse foreman that she'd forgotten to press send. It hadn't bothered him at the time. It had only been a question about the dog and she had even shown him the reply she had typed out but not sent. But had she in fact been distracted by something, or someone, else?

Something was going on and he wanted to know what it was. He charged at Luke, grabbing him by the throat and pushing him against the wall. The younger man struggled, but he was no match for Michael, who was filled with such anger he felt like he might spontaneously combust.

'Have you been fucking my wife?' Michael snarled. His head was telling him that it couldn't possibly be true, but his anger was clouding his thinking.

Luke glared at him. 'No!' he snapped.

Michael was distracted momentarily by the office door opening. Looking up, he saw Grace walking in, with a look of horror on her face when she saw he had Luke pinned to the wall.

'Michael!' she shouted. 'What the hell are you doing?'

In the background Glenda cackled. 'Oh, this is even better than I thought it would be.'

Michael stared at his wife. She was the love of his life. She was quite literally his other half. How could she have done this to him? To them? He felt like his heart had been ripped from his chest. Suddenly, all the fight in him was gone. What was the point of anything if he didn't have her? He released Luke from his grip and let his hand fall to his side. 'What the hell is going on between you two?' he said to Grace.

She stared at him blankly and he had to give it to her, she was playing her part well.

'Nothing is going on. What are you on about?' she asked as she looked between Michael and Luke.

'There's nothing going on between us,' Luke croaked as he rubbed the red skin on his throat.

Michael turned to glare at him and pointed in his face. 'You just shut the fuck up right now,' he spat.

Grace walked towards the two of them. 'Why on earth

would you think there's something going on between us?' she said to Michael as she reached him, placing her hand on his arm.

God, she was so bloody convincing. 'Because she said so.' He indicated Glenda.

'And you believe her?' Grace snapped.

'She said she has proof,' he went on.

'Well, I'm telling you she hasn't, because there is none to have,' Grace replied.

'I never said they were fucking,' Glenda piped up from the corner and they all turned to face her. 'You jumped to that conclusion all on your own,' she added with a grin.

Michal spun around to stare at her. What the fuck was she playing at? He felt like his heart was about to pack in. 'Then why? What?' he asked as he shook his head. What the hell was going on? Deep down, he had known Grace would never cheat on him, but what was this old crank on about then? His head was starting to throb as the blood continued to thunder around his body.

'You spiteful old cow,' Grace said as she walked towards Glenda. 'What the hell are you up to?'

Glenda looked between Grace and Luke. 'So you really don't know? Neither of you?'

They both stared back at her. 'Know what?' they replied in unison.

Glenda started to laugh uncontrollably at this point. 'Oh my God, you two think you're on top of the world, but you're really thick as pig-shit, aren't you?'

Grace walked towards Glenda and brought her face closer to the older woman's. 'You think you're safe because these two gentlemen would never hurt a woman? But I'm more than happy to,' she snarled. 'Now tell me what the fuck you're on about or I will slap the two remaining teeth you have out of your head.'

Glenda shrunk back in fear. 'It's not my fault your husband was so quick to assume you'd been carrying on behind his back,' she sniffed.

'Oh, but I'll bet that was exactly what you wanted him to think, you nasty old cow. Now what is it you think you know?'

Glenda looked up at her. 'I thought you would have worked it out already. The resemblance is uncanny. He's your brother.' She nodded towards Luke, who stood there with his mouth hanging open. Grace looked at him and then at Michael, and then back at Glenda. 'What?' she snapped.

'I said, he's your brother,' she sighed as she reached into her handbag. After a quick rummage around, Glenda handed her an old worn photograph. Grace looked at it and felt her heart constrict. It was a picture of a pregnant woman, whom she assumed to be Luke's mother. She was standing with a man, their arms wrapped around each other's waist, and both of them beaming proudly for the camera. There was no mistaking the man in the picture – he was Pete Sumner, Grace's father.

Epilogue

Grace perched on the edge of the desk in Jake's office in The Blue Rooms. She had felt like she'd been punched in the gut when Glenda had shown her that photograph earlier. The man in it was unmistakeably her father, but despite that, in some ways she hardly recognised him. He'd obviously had another life that for some reason he had kept entirely secret from her. Why had he done that? It had rocked her to her core. Looking back on her childhood, her dad had been her one constant. He had been her hero. They had been so very close. Except they quite obviously hadn't, had they? Had it all been a lie? He had looked so happy in that photograph. Why wouldn't he have wanted to share that with her?

She had stood there holding the picture in her hands when Luke had walked up behind her. 'That's my mum,' he muttered.

'And that's my dad,' Grace added. Although now he was *their* dad and that realisation floored her. Had Luke known? She'd barely had time to process anything when Michael's father Patrick burst into the room.

'Michael,' he'd started to say and then he'd looked up at Grace and Luke and stopped talking, his mouth hanging open in surprise. Had Patrick known all along? He had been her father's friend back in the day, but he'd been in prison when her father died before Luke was born.

'Something you'd like to share with us all, Pat?' she'd asked him.

Ten minutes later, Patrick and Luke had been able to piece together the story of how Luke's mum Maggie and Grace's dad Pete had met. Maggie had been a rep for the brewery and had met Pete on one of her visits to The Rose and Crown. From what Luke recalled his mother telling him, they had quickly fallen for each other and Maggie had become pregnant a few months after they'd met. Pete had died when Maggie was six months pregnant, leaving Grace an orphan and Luke without a father.

Grace's head spun with it all. There were so many questions she needed the answers to, but she wasn't sure if they could be answered. The two people who knew what had really happened were both dead. There was a chance that Glenda knew more than she let on. She had found the photograph in Maggie's things after she died, or so she claimed. But Glenda had been told to get lost and thankfully she'd obliged.

Luke had looked as baffled as she felt and Grace knew that he must have dozens of questions himself. He'd told them that he had no idea who his father was. All his mum had ever told him was that he'd died when she was pregnant and had owned a pub. Grace believed him, but she didn't know how this would change things for their family. Where would he fit in the new order of things now that he was her half-brother?

That had all happened less than an hour ago and now Grace was alone with Michael in Jake's office. She watched her husband, who sat on the large leather chair. He ran his hands through his hair with a sigh and she wondered what was going through his head.

'Did you honestly think there was something going on between me and Luke?' she asked him.

Michael looked at Grace. His wife, who had never given him any reason to doubt her during their entire marriage. The woman he loved more than anything in the world. 'Of course not. Not really. But me and Luke had been talking about him seeing someone and I guessed she was married because of how he was acting. Then Glenda said there was something between you two and I just jumped to a conclusion.'

'That I'm cheating on you? That was the first conclusion that came to you, was it? Not that Glenda was trying to cause trouble? What have I ever done that would make you think that?'

He looked at her. 'Nothing,' he said quietly.

'Then why don't you trust me?'

'I do,' he said as he stood up. Putting his arms around her waist, he pulled her to him. 'Of course I do, Grace. I told you, Luke was acting weird when I asked him who he'd been seeing. Then she asked me if I knew about you and him. My brain just went there. I didn't think. I just reacted. It was the heat of the moment.'

'A heat of the moment that had you throttling Luke?' she snapped.

'I know,' he said as he brushed a piece of hair behind her ear. 'I'll apologise to him.'

Grace shook her head. 'You're an idiot,' she said, and he noticed the hint of a smile playing on her lips.

'But a lovable one?' he said as he placed his hand under her chin and lifted her face to his.

She did smile then. 'Hmm. It's a good job, isn't it?'

'I love you, Grace,' he said, his voice thick with emotion. 'When I thought…'

'I know,' she replied. Then she pulled his face to hers and kissed him as he pushed her back onto the desk. Soon his hands were lifting the hem of her skirt, pushing the material up over her thighs. 'You really want to do this here? In Jake's office?' Grace breathed in his ear.

'Yes,' he growled. He wanted to forget what had had happened in the past hour and he suspected she did too – at least for a while.

'Someone might come in,' she added.

'They'll knock.'

'You're a bad influence on me, Carter,' she said as he trailed kisses along her throat.

He lifted his head and smiled at her. 'I certainly hope so.'

Acknowledgments

As always, I would like to thank the wonderful team at One More Chapter for believing in me and bringing these books to life, most especially Charlotte Ledger, Kim Young, and Jennie Rothwell, whose support of The Bad Blood series has helped it go from strength to strength. I'd also love to thank my amazing editor, Emily Ruston, who understands my characters as well as I do. My books are so much better for your expert input.

Most of all, I'd love to thank all of the readers who have supported me and who have bought or read my books. You have made my dreams come true.

I couldn't do this without the support of other authors too, and the crime writing community are a particularly lovely and supportive group of people. But, I'd like to give a special mention to Mary Torjussen, Edie Baylis, Noelle Holten and Mel Sherratt, for always being willing to lend a listening ear.

To all of my friends who put up with my constant

writing chatter. There are too many to mention, and I love you all! A huge thank-you to my family for their constant love and support.

And finally, but most especially, to Eric – who supports every crazy decision I make, and my incredible boys – who continue to inspire and amaze me every single day.